A MAN OF HONOR:
THE LIFE AND DEATH
OF YUBA KASAI

A MAN OF HONOR:
THE LIFE AND DEATH OF YUBA KASAI

MUZAFFAR A. ISANI

PARTRIDGE

To order additional copies of this book, contact
Partridge India
000 800 10062 62
orders.india@partridgepublishing.com

www.partridgepublishing.com/india

PREFACE

Let me state at the outset that the inspiration for this book is the classic work of Thomas Hardy, '*The Mayor of Casterbridge*'. The storyline follows the broad contours of that great work, incorporating key elements of the basic plot. Nevertheless, with manifold digressions in the situations and settings and an addition to the cast of characters, the present work stands apart from its source. In the final analysis, the plot too will have acquired a distinct basis and even a distinct intent.

It is not unusual for an author to adapt a theme or a plot from another source. Indeed, it is a familiar literary phenomenon and some well-known works have followed the storyline of another quite diligently. As a case in point, my reader may call to mind a popular tale of young lovers that various authors have told and retold since antiquity and that continues to hold interest in modern times. The best-known version of the tale is, without doubt, the one associated with William Shakespeare who has immortalized it for eternity as *'Romeo and Juliet'*. The genesis of Shakespeare's work is probably an obscure Italian novella rendered into English in verse by Arthur Brook around 1562 as *'The Tragical History of Romeus and Juliet'*. William Painter retold the same in prose as *'Palace of Pleasure'* in 1567. It was almost certainly from the latter work that Shakespeare adapted his version of the tragic love story, written between 1591 and 1595. The plot employed by Shakespeare is quite similar to that of Painter. In fact, during that period, Italian novellas were a popular source of plots for many writers of English novels and dramas, including several other works of Shakespeare.

More to the point, no modern interpretation of an Aristotelian tragedy is free from the influence of the works of Aeschylus, Sophocles and Euripides, the only complete texts of the Greek tragedies to have survived. The inspiration for Hardy's classic too is the Greek tradition. It exhibits many similarities to Sophocles' *'Oedipus Rex'*. Each recounts and dramatizes the rise and subsequent fall in the fortunes of a single protagonist. The tribulations of the protagonist in both works stem from some innate flaw in his disposition, though he might possess many other redeeming qualities. Hardy has borrowed characters and situations from other sources as well. The extreme polarization in the relationship between the mayor and his young friend is clearly reminiscent of the relationship between Saul and David in the biblical tale. Nevertheless, Hardy has rightly been credited with creating, perhaps, the most valid and meaningful modern revival and adaptation of that genre.

Let me now say a word about the motivation for the present work. The incident that defines the life of Hardy's protagonist—the selling of his wife at a country fair in a drunken frenzy—is so implausible and of such quaint reckoning that it more or less stretches the limits of the reader's imagination. In 19ᵗʰ century rural England, the setting for Hardy's work, such an incident would be quite improbable if not altogether impossible. Yet, its replacement by another more plausible cause would have lessened the immensity of the wrong for which Hardy's protagonist suffers his misfortune. However, such incidents occur with some regularity in certain parts of the world even to this day. The theme then seems perfectly credible in the social and cultural milieu of those societies and begs further introspection. In such societies, there is a remarkable confluence of the fault lines in social norms and the foibles of human character that engenders heightened and sometimes confused emotions, which can prove hard to contain. The events and emotions encountered in this book may at first glance seem incongruous or even absurd but there is a latent truth hidden in their fold.

The tragic story of a powerful man ruined by innate flaws of character is a fascinating indictment of the frailty of human disposition. It also lays bare the extreme ambiguity of communal values in certain societies. Hardy's protagonist suffers a mere misfortune even though his milieu would construe his act to be unnatural and would condemn it unequivocally. The consequence of a similar act perpetrated by the protagonist in the present work is a tragedy of far greater immensity even though in this case society has pointedly sanctioned the practice; such then are the dangerous crosscurrents of contradiction that are manifestly extant in those communities. There is then scant distance between misfortune and tragedy in such cases. The premise is straightforward but nonetheless compelling and, I hope, thought provoking.

In the end, let me admit that I did not really set out to write a novel. The work evolved from a casual exercise to sketch the theme of Hardy's classic as an entirely innocent undertaking. Before long, I found myself knee-deep in a morass from whence this handiwork then emerged inexorably. Nevertheless, I must confess that my gratuitous foray into an uncharted territory has at times been a labor of love and at other times a tedious exertion but its fruition has been an indescribable pleasure. If it does not merit well-disposed appreciation, so be it. It is my product, good, bad or indifferent and I own it unapologetically. In any case, I cannot escape the consequence of my temerity and therefore, I have emphatically laid bare the genesis of my endeavor to let the reader determine the extent of its authenticity. The norms and practices of the arts and the great artists clearly warrant accessing another work for inspiration and, indeed, for valuable quotes. I have duly exercised that warrant.

CHAPTER 1

It was early morning and the sun, though yet barely visible, had begun its advance over the village. An early spring chill enveloped the morning as a gentle breeze grazed the lush green stalks of the wheat crop on the outskirts of the village. The cold was of no real concern to the country folk who were constrained to toil in the fields at dawn anyway. On the contrary, the embrace of a crisp morning signaled the joy of life, the joy of simply being alive for another day. In any case, the latter part of the day always promised to be warm, cheering the heart in anticipation. However, this day the chill was palpable in another sense too. There was expectation in the air of an impending hazard and so, there were few if any farmhands doing their chores in the vicinity that would presently be the venue of a grave calamity.

Predictably, horrific cries soon ruptured the serenity of the breaking day as an unruly swarm of men emerged from the dark shadows of the eucalyptus trees, dragging a terrified young woman by the neck. The woman kicked

1

and screamed as at least half a dozen men, all wielding axes, pushed her into the wheat fields. They attacked the woman with great ferocity, taking turns in heaping blow after blow on her increasingly limp body. The screeching shrieks soon subsided to a whimper before finally giving way to an eerie silence. Then a young man, no more than 17 years of age, emerged from within the crowd, a butcher's knife gripped firmly in his hand. He bent over the lifeless body of the young woman and slit her throat with a single swipe of the blade. The woman had clearly died before the young man administered the coup de grace. Yet he participated in the orgy with unbridled enthusiasm.

The savagery of the depraved crowd was unbelievable. The woman was hacked to death in a decidedly pagan ritual when a single bullet in the head would have produced the same end in a somewhat more benign manner. The agonizing howls of the victim were to no avail. Passersby who chanced upon the foul deed had no inclination to act and chose to look the other way or simply scampered away. They saw no reason to risk bodily harm or even death over a matter that was of little concern to them. In any case, the perpetrators completed their sadistic chores unhindered. They then bundled up the body of the unfortunate woman in a hessian rag and threw it in a shallow grave in the village burial ground. There were neither any grieving pallbearers nor any sorrowing mourners. It could not have been otherwise for the perpetrators of the horrendous act were the girl's own family members and clansmen. They had planned the act days in advance and everyone in the village had known of the plan. However, the other villagers perceived it as an internal matter of the family and saw no cause to obstruct their design. Many may even have privately applauded the propriety of the act that the family had evidently carried out in the name of honor.

The heinous crime was committed in a village located in a region that could best be described as a wasteland of humanity. The community was an eclectic and often explosive mix of clans of different castes, religions and sects. The relationship between the clans was far from harmonious and often erupted in violence, usually over petty matters. There was little if any social intercourse between them. Yet, there ran a common thread amongst the clans; they all adhered slavishly to a dubious code of honor. The notion of honor, though vague and ambiguous, played an overarching role in the social organization of those communities. The most insidious operation of the code was the so-called honor killing. It was imperative, indeed mandatory, for a family to purge the stain of a dishonorable act of a family member by killing the offender. Dishonorable acts of every definition were commonplace but the act that attracted the wrath of the community most often involved an illicit relationship between a man and a woman. Even then, the ire of society fell unduly on women, both those who were said to have desecrated themselves by their alleged immoral act and those who were simply unaccompanied by luck at the time of their birth. Its application was far more relaxed for men who might have ravaged those dishonorable women to satisfy their own lust. They could simply answer for their misdeed by compensating the family of the victim. Honor killing was therefore a ritual reserved mostly for women, though occasionally a man could become a collateral target. The blood libation ostensibly cleansed the family of the disgrace.

Such then were the mores of the society that the unfortunate woman in question inhabited. Her family wasted her life wantonly for the sin of violating the sacred code of honor. She might have had the temerity to love a man in the village but her family saw it as a relationship borne of depraved lust. If it was not bad enough for the girl to have committed such abominable immorality, the fact that the man happened to be from a different clan made it even worse.

In matters of such nature, there was neither any need for an investigation nor the necessity of affording the offender an opportunity to mount a defense. By the very operation of the code of honor, suspicion was tantamount to guilt and the luckless woman was condemned to death. The woman's clan got ready to carry out the sentence forthwith. The unsavory task customarily fell to the lot of the father or brother of the offender, notwithstanding the love that might have existed between them prior to the event.

The gruesome murder of the young woman went unreported as all such matters usually did and neither the police nor the justice system thought it worthy of further inspection. That was not the end of the matter though. There was the issue of retribution against the dead woman's lover. The star-crossed lover fled the village to give his family a chance to negotiate a deal with the aggrieved family before they could set upon him. The dead woman's family may not have had the desire for vengeance but they perceived an opportunity for gain. They could make the lover's sister the bargaining chip for his life. In the perverse traditions of such societies, girls were the favored coinage for the payment of compensation, or reparation if you will. Thereafter, an assembly of elders convened to adjudicate the matter between the two families. The assembly awarded the sister of the dead woman's lover to the offended family as compensation. The 15-year-old girl in question would henceforth be the property of the dead woman's family and her ties with her own stood severed irrevocably. The parents of the girl too were keen to give up their daughter, relieved that the bargain would spare the life of their son. In any case, they had no recourse against the decree. The family that thus came to acquire the girl could do with her as they wished. In the event, the family elected to give the girl in marriage to the brother of the dead woman, the same young man who had sprung out of the crowd to slit the throat of his sister. Immediately thereafter, 17-year-old Yuba and 15-year-old Jannat became man and wife. At the end of a perfunctory marriage ceremony, the family left the adolescent groom and his pubescent bride to their unceremonious devices to carry out the conjugal rites in the best manner they could, perhaps awkwardly and without grace.

Though Yuba and Jannat both lived in the same village, they were of different clans. Yuba's clan was of the lowliest caste, the *kasais* or butchers. They were also engaged in the preservation of skins, which earned them an even more derogatory sobriquet of *chamars*. Yuba's family was poor, indeed the poorest of the poor in their poverty-ridden village. The two-room mud hut with the ragged thatched roof that the family lived in was proof enough of their poverty. Jannat's family was just as poor. However, as cultivators, her clan was a notch above that of Yuba in the strict social hierarchy of the village community. The cultivators too held the lowly *chamars* in disdain. It was unlikely that the lives of Yuba and Jannat would have intertwined beyond casual acquaintance but for the happenstance.

The fate that befell Jannat was neither surprising nor difficult to divine. It was always on the cards. Her ordeal was actually quite mild by the prevailing standards. Some may even have considered her lucky. Under different circumstances, several male members of the family that had come to acquire her, would have raped the poor girl serially and then left her to her own devices. Her implied good fortune was due largely to the penury of the *kasais*. They could not afford to squander their capital on a gratuitous escapade. Instead, they made the most of their acquisition and put the girl to good use. Providence had spared Jannat the indignity for now, perhaps to inflict a greater one at a future date.

CHAPTER 2

Jannat's move to her husband's house was hardly auspicious. Yuba tortured her both physically and psychologically from the first day. Indeed, his elders had instructed him to do so, lest the young bride developed wrong notions about her status. Jannat found herself in a trap from which there was no escape.

An even worse fate lay in store for her. She soon earned further indignation by giving birth to a baby girl. Yuba, the 18-year-old father of the baby, was livid. The birth of a boy would have been cause for great revelry, a hand on which the father could depend on as he grew into old age. But, a girl could prove to be a burden, a mouth to feed, good only for the bride-money she would bring in at puberty. Besides, girls could easily cause dishonor and disgrace for the family. A thought crossed Yuba's mind at once. He would have to evaluate his future with the woman if perchance she were to give birth to another girl. For Jannat too it was a matter of some concern. The birth of a boy would have elevated her status within the family and might even have brought about a change in her husband's attitude towards her. She too was disappointed. Yuba might have seen the baby girl in an unbecoming light but he named her Noor, the dazzling light, though it would be hard to believe that he understood what it meant or that he even intended to impart the connotation. After all, the meaning of Jannat was rapturous paradise, though Yuba saw nothing in her person but torturous hell.

For now, though, there were other more pressing matters for the young and strapping Yuba. He was a man with burdensome responsibilities, having encumbered himself with a wife and family. With work hard to come by in the village, Yuba's frustration had become more marked with each passing day. Jannat and the baby were now beginning to be an unbearable burden, a millstone around his neck. In time, the need to search out better prospects became more pressing. He could no longer afford a facile existence in the village. He would have to leave his familiar moorings to find work elsewhere. However, a dilemma confronted Yuba as he contemplated his move out of the village. If he were to venture out, he would have to go alone. Carting his wife and child along would be a gravely cumbersome arrangement for the young man seeking work in an unfamiliar and uncertain world, with the prospects of a livelihood unclear. The immense burden, not to mention the responsibility, would be at counter purpose to his mission.

Yuba had no lodgings of his own and lived in the mud hutment that belonged to his father. He wanted to leave Jannat and the child at his father's home, at least until he could find work and earn enough to rent a room. His father, however, put his foot down. He had been providing for Yuba's family for the most part but he was not prepared to carry the burden any longer. He could scarcely scrape together enough for himself. In fact, his lot was hardly above that of the indigent and the beggar, both of whom abounded in the village. Besides, Jannat was not family. She had come as reparation for the crime of her brother.

In the midst of this spat between the father and son, the father announced one day that Yuba and his family would no longer be welcome at his home unless Yuba began to contribute towards the upkeep of his wife and child. He ordered him to move out of the house immediately. His father's edict finally cast the die.

CHAPTER 3

The extenuating circumstances of his life had led Yuba to acquire a fondness for alcohol. In spite of the destitute nature of his existence, he spent what little money he earned to satisfy his habit. Alcohol was a proscribed commodity throughout the country but there was never any shortage of a lethal variety distilled locally. On days when he managed to earn something, Yuba walked down the dirt road from his village to a small town on the main highway, where a dilapidated shack on the outskirts of the town served as a tavern of sorts. The popularity of the shack was quite evident from the sizable presence of an ardent clientele that thronged the place on any given day. It was mostly a frivolous contingent as was to be expected; laborers lucky enough to have earned wages for the day, peasants from nearby villages done with their day's chores, taxi drivers who stationed their vehicles at the local petrol station and even a stray soldier or two out on a well-deserved furlough. Yuba felt quite at ease with the forlorn company that frequented the shack.

A local thug, who had long since passed the prime of his life without having experienced any solicitation from his conscience, ran the popular watering hole. The thug, whose real name was lost to all, went by the grandiose appellation of Sheeda Pistaul, the second part of which was clearly a vernacular reference to his readiness to whip out a pistol at the slightest provocation. The establishment could not naturally have existed without the acquiescence of the police who would have been most upset had Sheeda decided to atone for his life's work. The police received a fair amount of reward for providing Sheeda the protection that was so vital to his nefarious activities, the sale of alcohol being one of less disrepute compared to the others in his portfolio. Sheeda had spent his entire life in immoral pursuits and had earned his stripes the hard way, having been in and out of prison regularly. In time, he had acquired notoriety far beyond the confines of the town in which he operated.

CHAPTER 4

Yuba was in a foul mood on the day his father ordered him out of his house. Ironically, he had come by some work on the very day of his father's ultimatum and it might have saved him the ignominy had he decided to compensate his father with even a part of the day's wages. He preferred instead to spend what little money he had earned to satisfy his habit in the comfort of the degenerate company. In fact, he chose to ignore his father's directive altogether, sensing no peril in it and headed straight for the shack. Yuba seated himself on his favorite perch and ordered the usual. As always, Sheeda was reluctant to serve him until he made the payment up front. Yuba surprised the gathered company by displaying enough money to last him the evening.

After finishing the first drink, Yuba ordered a second and so it went, each time signaling for a stronger potion. The effect of the indiscriminate consumption was soon apparent. Still, there seemed no end to Yuba's voracious appetite for alcohol. He was now beginning to get loud and started interacting with the others in the shack. At the end of the first drink, he was somewhat serene, at the second he was jovial, at the third argumentative but by the fourth he had become overbearing, even quarrelsome—his conduct signified by the contortions on his face and the occasional clenching of his teeth while pounding the table with his ample fist. The fiery spark in his dark, glowing eyes rapidly began to assume ominous intensity.

The conversation amongst the degenerate lot at the shack soon took on something of a philosophical turn, as it usually does amongst those who have imbibed in surfeit. The ruin of good men by bad wives formed the main theme that the inebriated company elected to dilate upon that evening. Yuba was the most vocal of the interlocutors and he pointedly chose to make his own condition the focus of the discussion. He rendered a bitter account of how his early imprudent marriage and familial responsibilities had extinguished his youthful energies and frustrated his aims and ambitions.

"I haven't a cent to my name, yet I am as experienced a man as any in my trade. I can skin animals with greater finesse than any man that has ever wielded a butcher's knife. If I were a free man, I would be worth a tidy sum in no time. Alas! I have to carry the burden of a useless woman at the prime of my energies. And as if her sloth was not enough, she has produced a girl to add insult to my deep injury."

Yuba's reference to his supposed ample skinning skills was accompanied by an audacious display of the butcher's knife that he carried by his side constantly, more on account of his belligerent disposition than for professional reasons. His demeanor assumed an arrogant air as he continued with his vain incantation. His tantalizing avowal of his skills, however, soon gave way to denigrating his wife's merit.

Indeed, he contrived his method carefully to highlight the value of his skills in relation to the worthlessness of his wife and the hurdles she posed to his ambitions. His wife was to him a wicked problem that he was determined to addressed urgently. He paused for a moment, gesturing at the expressionless faces of the debauched company as if he expected some useful ideas with which he could resolve his dilemma. He then continued with his invective with supreme vulgarity.

"Am I wrong in saying that men who don't want their wives should be able to get rid of them? Do we not rid ourselves of animals who have outlived their utility? Yes, indeed, one should and I too would rid myself of my useless wife this minute but I must recover her cost. She has come as compensation for the dishonorable death of my sister and so I will hand her over to anyone who is willing to make an adequate payment."

In an amazing coincidence, Jannat entered the shack just as Yuba delivered those foul words. It seemed as though the contrivance had an impetus from an apostate of all that is virtuous. The poor soul knew nothing of her husband's evil resolve or the inopportune moment she had chosen for her excursion. As a matter of fact, she would not have had the courage to intrude upon the vile man's sanctuary now or ever except that the matter at hand could not wait until he returned home; Yuba and Jannat no longer had a home. Yuba's father had thrown Jannat and the child out of the house. Jannat gathered her meager belongings in a bag that she was presently carrying and left immediately. She naturally had to communicate her situation to her husband at once. She knew Yuba had earned some money during the day and would have headed straight to the shack; he had never made a secret of his fondness for the thug's concoction.

Yuba was livid, not at his father or the fact that he had thrown his wife out of the house but at Jannat's intrusion in his forbidden haven. It was the last straw.

"How dare you come here to rob me of the few moments of peace I enjoy with my friends? I have had nothing but bad luck since the day I set my eyes on you. My father would never have thrown me out of his house but for you. You have scandalized me again."

"Please, Yuba, you can deride me all you want but right now you have to come to the village and settle with your father. It is almost evening. Where will we spend the night?"

Yuba was deaf to her earnest entreaties and was apparently unmoved by the seriousness of the matter of which Jannat had come to apprise him. Instead, he continued to harp on the subject of his burden with added vigor and unfeigned disparagement, as if the matter was of no concern to him. In a blatant display of crass insensitivity and indeed shamelessness, he now offered Jannat in person to anyone who would have her, for a price of course.

"Here she is my friends, the jewel in my crown that I was talking about earlier. She has made herself available for you to size her up before you bid for her. You do not have to take just my word anymore. What you see is what you get.

Seeing that Yuba was now nearly senseless and would not be bothered with her predicament, Jannat turned around to leave. Yuba jumped to his feet, caught her by the rear of her shirt and dragged her down to the seat next to him. In the process, he almost dislodged the baby she was carrying on her slender hips.

"Is there no one here who will relieve me of my burden? Am I asking for the moon? I repeat I would gladly part with this woman if someone would pay for her. Now is your chance before I withdraw my offer."

There was a sudden roar of laughter as the merrymakers inside the shack presumed that the man's offer was in jest. All the same, Yuba's diatribe was tantamount to an invitation for others to ridicule the young wife. The odd bunch of men imbibing the harsh country liquor were now on the verge of senseless impudence and started staring intently at the woman, who, though unremarkable in appearance, was by no means unpleasant. Someone from the far end of the shack responded approvingly after taking a measure of the besieged woman's attributes.

"There are men who would gladly take her, you know. She is a fine specimen of womanly attributes."

A chain-smoking man in an attire that betrayed his urban essence joined in to endorse the man's appreciation of the woman's personality.

"True. I have worked as a driver among refined families in the city and I say that she may have qualities that bear bringing out."

The unexpected praise of his wife took the young husband by surprise. He was half in doubt over his own evaluation of her qualities. However, he quickly returned to his harsh mood.

"If that is so, now is your chance."

Then in a resolute and determined manner and with a touch of cynicism, he added a vulgar sales pitch.

"I am open to an offer for this priceless treasure. The woman is no good to me but she will make a fine companion for one who has no ambitions in life. I guarantee fair value for a fair price, if you know what I mean."

He supplemented his last words with a wink of his eye as if underscoring an implication that he could not reveal in public. The young woman was by now in a grip of anxiety.

Turning to her husband, she implored him to desist from his folly, still restraining her tone to a prudent whisper.

"You have talked a lot of such like nonsense before and treated it as a joke. A joke is a joke but you are going too far this time."

Yuba stood up with a lurch, incensed at his wife's injudicious speech. He grabbed her by her hair and yanked her off the seat in a daring display of perversity. Jannat tried to free herself of his stranglehold but with a baby to hold on to, it was futile. Yuba continued with his contemptuous oration with undisguised rage, aimed now at Jannat but obviously meant to serve as further confirmation of his objective.

"I know I have said it before and I've always meant what I have said. You were never part of the family. You came as compensation and I am entitled to dispense with you as I wish. I have every right to sell you."

The assembled company neglected to respond to the offer, preferring to guzzle down even more of their country brew and dropped the subject for the moment. Seeing a lack of interest in the gathered company, the husband quietly took his seat again pulling his wife down with him. Then he went on consuming ever more heavily, though he was young and so strong-willed that he still kept up a reasonably steady appearance. However, he was relentless in his mischief and later picked up the topic again.

"Here I am waiting for an offer. The woman is no good to me. Who will have her?"

The company had degenerated completely by now and the renewed offer met with another appreciative laughter. The woman, imploring ever more fervently and anxious beyond endurance, whispered yet again.

"Come, come, it's getting dark. If you don't come along, I am leaving without you."

She waited a few anxious moments but the man did not respond. Instead, he repeated his query.

"Who will have her?"

The woman's manner changed. Her face grimaced and her fist tightened.

"Yuba, this is getting serious, too serious."

The husband paid no heed to her words and continued with his nonsensical harangue, now ignoring her entreaties completely. He pressed on with his offer, shouting almost fiercely.

"Is there no one here who will take this useless woman off my hands?"

Finally, the woman reacted and addressed the gathering, shouting fiercely for everyone to hear, loud and clear.

"I wish someone would release me from my miseries because my man is not to my liking either but he is not man enough to let me go honorably."

She then turned to her husband and addressed him most emphatically.

"Why don't you divorce me and be done with my presence in your life? No, you will not let go of me unless someone pays you a price for me. You pretend to be a man of honor but in reality, you are just a pimp. You aim to extract a price for my flesh."

Jannat's insinuation of an ignoble purpose took Yuba aback and his face flushed up with discomfiture. Nevertheless, he quickly regained his wits. He ignored the essence of her spiteful riposte and pounced on the more meaningful part, as if sensing an opportunity.

"So we are agreed upon that, gentlemen, you all just heard her. It is an agreement to part. Why, she may take the baby if she wants and go her way. I will settle for a modest sum of money as her price."

The crowd became boisterous as they awaited an eventful outcome. There was excitement in the air. Seeing the young woman's predicament, an elderly man tried to nudge the indolent company towards sanity. Alas, his lonely voice resounded aimlessly in the dissolute wilderness of the shack as the inebriated company chose to ignore him. Instead, everyone joined in the chorus with the now witless husband egging them on to crass action. The young woman seemed to resign to her fate as she bowed her head in absolute indifference, sobbing lightly. For all the prevailing depravity, no one in the gathering really expected the husband's exhortations to come to fruition. Yet, the puerile assembly engaged in the theater of the absurd was unaware of an ominous presence in their midst.

At some point during the proceedings, a man had slipped in virtually unnoticed and was sitting unobtrusively in a darkened corner of the shack. The man was clad in crisply laundered clothes in contrast to the soiled, stained and generally ragged attire of the regular patrons. A manicured stubble accented his face along with viciously long handlebar mustache. An abundant application of pomade kept every strand of his deep black shoulder-length hair in place. A shawl slung rakishly around his neck displayed a heavy gold chain through an opening, while a large gold ring and a flashy watch further adorned his person. A slight bulge at the hip would no doubt have revealed itself as a pistol on closer inspection. The man had sat watching the shenanigans of the inebriated company unobserved by the rest. Now for the first time during the course of the evening, he joined in the proceedings. He addressed the husband directly, in a tone that was at once taunting and designed to provoke. The crowd turned around to face him. The man was obviously a stranger in those parts and none of the regulars seemed to know who he was except, perhaps, Sheeda who notably stayed by his side during his purposeful reproach.

"I suppose it is none of my business but I have been listening to your diatribe all evening. If you were to treat your wife in this manner in the privacy of your home, no one would have the right to confront you as I do now but you are creating a public nuisance by inflicting such brutal indignity on the poor woman in public. You do not even care that she is the mother of your baby. If you were an honorable man, you would part with her honorably. You should divorce the woman lawfully and not engage in this vulgar public demonstration."

The show of such unnecessary audacity by a complete stranger startled Yuba. He stared long and hard at the man and it seemed for a moment that he was reaching for his omnipresent butcher's knife. Yuba's action provoked a reaction from both Sheeda and the man, as they too seemed to reach for their weapons. Yuba backed off, preferring to engage the man in a war of words instead.

"You say that I should divorce this woman and let her go her way?"

The stranger's personality and demeanor did not quite instill confidence in the righteousness of his vehement oratory though the clueless company could not have seen through it. None of those present could have understood his purpose as he continued almost casually.

"Yes, I do. That is the only decent thing to do if you cannot live with her. But I can tell that you are incapable of decency."

Yuba was uncharacteristically calm in the face of the provocation. He became thoughtful, contemplating with great care his next move. He looked at the man stupidly as he searched for a response.

"I think he is right. I want her out of my life and I think I will let this conscientious man do a worthy deed. My good man, are you willing to pay for her? One million and she is yours but let me tell you clearly that I will bear no responsibility for her future condition or that of the baby. And I will divorce her without further delay and all these fine folks shall bear witness to it."

Yuba had clearly quoted the figure randomly. He might have imagined it as the ultimate level of riches, one that he could not even envision in a dream. He did not really expect anyone to respond to what was by his own reckoning an outrageous demand and he certainly did not expect a counter-offer. In fact, he might have aimed his demand at warding off the stranger but the stranger had obviously come armed with a nefarious design.

"For three hundred thousand I can relieve you of your burden right this minute."

For a few seconds that seemed to last an eternity, the degenerate company descended into utter confusion. A mortal silence followed as Yuba tried to digest the man's response.

"You say you are willing to pay three hundred thousand?"

"Yes, I do."

Yuba stared at the stranger. He was half in doubt over the sincerity with which he had made the offer. He did not really know that Jannat was worth that much or else he might have transacted her a long time ago. Yuba was suddenly alert to a lucrative opportunity. He summoned his vilest bargaining skills to negotiate the sordid deal.

"Come, my good man, three hundred thousand will not even fetch three good buffalos. I will accept no less than one million. Take it or leave it."

The man walked towards Yuba, pulled out some currency notes tied in a bundle and threw them on the table. He then addressed Yuba in a harsh tone as if chiding him for the unnecessary sloth in carrying out the transaction that he had himself initiated.

"Five hundred thousand are all I have. Pick up the money and get on with the divorce or else just shut up and take the woman home, if you have a home, that is?"

The sight of the money seemed to take the spectators aback. An air of seriousness suddenly engulfed the proceedings and all eyes became riveted to the major actors in this surreal drama. Up until then, the spectators had assumed that despite his tantalizing declamation, Yuba was not in earnest. They had assumed that being out of work the man was frustrated and had vented his frustration on his wife. They were in no way prepared to see this mirthful action taken to the extreme.

Soon the jovial frivolity of the scene departed and a lurid color filled the air. Yet another silence descended upon the proceedings in anticipation of the outcome of the intense drama that was now unfolding before them. The sound of the woman's crackling voice finally broke the silence as it cut across the chill now enveloping the shack. She looked straight at her husband with a defiant look. Her normally low dry voice now reverberated around the shack as she addressed her husband in a manner of an ultimatum.

"Before you go any further, listen to me. If you so much as touch that money, the baby and I go with this man. It is not a joke anymore."

Yuba started shouting determinedly, as if resenting her suggestion.

"Of course it is not a joke. I take the money and the man takes you. That is plain enough. That is how it is done in these parts."

The elderly man in the midst of the loutish company interjected once again to caution the young man on the immensity of his decision, which he was rendering so casually.

"I wish you would give it another thought, son. This is not a decision you ought to be taking in your present state. She is clearly willing to stay by your side. You could at least wait until the morning so that you are in a better position to understand the implications of your action."

Yuba dismissed the elderly man's suggestion summarily.

"How dare you question my condition? I am as sober as a man can be."

The prospective buyer of the human cargo too had some concerns of his own and aired them artlessly, concerns that should have been a dead giveaway of the man's purpose.

"The woman must be willing. I will not take her if she does not cooperate. I don't want the police breathing down my neck."

"She is willing, provided she can have the child. She says so every day and even repeated it here earlier."

However, the stranger preferred to inquire from her directly, unwilling to rely on the husband's word.

"Is that correct?"

The woman paused for a moment. Then, glancing at her husband's face and finding no repentance there, she answered softly but defiantly, her defiance borne more of crude simplicity than measured conviction.

"Yes, that is correct."

"There you are. The bargain is complete. I will repeat the solemn words of the divorce and the deed shall be final."

Yuba took the money and pocketed it with an air of finality. He then proceeded to pronounce a verbal divorce, which is all it took to sever the relationship of man and wife. The baffled spectators served as mute witnesses. To all intent and purpose, the stranger owned Jannat from that moment on. He turned to her and addressed her abruptly, as if issuing an edict.

"Come along and bring the baby too. You are now my responsibility."

The woman deemed Yuba's shenanigans a binding arrangement and immediately reconciled with her new status. She at once concluded that she was now the chattel of the man who had paid for her. The prevalent customs and social mores reinforced her notions. In any case, the pronouncement of a divorce had sealed her fate. Jannat was no longer Yuba's wife. It did not matter to her that the husband was drunk to the point of being senseless and that under the circumstances she may not even have been validly divorced. One could hardly have blamed her though. She was of a peasant stock from the backwaters of society and barely literate, both decidedly less than conducive to erudition or to enlightened thinking.

Jannat looked at the man who had paid for her, picked up the baby and followed him as he made his way towards the door of the shack. On reaching the door, she turned around to face Yuba one last time. She pulled a base metal ring off her finger, flung it across the shack in the direction of her now ex-husband and addressed him for a final rejoinder.

"Yuba, I have lived with you the past year or so and I have borne the brunt of your foul temper with patience. You blamed my presence for your miseries. Now that you have plucked the thorn from your side, I do hope, for your sake, that you will overcome your present status in life. I am no longer your wife now. I too shall try my luck elsewhere. It has to be better for the baby and me."

So saying she stormed out of the shack sobbing bitterly, barely able to hold the baby. The man followed her, glancing at Sheeda on the way out, a cursory but meaningful glance.

Yuba rose and walked mockingly towards the entrance of the shack with the careful tread of one who is conscious of his inebriation. Others followed him, staring at the dark human shadows in stunned astonishment as the threesome vanished into the gloomy night. Not a single person amongst the degenerate lot tried to stop the bizarre drama with any vehemence. They simply froze in imbecilic inaction and allowed the crime to take place unchecked. The husband handed over his wife and child to a perfect stranger without concern for their welfare. Under different circumstances, the same man would have killed both his wife and any marginally suspected paramour at the slightest hint of impropriety between the two.

After a few moments of inexplicable taciturnity, the antecedents of the stranger provoked the curiosity of the onlookers. The stranger had arrived stealthily and unnoticed but walked away with a human cargo in plain view of all who cared to watch him.

"Who is that man? Where did he come from?"

"God only knows! Without a doubt, he is a stranger here. I did not like the look of that man. If you ask me, he is not a good man. Can anyone purchase a woman as if she were a farm animal, except for an evil purpose?"

"Poor woman, she did not deserve the treatment she got from her husband."

"She seemed like a perfectly respectable woman. What more could a man want. I marvel at the woman's naivety though. Her response to the situation was beyond explanation. She walked off with a perfect stranger in the middle of the night with a child in her arms, not knowing what lay ahead of her. It is so amazingly simple-minded."

The elderly man again addressed the husband, trying to goad him into action.

"You must go after her and bring her back."

The former husband of the wronged woman fumed at the man, resenting his uncalled-for advice.

"Mark my words; I will not go after her!"

He then returned doggedly to his seat and started flaunting his newfound wealth, ordering a round of the formidable brew for everyone present in the shack. In an amazing display of callousness, the degenerate company continued to relish their drinks. As the evening wore on, there was no further introspection of the event. It seemed as if nothing extraordinary had occurred in the premises at all. The customers soon started thinning away and Yuba too could no longer stay alert. He stretched his elbows forward on the table, placed his face on his forearms and began to snore. Sheeda Pistaul, who was in some ways the original source of the entire mischief and largely if not solely responsible for the grave wrong, was the only one left and seeing that it would be impossible to awaken the wrecked man, he left him alone in the shack. Yuba's loneliness was a metaphor for the moral abandonment of those who are ordained to eternal damnation.

CHAPTER 5

Yuba emerged from his languor as the morning sun was streaming through the crevices of the door and windows of the shack. His head was throbbing wildly. He tried to open his eyes but shut them again, unable to bear the gaze of the sunrays. He laid motionless for a moment before finally prying open his eyes. The backdrop terrified him; he could not figure out why he was not in his own bed and even wondered why Jannat was not at his side. An empty glass on the table caught his attention but he could not recall having made use of it. As he looked around the room, a shiny object on the floor met his gaze. He picked up the object and recognized it as the ring he had once given to his wife. A somewhat muddled picture of the previous night began to come back to him. He instinctively put his hand in his pocket and dragged out some currency notes. There was no need for any further verification of the misadventure of the previous night. Shorn of the alcohol-induced bluster, the enormity of his action suddenly descended upon him forcefully. Yuba seemed to freeze completely, as if struck by sudden paralysis, staring absently at nothing in particular.

Yuba had never really considered Jannat any more than an unnecessary appendage with which the clan had saddled him. The relationship between husband and wife was utterly devoid of love or respect. However, the baby was a different matter altogether, she was flesh and blood, kith and kin. Moreover, the question of honor never failed to spring up where girls were involved, even one who was barely 2 months old. He started fretting over the dishonorable fate that might befall his little girl away from his watchful eyes. The thought at once seized him with an urgency to undo the wrong. Yuba's stance was obviously contradictory. He had been so distant and indifferent to the baby that he would not have been able to recognize her without the mother. Besides, he had made the baby a part of the deal knowing very well even in his drunken state that he would not be able to look after her once his wife departed.

"Good Lord, what have I done? How did the devil possess me thus? She is gone, gone for sure and she has taken my baby with her. I must find her, I must. How will that stranger treat my baby? I cannot permit my baby in the hands of another man. It is a most dishonorable situation."

Yuba emerged from the shack onto the garbage-strewn lane and at once began the search for his wife and child. He headed towards the town, his mind totally engrossed with the events of the previous night. He was surprised and nettled that his wife had been such a simpleton and had taken him so literally. He found it convenient to put the blame of his predicament entirely on the woman as he mused angrily within himself.

"Why did she not try to stop me with any degree of vehemence? She knew I was not in my senses. She should have known better than to put me in this disgraceful situation. It was so like her to show such idiotic simplicity. That weakness of her character has done me more harm than the bitterest temper of mine could have."

It was beyond him to think reasonably with his self-centered certitude. He could not for a moment consider that he had, perhaps, driven her to a point of no return, that what he saw as idiotic simplicity was more on account of the mental torture he had continually inflicted upon her than that of deficient genes. Upon calm reflection, he concluded that there was no point in apportioning blame. He could not annul the foul deed by thoughtless reflections on its source and so he resolved to find his wife and little girl and put up with the shame. He may not have come around to admitting that the wretched situation he had landed in was of his own making but he knew that he would have to bear its consequences.

Yuba started by making inquiries around town, hoping to come by someone who might have seen the stranger and who might at least be able to identify him. However, the perplexing nature of his undertaking soon became apparent. Though he went through the length and breadth of town, he could find no clues whatsoever about the identity of the man, much less his whereabouts. The town was located on a highway and many strangers passed through it each day. The man too was obviously a stranger there. Yet the truth of the matter was that Yuba could not pursue his quarry too vigorously for fear that he would have to disclose the details of his conduct during his night of infamy. In his desperation, he sought out the elderly man who was at the shack with him during the incident, as he remembered his protestations over the matter. The elderly man led him to believe that the stranger had provoked him into action and that Sheeda

Muzaffar A. Isani

was somehow complicit in the matter. The elderly man's incrimination alerted him to the likelihood that the thug at least knew who the stranger was. Yuba had avoided Sheeda during his initial inquiries out of sheer embarrassment. Now that he had hit a dead end, he realized that a visit to the shack was his only hope of finding the man.

It was late in the morning as Yuba entered the shack. Fortunately, Sheeda was alone or else the presence of the regular company would have proved discomfiting. Sheeda greeted Yuba most decorously, as if welcoming a valued patron. He knew well that the man was loaded with cash.

"Oh! Come, come, my dear Yuba. You are a bit early, are you not? So when did you leave the premises last night? It must have been in the morning. But never mind, come and have a drink, the first one is on the house."

Sheeda did not refer to the shenanigans of the night before, pretending to be unconcerned or even worse, uncaring. In fact, he had every reason to stay off the subject though he did not really know the exact purpose of Yuba's untimely visit and so, he continued with his small talk. Yuba was not amused with Sheeda's small talk.

"Sheeda, I am not here for a drink. I think you know why I am here so early in the day. I want to know where I can find the stranger who took away my wife and child last night."

"I thought you carried out a voluntary transaction with the stranger last night. Why then are you looking for him? Did he short-change you?"

"Cut out that bullshit, Sheeda. You know that the man took advantage of my state. You must understand that I am desperate to undo the wrong. So just tell me who he is and where I can find him. I need to know right away."

"Why are you snapping at me, my friend? What did I do to deserve your hostility? It was entirely between you and the stranger. So where do I figure in your problem? In any case, I have no idea who the man was. Many strangers patronize my establishment and I could not possibly know them all. This is not exactly a respectable place, you know, and many of my patrons are unsavory characters but I cannot afford to discriminate. I run an illegal joint, remember. I had no idea that your action, advertent or inadvertent, has caused you such regrets. I must tell you that I am really sorry for your loss but I cannot help you."

Yuba could see through Sheeda's mock commiseration. He too was now convinced that Sheeda was somehow complicit in the affair and hurled grave accusations at him.

"Sheeda, I have inquired all over town about the man but no one seems to be able to identify him. No one has ever seen him in these parts before. He could not have just walked into the shack unless he knew you. Frankly, I suspect that you may have acted in concert with him to herd me into that madness, but right now the question of your complicity is unimportant. I just want my wife and child back. All I am asking of you is to lead me to the man and you are off the hook."

Sheeda was livid at the bald-faced accusation of impropriety by one who was still wet behind his ears. He at once gave up the pretense of detachment and reacted with the most violent diatribe.

"Wait a minute boy, I am not going to stand here and listen to your absurd notions. You are a dishonorable man. The manner in which you shamed your wife in front of strangers was sickening. You offered her to everyone as if she was a common whore and you her pimp. You pocketed the money that the stranger gave you for your wife and you divorced her publicly. He had every right to take her wherever he wished. I have told you that I have no idea who the man was. In any case, I do not have to address your concern. Now, let me give you one last word of advice. If you ever come back to my place again, I will wring your neck."

Yuba started trembling with rage at the harsh broadsides that Sheeda had directed at him, denying him even the thin veneer of respectability he might have enjoyed hitherto. He responded to Sheeda's diatribe with invectives delivered in the most stringent manner and with the choicest expression at his command. Sheeda was not about to take Yuba's insults lying down. He took out a pistol from the folds of his loose pantaloons and fired a shot. The bullet grazed Yuba's shoulder. Yuba lunged at Sheeda in a flash, throwing him off balance. Sheeda fired another shot but it went wide off the mark. Yuba grappled him to the ground and pinned him down in an instant. The pistol slipped out of Sheeda's hand and he lay helpless against the brute strength of the young man. Yuba whipped out a knife and held it to Sheeda's throat.

"I swear I will kill you this very instant if you do not tell me about the man."

The thug was reduced instantly to groveling and pleading for dear life when only a few moments earlier he was arrogant and irreverent. He cringed at the sight of the butcher's knife in the hands of the young man. Sheeda had no idea how adroit Yuba was with the knife and how vicious he could be when he fancied its use or else he might have groveled even more vehemently.

"I know nothing about your wife and child. I swear I am telling you the truth. I do not know the man except that he comes here occasionally from the big city. He drives a taxi and passes through town when he has passengers. I do not know of his antecedents; I swear to you. I would never commit such a scandalous outrage against a friend. We are practically friends. Take pity on me. I am a poor man. I am only trying to provide for my family. Please do not harm me. I am begging you."

Yuba's apprehension rose greatly on hearing that the stranger was a taxi driver. He was now convinced that the man had driven his wife and child away during the night. That, he surmised, was the reason why no one had seen him around. He stared menacingly into the eyes of a terrified Sheeda. It seemed he would slit his throat and he did press his knife hard on his jugular, leaving a bloody mark on his neck. He was convinced that Sheeda knew more than he had declared. Nevertheless, he loosened his grip while pushing the thug's head back to the ground. He then stood up, turned around and left abruptly. Sheeda caressed his neck with his hand and observed his blood stained fingers. He muttered something under his breath, got up and flapped the dirt off his clothes. The man stood thoroughly humiliated for the moment but lived to fight another day. Yuba had acted on an inexplicable instinct in releasing Sheeda, a move he could regret someday.

CHAPTER 6

Yuba knew that the story of his misadventure would eventually reach the folks in the village, not that it was likely to shock or disturb anyone. They would soon forget it as another incident of no consequence. Even so, he thought it might be unwise to go back just yet. Moreover, it was highly unlikely that his father would admit him into his home again, which was an added reason for him to stay away. More to the point though, he had all along planned to seek work beyond the confines of his village and so he decided to leave for the city without further ado. In this way, he could also carry out his search for Jannat and the child, if indeed the taxi driver had transported them there.

The bus that Yuba boarded foretold the imminence of painful partings for many of his fellow passengers, as the poorest left their homes in the countryside to journey on to the cities; some back to the drudgery of unfulfilling labor, others venturing out for the first time in search of work. Those who had no familiarity with the world beyond the one they were leaving could not have been without anxiety. Yuba too was leaving the familiar surroundings of his village for the trials and tribulations of the city for the first time. His situation in life--the poverty of his household and the unusual circumstances of his own making--was leading him away from the barrenness of the village towards the fecundity of the city, where a small contingent raised on privileges thrived on the miseries of the deprived multitudes. It is a law everywhere, in rich societies and in poor, that although the needs of all human beings are nearly equal, the affluent have disproportionately bigger desires. The provision of luxuries desired by the rich enable the less fortunate to earn their necessities. Yuba too wished to earn at least his necessities.

Yuba had embarked upon the journey with an equal measure of fear and anticipation. His fear was all too natural, the fear of the unknown, for he had no way of divining his future, no way of knowing what lay in wait for him, no way of telling how he would fare in life. However, it was anticipation that was the more damning emotion. He was ambitious enough to anticipate more than just necessities but a feeling of disquiet at the eventual outcome overshadowed that ambition. He could only hope for a well-disposed outcome but hope can be as evanescent as it can be inspirational. Yet the ways of the world are at times vividly incomprehensible. Fortune does occasionally smile on the wretched of the earth but only after wrenching the last thread of humanity from their spirit and even eviscerating the soul of its pith.

As soon as he arrived in the city, Yuba started a quixotic search for a needle in a haystack; a search for his wife and child in a city inhabited by millions. He never really entertained a realistic chance of succeeding. He knew nothing about the city and he knew nobody in it who could help him in his mission. The very largeness of the space that circumscribed the gargantuan human habitation overwhelmed him. During the course of his impossible undertaking, he encountered a great deal of hostility. A man of his status, so evident from his appearance, had no business roaming the mean streets, seeking relief. If he thought he was entitled to some sympathy because of his lacerated emotions, the attitude he encountered on the streets quickly disabused him of the notion. Naturally, therefore, here too his search yielded nothing. During his search, Yuba could seek no gainful employment and survived only on handouts or on occasional odd jobs. It soon became clear to him that he would have to seek work in earnest and so he would have to give up his quest for now, though in truth he would never entirely abandon it. He would continue the search for his wife and child for the rest of his life.

Yuba might have assuaged his guilt somewhat by pretending to continue with his search but he could not unburden himself entirely by such measures. He would have to subdue his conscience and contrive peace and quiet if he were to survive the emotional upheaval of his evil action and carry on with life. He would have to placate his mind by seeking divine intervention to guide him towards a just deliverance from his sins. That would at least soothe his remorse and allow him to function in an ordinary way.

Yuba was not a religious man in the conventional sense. Those who are untutored embrace religious beliefs only superficially, for one cannot acquire esoteric beliefs intuitively. Uneducated village folks put greater faith in the divine powers of dead saints whose opulent monuments evoke majesty more readily than the cryptic name of God. The city that Yuba found himself in was home to a saint who was known far and wide, known even to village folks, though those folks could never hope for a chance to be in attendance at his shrine in the ordinary course of their lives. Fortuitously, Yuba had just such an opportunity and so, as the light of day gave way to the haziness of dusk, he trudged wearily to the shrine of the saint even as the muezzin's call to the faithful reverberated in the air. There he sat for many an agonizing moment, contemplating, meditating and praying, all the while begging for forgiveness. Then, with the saint as his witness, he took an oath never to indulge in any intoxication for the rest of his life. There, with the saint as his witness, he also pledged solemnly to make amends of his actions and to recompense his wife and child in the best way he could, whenever, wherever, and in whatever condition he may find them. He sought the blessings of the saint to grant him the fortitude to carry out his solemn pledge and he sought the benedictions of the saint to accord him the strength to persevere through further impediments in life.

Yuba had no money to spare for food or for lodgings of any sort, for he had pledged on the call of his conscience at the very onset of his guilt, not to spend any more of his sinful gains. He stood in line for the handout of the curried rice that was always on offer at the shrine and then, having satisfied his hunger thus, he lay down on the pavement alongside vagrants and drug addicts, crestfallen and bone weary. As the darkness of night engulfed him in its embrace he finally fell asleep, obscuring the grim episode that had led him to this pass and hoping that the brightness of the rising morning would signal a new beginning to his life.

CHAPTER 7

Yuba woke up at daybreak and for the first time since he committed the disgraceful act, he started looking for work in right earnest. He found himself in a strange land. Never, in all his waking hours or even in his wildest dreams, had he imagined that he would hazard so far from home. He had heard of people who had ventured out in quest of a livelihood and had vanished in the squalor of the city. His brother Ibrahim, elder to him by a few years, had been lost to the family in just such a manner. Now an entirely improbable chain of events had planted him in the belly of the beast. Fate had enticed him to a destination where he could yet rue his monumental indiscretion.

Yuba wandered around the streets of the city almost in a daze. He was desperate for work but work was hard to come by. He would occasionally manage a stint as a casual laborer and on those days he earned enough to feed himself. On other days, he was a grateful guest at the shrine of the saint, fending off hunger with a handout. After many weeks or even months of demeaning privation, he managed to land a job at the municipal slaughterhouse on daily wages. He worked hard to make the most of the opportunity, returning after each workday to the pavements and parks for a much-deserved night's sleep. When the going was good, though, he sometimes indulged in the luxury of renting a bed in the open-air lodgings near the railway station. With the passage of time, his situation stabilized and he became far more comfortable, even managing to rent a small room that he could finally call a home.

The time that Yuba spent at the municipal slaughterhouse was most auspicious. He worked diligently and began to further hone his craft. Soon, his prospects started soaring like a rising moon, owing in no small measure to his own effort that was far in excess of normal human endurance. He progressed from butchering and skinning animals to dealing in hides and skins. He would facilitate leather-tanning companies in their purchases from the slaughterhouse and assist them in making the right selection. It was a natural progression for a man who, though largely unschooled, had plenty of native genius.

As soon as he freed himself from the straitjacket of consuming poverty, Yuba developed a burning ambition to ameliorate his lowly existence. He soon started trading in hides and skins on his own account. He would buy small quantities on credit both from the slaughterhouse and from itinerant dealers from beyond the country's borders and supply the same to tanneries, attaining an appreciable volume of trade in this manner in a short period. His success was even more remarkable because he was apparently straightforward and honest in a milieu where deceit and duplicity, dishonesty and fraud were commonplace. Even so, he was never naive enough to assume that luck was just another name for hard work. The values and ethics he brought to his business dealings were the values and ethics of the underclass in society, no more, no less. Life was all about survival and survival was only for the fittest. He gave no quarter and expected none. Even his innate notions of honor could not prevent him from using his native cunning, which in his system of values simply passed for clever tactics not chicanery. He learnt where, when, and how to use the wicked ways of the world to his advantage without actually perpetrating an iniquity. However, his biggest assets were his firm grasp of the fundamentals of his trade and his business instincts. He had acquired a knowledge of skins and hides that was as thorough as any man could boast of and he had an uncanny feel for the timing of sales and purchases.

Then, only a few years since the day he arrived in the city as an indigent living off charity, he hit a jackpot. The country was celebrating the festival of sacrifice during which the faithful slaughtered millions of goat, sheep and cow. As a result, a large number of hides and skins flooded the market in the aftermath of the festival. That year, the market was in a decidedly downward spiral. The country was suffering from a severe security backlash and foreign buyers of leather and leather products were reluctant to enter into new contracts. It landed a big blow to the leather industry that depended largely on exports, curtailing manufacturing activities tellingly. As a result, tanning companies and investors alike abstained from major purchases. The prices of hides and skins crashed spectacularly. In the midst of the disturbed market conditions, Yuba took a supreme gamble. He started buying even as prices continued to dip. He gambled not just on his own hard-earned money but also bought an inordinate quantity of the material on credit from sellers who were eager to offload alarmingly high levels of accumulated inventories. Yuba was relentless in the pursuit of his ambition and unmindful of the consequences of his extreme behavior.

Yuba's heedlessness paid off magnificently. Over the next few months, Providence conspired with him to hand him a bonanza. Prognosis of a severely cold winter in Europe forced foreign buyers to re-enter the market, filling the order books of the manufacturers and exporters of leather and leather made-ups to the brim. Prices of hides and skins began a steep ascent, soon reaching a level that the trade had not seen in many years past. Yuba was holding large stocks of the material at that opportune moment. In yet another uncanny display of brinkmanship, he bided his time to extract even more. He raked in tremendous profits in the bargain. More importantly, it enhanced his status within the trade and boosted his credibility. Henceforth, the power brokers of the leather trade would reckon Yuba as a force. Yuba the butcher had arrived on the big stage with a bang.

CHAPTER 8

Yuba was soon worth a small fortune; an eventuality he had foretold in his youthful arrogant boast. In the process, he built up a leather business that was an envy of the entire trade and a magnet for foreign buyers. Yet he would not rest on his laurels. He continued with his punishing routine, brooking no distraction from his work, not even taking the time out to enjoy his newfound wealth. He could have led an indulgent, or even a decadent life, as many newly enriched are wont to do, yet he stayed away from such temptations. He just would not squander time or money on frivolous pursuits.

His pre-occupation with his work was, in part at least, an effort to obliterate the memory of his inglorious past. There was no other way of accounting for his addiction to work and his acquisitive instincts. Few in society knew that an enormous weight of guilt hung around his neck like an albatross. He could neither live life to its fullest nor wither away in his shame. He was virtually consigned to the ranks of the living dead. The mystery of his past would soon become an enduring myth of his persona.

Yuba's rags-to-riches story may have read like a fairy tale but he had surmounted monumental adversities in life to author it. In the process, Yuba Kasai underwent a metamorphosis. He became Ayub Qureshi. Ayub, of course, was his given name all along whence Yuba emerged in deference to the rural tradition and custom of never articulating a proper name fully. Qureshi simply signified a common social transmutation from the countrified kasai or butcher. The transmutation was common to all lowly trades. Those who had made it in the world sought social status by casting aside the derogatory sobriquet associated with their trade.

Ayub's wealth did bring with it significant creature comforts as one could well imagine and even his frugal inclinations failed to restrain him from putting up a stately façade. A mansion in the most desirable quarter of the city and costly furnishings were now essential accessories of his lifestyle, as were the many expensive cars. One could suppose that the mild ostentation of his style of living was an obligatory allowance to his newly acquired status and, in some ways, an investment in business. It contrasted with the simplicity of his personal life and his adherence to tradition, both of which were remarkable in one who had suffered such thorough deprivation in his youth. In many other ways too, Ayub was different from those whose riches were of a similarly recent vintage. Not many of his ilk comported themselves with such dignity as Ayub did and not many abhorred flaunting their riches as he did. Yet he did spend copiously on his friends and was generous to those he perceived as needy. In particular, he spent liberally to feed the poor and the hungry and to provide shelter for the destitute and the homeless.

Material success also conferred on him an exalted status and prominence in his trade and in society. In time, Ayub became the unquestioned leader of his trade organization and its members elected him as its head twice over the years. In an ultimate accolade to his success, the business community at large chose him to head the country's chamber of commerce, recognizing his influence beyond his own trade. His stint at the head of the chamber brought him into closer liaison with the political power brokers and he soon made his way into the corridors of power. He had no compunction, nor did he see anything wrong, in spending money to acquire a seat in the upper house of the country's parliament. Ayub was not the only one to use the back door. In fact, the door was wide open to all comers who cared to bid. The money spent on such ventures was money well spent, as a business proposition, of course. Indeed, the very basis of big business in the country was the opportunistic conjoining of politics and business and it never failed to ensure lucrative returns. Ayub too was full of ambition and wanted a piece of the action.

CHAPTER 9

Coincidently, Ayub's wronged wife Jannat had also come to acquire a dwelling in the same city; a coincidence contrived, perhaps, by the same force that had guided her to the shack that fateful evening. In fact, even though Ayub had failed in his effort to locate her, she had probably been in his proximity since the day of the incident. The small flat she lived in was located in a middle-class neighborhood, far removed from the resplendence of Ayub's newly embraced world. The décor of the flat, if one could even refer to it as décor, clearly betrayed the tenants' gender, for the only other occupant of the flat was Jannat's now grown-up daughter, Noor.

Though still short of her fortieth birthday, Jannat came across as a middle-aged woman, pale, weak and slightly wrinkled. Her face carried a certain sadness that seemed deeply embedded in her psyche. Jannat's life had been a constant struggle to keep a roof over her little girl, to feed her and clothe her and to afford her a measure of dignity.

Never one of strong constitution, she had grown frail to the point of constant ill health. Her face, once demure though never handsome, was now marked with creases, caused not by age but by constant anxiety. She nevertheless displayed the same serenity that was so clearly the hallmark of the unfortunate woman twenty or so years earlier.

The circumstances of Jannat's life were neither simple nor straightforward and certainly not of such peace and quiet as Ayub had devised for himself. The incident of her separation from him had caused a grave harm to her, landing her in a most disagreeable situation. That part of her life though had always been off limits to others. Jannat had borne her burden with dignity and she had no desire to expose her misfortune to ridicule, or even worse, to insulting innuendos. In time, she did experience a fortunate break though. Happenstance steered her into another episode of marriage, just as happenstance had led her into a marriage with Yuba the butcher. Fortuitously, she had met and married an older man of adequate means. Her years as a wife in her second coming were about as much as she could ever have asked of providence. She could never trivialize the consequences she had to suffer because of the appalling manner of her separation from her husband but the serendipity of her subsequent good fortune seemed, at least on the surface, to make up for it. Her new husband provided Jannat with security that she so desperately yearned for and a level of comfort that she had never known in life. It gave her great pleasure to see her little girl grow in circumstances she could never have imagined.

Noor cherished her father and was constantly by his side. He too in turn showered her with love and affection unhesitatingly and provided her with everything that a girl of her environment could ask for, perhaps more. She started school at the normal age, a prospect that might have been unimaginable given her mother's circumstances, breeding, and acquirement. In fact, she soon began excelling at her studies and might even have gone on to college and university when the unthinkable happened. Her father died suddenly, leaving Noor, then barely 15 years of age, devastated.

Jannat had become accustomed to the vagaries of her existence and took the death of her husband in her stride. The sadness of the loss, never particularly poignant for one who had grown incapable of loving a man, soon abated and even his memory began to fade. In many ways, the fading memory of her husband also contributed to the fading of the memory of her ignominious past that continued to torture her weak conscience. In any case, she thought less and less of her husband as she became more engrossed in raising Noor.

The death of her husband had left Jannat once again in financial straits, rough waters that she had to negotiate without visible support. For the most part, she relied on the savings she had accumulated during her marriage, a feat that required considerable dexterity and entailed great personal deprivation. The fact that she owned the flat that was now in her occupation no doubt mitigated her situation greatly. She was more grateful to her husband for that single source of security than for the numerous other contributions to her life. Her thoughts, however, were never far from the harrowing prospects of the day when she would use up her meager resources. She knew she would have to do something to supplement her savings. Without education or experience of work in her past, she was in no doubt about the bleak prospects that awaited her.

Jannat's vigil over her daughter was a lonely one, fraught with anxiety. The vision of Noor growing up in the shadow of her penury heightened her concern. If the prospect of an unlettered woman earning a living was daunting, the very notion of a single woman with a grown-up daughter, living alone without adequate means, was positively frightening. However, Jannat had faced far greater adversities in life and the challenges that confronted her now did not daunt her at all. She was from the peasant stock and had the tenacity and native cunning that nature had so liberally endowed the peasantry. The original ground for Yuba's contempt for Jannat was her supposed simplicity but he had never really had the opportunity to fathom the depths of her inordinately alert native senses. She was never as simple as Yuba had supposed her to be. Moreover, the hurts and injuries she had suffered in life had imparted to her the skills to survive the harshness of a harsh world. Jannat somehow managed to see Noor through to her eighteenth birthday, as she completed her twelfth year of school. Through it all, she maintained the bearing of a respectable widow.

Noor, now nearing 20 years of age or thereabout, had developed into womanhood early. Her face, though somewhat incomplete in its maturity, possessed the makings of a handsome woman. Sadly, the burdens of her strained circumstances had robbed her of youthful exuberance. She was a pale, almost self-effacing presence, yet blessed with an unrestrained radiance of spirit. The sight of the girl made the mother sad. She had seen how the young woman had striven to better herself. Unlike other girls in similar straits, the daughter had a desire, though quite repressed, to acquire a better station in life. Jannat groaned as she realized she could not assist her daughter in her pursuit. Their situation demanded that Noor abandon further schooling for the mundane task of earning a living, and so she went out into the world to seek work as she turned 18 years of age. For the present, she had to be content with a job at a local hotel apprenticing in event management and doubling as a guest relations person, much to the consternation of the mother who tended to look at the job as somewhat undignified. She thought it exposed Noor to lecherous advances. Nevertheless, the job did provide the young woman with the opportunity to meet and mingle with a certain class of people. The cream of local society frequented the hotel and many foreign executives too stayed there during their visits to the country. The job provided her with an opportunity to learn the ways of the genteel society. In any case, with Noor now bringing in a regular paycheck, mother and daughter were at least assured of a minimally adequate living. Thereafter, Jannat's life became more tranquil.

CHAPTER 10

Ayub's working day invariably started at the tannery where he spent a couple of hours before repairing to his office in the business district of the city. This day too he left home for the tannery as usual but there was a distinct change in his demeanor. During the drive through familiar streets, he looked visibly perturbed. His face, which expressed his inner most feelings at the slightest provocation, bore a decidedly disturbed look. This time too, the expression on his face was not without provocation.

Production at the tannery was in the throes of a serious problem that was causing grave losses for the business. Hides and skins were normally prone to attacks by certain types of viruses while being processed into leather but the virus was always and quickly subdued, causing little or no loss to the material. Now, a pervasive strain of virus had entered the production process, the like of which the tannery had never encountered before. The production staff had been battling this mysterious contagion but for all their collective expertise, they could not understand the nature of the virus. They watched helplessly as the virus destroyed hides and skins worth millions until finally the company had to shut down production altogether till a solution could be found. The unnerving problem disturbed the schedule of exports and, predictably, importers started calling to cancel pending and future orders. It caused Ayub great consternation. He was particularly incensed at the factory manager who might have saved the day if he had addressed the issue at the onset.

Alam Mirza had been by Ayub's side for better than 15 years and had seen him through thick and thin during his ascent. He had done well by his boss in the past but the present problem was beyond his capacity though he would not admit it. He had never had formal training in leather technology and had learnt his craft on the factory floor. However, his haughtiness was such that he would acknowledge no one to be of superior knowledge to him when it came to the tanning process. He allowed no one to interfere in his domain, not even Ayub. Alam Mirza's attitude was beginning to exasperate Ayub.

As soon as Ayub reached the tannery, he made his way straight to the production hall. Alam Mirza had yet to arrive even though it was long past the start of the work day. Ayub huddled with senior technicians in Alam Mirza's absence to discuss the problem with them instead but none of them could come up with a convincing idea. Alam Mirza arrived in the midst of this exercise, to the undisguised annoyance of Ayub. The piercing gaze of Ayub's dark eyes greeted his arrival. Ayub addressed Alam Mirza rather sarcastically.

"So you found it convenient to finally come to work. Thank you very much."

Alam Mirza started muttering some excuses but Ayub was in no mood for mindless inanities. Alam Mirza was making light of a serious problem, failing even to give it adequate time when he should have been attending to it day and night. Ayub started hurling abuses at him in front of the staff present there. Alam Mirza reminded his boss of the past, which saw him go from rags to riches, and his, Alam Mirza's contribution to that success. Alam Mirza requested him not to use such harsh language, especially in front of the staff. Ayub perceived a taunt in the manner in which Alam Mirza addressed him and it produced an uncharacteristic reaction from him. He flew into a volcanic rage the like of which his employees had never witnessed before. Ayub had managed to suppress his rage, and indeed many of his more offensive character traits, during his steady ascent. Some of those traits were now beginning to surface at the first sign of a strain, giving a rare glimpse of his true nature. Then, in a moment of extreme impetuosity, he dismissed Alam Mirza from his employment rather unceremoniously. Alam Mirza had been an important cog in Ayub's establishment for the better part of its existence. His departure at this crucial juncture was ill-advised, notwithstanding his lack of success with the present problem.

Ayub left the factory for his city office immediately after his disconcerting encounter. As he settled down in his chair, he regained his composure and the agitated expression on his face slowly gave way to a calm and composed demeanor. Indeed, a look of smug satisfaction appeared on his face. He immediately issued formal orders to his staff for the termination of Alam Mirza's services. The sacking of Alam Mirza naturally did not provide a solution to his immediate problem. Ayub had killed the messenger but the message lived on. He, therefore, got down to the serious business of consulting his senior office staff to address the company's production woes and to find a replacement for his factory manager.

CHAPTER 11

The problem at the tannery and the firing of Alam Mirza coincided with the annual exhibition of leather and leather products organized by the representative body of the leather trade. As chair of the body Ayub could not naturally absent himself and so, despite his business distractions he made himself available at the local hotel that was the venue of the exhibition. It was an important event in the business calendar of the city, readily graced by the very highest-ranking political personalities, often featuring the country's prime minister or the president. All major and minor companies in the trade participated in the annual event to display their products before the large number of local and foreign buyers who attended. One of the larger stalls in the hall was that of Ayub's company, as usual.

The three-day exhibition ended after the formalities of the closing ceremony. After seeing off the chief guest, Ayub sat down in the hotel lobby, greeting visitors and fellow exporters alike. His principal foreign agent who was in town for the exhibition soon joined him. Before long, the two were engaged in deep conversation, having dispensed with the rest. The agent had been instrumental in the expansion of Ayub's exports overseas during their long association and had in turn profited from it. The state of Ayub's business had begun to put a strain on their relationship and he wanted to get out of his binding contract. Ayub argued vehemently that his problems were temporary and that he would surmount them soon but the conversation between the two ended abruptly on what seemed like an inconclusive note. The agent got up to leave. Ayub stood up, shook hands with the man and sat down again, engrossed in his thoughts. The events of the last few days had weighed heavily on him. The firing of Alam Mirza, his long-time manager, had only accentuated his attention on the losses that he continued to incur. Now the agent on whom he had relied for so long for procuring overseas business seemed to be turning his back on him. Alam Mirza and his main foreign agent had together taken Ayub to great heights and their simultaneous departure was ominous.

Ayub was so deeply engrossed in his thoughts that he was oblivious of a young man, 30 years of age or thereabouts, trying to seek his attention. Ayub was a reserved person and not easily accessible to strangers. If the young man had known Ayub's nature, he may not have taken the liberty of approaching him at all.

"I beg your pardon, sir, could I have a minute of your time."

"Why? Do I know you?"

"No, sir, you don't. I too have never laid eyes on you before but I know you well by your great reputation. You are Mr. Ayub Qureishi, are you not?"

"Yes, I am. But how do you know me?"

"Honestly sir, any person connected with the leather trade, as I am, has heard of Ayub Qureishi."

"Is that so?"

The young man's generous remarks obviously elated Ayub and broke the ice somewhat. Even so, the reticent older man would not lower his guard completely. He took a measure of the young man who was clad in a suit and tie. He seemed educated and urbane, a marked contrast to the older man. The two entered into further conversation, with Ayub seeking to discover the young man's background in the first instance.

"Well, who are you, and what is your purpose in approaching me?"

The young man introduced himself as Shahzaib. He informed Ayub that he had come to town to attend the exhibition on behalf of his employer and that he was a leather technician. Having introduced himself thus, he went on to state his purpose in the same breath.

"I must apologize for eavesdropping on you but I was seated so close to you that I couldn't help listening to the conversation between you and your companion. I understand very well the problem you were discussing. We encountered a similar problem at our tannery some time ago. I think I have a possible solution and wouldn't mind sharing it with you."

Ayub was highly skeptical of the motives of the young man for approaching him in such a brazen manner for a purpose that, to his mind at least, seemed to reek of dubious sincerity. Ayub's first reaction to any gratuitous offer was always one of skepticism. He hesitated for a moment but then invited the young man to have a seat. There ensued a long discussion between the two. By the end of the discourse, the young man had clearly impressed Ayub not only with his knowledge of the tanning process but also with the intricacies of the leather trade.

"I am impressed by your knowledge. If what you say holds true, I could avoid losses amounting to millions. But why do you favor me with such valuable know-how?"

"I have heard of your reputation in the leather trade. You, sir, are a living legend for all those who aspire to succeed, not just in the trade but also in life in general. It is an honor simply to be in your presence."

Shahzaib spoke those words with evident sincerity. He obviously admired Ayub Qureishi, the legend but it was not within Ayub's cynical endowment to understand such impulses. He had lost his innocence a long time ago and would not now be stimulated by sentiments that had become alien to his nature.

"But surely you must have a motive, a reason, an aim, an intention. Why would you dispense with your capital unrequited?"

"You seem to be in some difficulty and the process I have suggested is not within the grasp of our barely educated technicians. I merely wished to share my knowledge with you, as indeed I would with any other person who was facing a similar problem. I doubt if you have qualified professionals to put my suggestions to any use but if you have even one, I can assure you that it can be of considerable help in alleviating your problem."

"You are right. No one in my establishment has the skills to carry out the process. Perhaps, you can demonstrate it at my tannery. I have a fine laboratory for just such a purpose, one that I can rightly be proud of, though I dare say we hardly ever put it to good use. I can compensate you for your time and expertise."

"I would gladly do that tomorrow, as I will be in town for the day with nothing to do. I must tell you though that I am not seeking any compensation from you, sir, and I most emphatically will accept none. Your tannery is the finest in the entire country and I quite relish the thought of visiting it. That is compensation enough for me."

"Agreed, I shall send a car for you tomorrow. It will be at the hotel at nine in the morning."

Just as the two men were gearing to leave, the hotel manager accompanied by a young woman guest relations officer appeared at the scene and introduced himself and the young woman to Ayub. The two seemed to take no particular note of the younger man. The manager sought Ayub's comments on the hotel's arrangement for the event and was relieved at the expression of satisfaction. The manager requested Ayub for permission to take a group photo, a practice quite common in upscale hotels. Ayub readily consented and the foursome posed for the picture. Ayub and the hotel manager stood with each other in the center while the young man and woman occupied the flanks.

Chapter 12

Noor returned from work late that day, to the usual uneasiness of her mother. Though visibly exhausted, she could barely mask her excitement. Conducting the expo at the hotel had been an experience she would not soon forget. She was at no loss for words as she apprised her mother about her day's work in animated tones. Noor fished out some photos of the event from her handbag and virtually thrust them in her mother's face, imploring her or even daring her to take note of her accomplishment. Jannat looked at the photos with a detached air as Noor identified each individual with his name. It was apparent that they were not of much interest to her but, as the images flashed past her vision one of the photographs seemed to catch her attention. It was the one in which Noor had posed with Ayub Qureishi along with the hotel manager and the unknown young man. She looked more attentively at it, narrowing her focus now to Ayub Qureishi's face. It was as if she was jogging her memory, trying to recognize the man. She asked her daughter to repeat his name.

"Ayub, Ayub Qureishi. He is a wealthy industrialist."

Jannat would have dismissed the matter at that but for the fact that Noor continued to dilate unnecessarily on the virtues of the man, expressing her acclaim for the object of her immediate attention with obvious admiration.

"He is said to have come to the city from some backward village, not far from here, and started life as a lowly butcher. I, for one, cannot help admiring him. To rise from such humble beginnings and make it to the top is nothing short of a miracle in our society. We may not have a formal caste system but our society is no less hidebound. A victory in the face of such ingrained adversity must arouse a deep sense of admiration."

Noor's long-winded recitation of the man's background— the name, the caste, the fact that he was from a nearby village—prompted greater curiosity in Jannat for the man. After all, she too had had an association with a butcher once, a butcher named Yuba whose given name was, in fact, Ayub and she too had originated from a nearby village. The photograph merited more reflection. Jannat took possession of the photos from her daughter as Noor walked away casually, having unwittingly evoked her mother's interest in the man. She could never have guessed the nature of her mother's curiosity.

Jannat sat down on the edge of the bed, took out the photograph of her interest from the pack and started scrutinizing it. She was obviously seeking signs that would identify the man in the picture as Yuba. She could make out a faint resemblance to him though she could not be sure. Nevertheless, the face did create enough doubt in her mind for her to persist with the visual inspection. At long last, Jannat saw enough tell-tale signs in the image of Ayub Qureishi to convince her that the man was indeed the same that had visited upon her the grave indignity, the man who had sold her and then divorced her in such a shameful manner in public. The reprehensible event of her life had engraved Yuba's face in her memory so that even the thick beard and the deep creases could not disguise him sufficiently. Jannat had no doubt that she had stumbled upon her past.

Jannat deliberated over the implication of her discovery. Confused thoughts crossed her mind, creating a whirlwind of bewilderment. She had never imagined on the day of her separation that she would ever set her eyes on Yuba again but she had never been able to completely erase his memory and that of the disgraceful act he had perpetrated, an act that had caused her such immense suffering. Up until that point, Jannat had no way of knowing where Yuba had drifted to after separating from her. Nor did she have any idea of how he might have gone on to fare in life. Now her daughter's narration had alerted her to his good fortune. She was naturally curious to find out more about him, though the fear of resurrecting the demons of her past dampened her interest somewhat. Surely, she thought, she would be embarking on a fool's errand if she were to dig deeper. Jannat was never one to take up unwarranted challenges. Her instincts would have her ignore her latest incitement without further incident and to continue with her life as she had been living hitherto. Besides, if Yuba had really become rich and powerful, it might be imprudent to accost him with a reminder of his past, a past that he had more than likely erased from his memory. Deep down, however, she had long nourished a desire to confront Yuba, to ask him why he had heaped such grave injustice on her even though she had been willing to live life with him in any manner he pleased. She suddenly felt stimulated by an improbable inclination to uncover the truth about Ayub Qureishi, at least to ascertain whether the wealthy industrialist was indeed Yuba the butcher. Therefore, she set about inquiring after the man, without a hint to her daughter. At that point, she was perhaps acting only out of curiosity.

CHAPTER 13

The morning after the encounter at the hotel a chauffeured car drove Shahzaib to Ayub's tannery and he immediately went to work in the laboratory. Ayub joined him later. The results produced in the laboratory seemed to vindicate the young man's insight into the problem afflicting the tannery. He later replicated the experimental procedure in the actual production process and the results were quite astonishing. Ayub's own technicians had been working on the problem for months, without success and at great financial cost. The young man had come up with a solution in a matter of a few hours.

His job done, Shahzaib asked for Ayub's leave. As he entered the car, Ayub slid next to him and the two drove off together. During the course of the day, Ayub had observed Shahzaib's way of working keenly. He had also tried to size him up as a person. On both counts, Ayub was convinced that no amount of inducement would be too great to entice Shahzaib to work at his tannery. Indeed, true to his impulsive nature, he became excited at the prospect of having the young man by his side and he wasted no time in bringing up the subject. He clasped Shahzaib's hand in his own, squeezing it off and on in a gesture suggesting an ardent resolve and made a brusque offer of employment.

"I have of late been looking for a factory manager and you are just the person I need under the present circumstances. It might seem untimely but I would like you to join me. Will you?"

The unexpected offer of employment took Shahzaib by surprise. He seemed to muse silently for a while, feeling somewhat suffocated by the constricted clasp of Ayub's hand. He then responded, slowly but purposefully.

"I am grateful for your gracious offer but I must decline it respectfully. I have a generous employer who has looked after me well for many years. I cannot now turn my back on him."

"I can no doubt find another manager but I have somehow begun to like you personally. I tend to remain distant from people but when a man takes my fancy, he takes it strong. You can name your terms and I will agree to them without a word. There it is, plain and simple. Will you at least consider my offer and let me know later."

"Let me be honest with you. It is not that I cannot leave my present job though I must say that I would not necessarily do so for the sake of more money. I hope I do not come across as rude or arrogant but I have a vision for the future, an ambition. I hope to start my own business, sooner rather than later. There is, therefore, no point in moving to another job at this time."

"I will not belittle your vision for the future. I too dared to dream and in the end succeeded far beyond my dream. I have no doubt that you will one day realize your vision. But for the present at least you can join me and if you should be disappointed in any way, we shall agree to part, amicably no doubt."

The young man's hand remained in Ayub's tightened grip as the car drove on to its destination. Shadows of darkness had now begun to descend on their faces but the bright lights flashing off and on revealed a palpable anxiety across those faces. Shahzaib sighed inexplicably as he started a sentimental monologue that did not really address Ayub's pleading.

"It is a great irony of fate that I should be embarrassed by such richness of opportunity. My father spent a lifetime in the same vocation and tried to rise above his menial status by working day and night but to no avail. Disillusioned and bitter, he soon started drifting from job to job and from city to city with extremely painful interludes of joblessness in between. Father's situation was at times desperate and led him to neglect his family in his despondence. With the passage of time, he abandoned my mother and me altogether."

The thought filled Shahzaib with raw emotions that threatened to burst out. He managed to suppress his feelings at once. However, the expression on his face continued to betray an intense bitterness. There was no doubt that he held his father in deep contempt. Ayub remained silent as Shahzaib gathered his composure and continued. He was calm and even reverential, as he now spoke of his mother.

"My mother, God bless her, was never one to wallow in self-pity. She took up the responsibility of raising me entirely on her own. She had a dream for my future and she struggled incessantly to realize it. She cooked, cleaned and did all kind of menial tasks so that she could put me through school, college and then professional training, never once wavering in her resolve nor ever shirking from her backbreaking routine. I will not lose sight of the purpose for which my mother put herself through such suffering. I have formed a vision of my future far exceeding that of my mother's modest expectation."

Ayub listened with rapt attention to the rhapsodic oration of the young man and felt a strange emotion of his own. He too had started life thoroughly deprived but no one had ever offered him a prop. Though the young man's circumstances were different from his own, he saw in him the same resolve that he himself had nurtured at the depth of his desperation. Oddly, Ayub also saw in the young man a vague resemblance to his older brother Ibrahim, or so he thought. His brother too skinned animals and was equally accomplished in the craft of preserving hides. He too had gone to the city to seek work, perhaps even in a tannery such as his own. Sadly, no one had heard from him or of him since. He turned to Shahzaib and reciprocated in the same impassioned manner that Shahzaib had demonstrated.

"You are a stranger and yet you look familiar. Your forehead is something like that of my poor brother Ibrahim and your nose too is like his. You know, my brother left to escape the bleakness of the village while he was barely in his teens and we never heard from him or even of him again. But never mind, I guess I am simply seeking a bond where none exists."

Ayub paused and took a deep breath. He was lost in a reverie for a moment or two, as if pondering over a painful episode of a distant past. He soon shook himself out of his trance, though he could not let go of his disturbing thoughts, and bared his soul before the young man.

"I have never felt so deeply emotional about one I know so little about and I cannot really explain my emotions cogently. I too have suffered in life but I had no one to comfort me. I have known the pains of hunger and the anguish of deprivation. I have even suffered the degradation of my soul. Yet, I soldiered on with only a dream by my side. I will never stand in the way of your vision. Indeed, I will assist you in realizing the expectations that your mother has for your future. So please join me."

It was a strange plea, quite inexplicable for one who was nothing if not pragmatic in the affairs of business. There was in it a profound commitment for the young man's future, a man who was yet practically a stranger. Ayub had suddenly let his guard down completely and in the process, he had placed the young man too in a most vulnerable state. Shahzaib did not know what to make of the man or the improbable state of mind in which he had placed him. It was almost as if Ayub was goading him into accepting his proposition and he did respond accordingly.

"I never expected this, I did not. Providence has brought me to this pass and Providence beckons me to stay. Should anyone go against Providence? No! I will turn my back on my old job and, at least for now, I will withhold my vision of the future. I will join you and be your man. The terms of my association are for you to determine."

"Then it is done?"

"Yes, it is done. I will join you as soon as I am able to take leave of my job. I must ensure that my parting does not cause my employer any inconvenience. There must not be any hard feelings on that count."

Ayub's face beamed with satisfaction that was almost fierce in its strength as he exclaimed excitedly.

"Now you are my friend!"

CHAPTER 14

Shahzaib returned a few days later and joined Ayub's establishment. He took over the running of the factory and immediately applied himself to the problem because of which he was hired in the first place. He soon succeeded in streamlining the manufacturing process, restoring production to its normal level again. In due course Shahzaib ensured completion of all pending orders, minimizing the delays to an acceptable level. New orders too started pouring in. The tannery was now buzzing with activity, a happy situation not seen in those premises for many months before the arrival of the young man. Ayub naturally took a great deal of satisfaction over his decision to persuade Shahzaib to join him.

With the passage of time, Ayub came to trust the young man to a point where he delegated many of his own responsibilities to him. Before long, Shahzaib had virtually taken over the general management of the company and was conducting all normal day-to-day business operations--dealing with customers, exporting finished goods, importing raw material, dealing with the human resources. In fact, he managed all aspects of the business except the company's accounts, which remained the sole preserve of Ayub. The job was quite a handful for anyone but Shahzaib proved equal to the task, carrying on quite cheerfully. He even managed to convince the buying agents abroad of the new potency of the business and was instrumental in luring some of them back into the fold. Ayub seldom questioned Shahzaib's business decisions. Indeed, Shahzaib gave him no reason to do so. He worked diligently and was honest almost to a fault, if one were to see it in the context of the values of a society that saw honesty as a fault. Ayub freed himself from the day-to-day operations of the company and concentrated on the larger picture, setting a strategic direction and overseeing its implementation. Oftentimes, though, Shahzaib was wont to diverge from the policy parameters set by Ayub but such was Ayub's growing reliance on Shahzaib that he would just as often tend to ignore such incidents, at least until his enthusiasm for the young man lasted.

In due course, Shahzaib was re-designated as the general manager. His expanded responsibilities required that he move to the main office in the city though he continued to manage the factory as well. The move brought Shahzaib in even closer proximity to Ayub, not just in his official capacity but also as his friend and confidante.

CHAPTER 15

Jannat's enquiries into the antecedents of the man confirmed beyond any doubt that Ayub Qureishi was indeed Yuba, her errant former husband. She discovered too that he was living alone; never having married since the questionable manner in which he had dealt with her. Moreover, he apparently led a lonely life, deprived of love or affection or even comforting company. Although no one could dilate on his personal life with any authority, she did come by enough information to surmise that he harbored a deep sense of remorse at some event in his life. The thought entered her mind that, perhaps, guilt still tormented him because of his action years earlier. She finally concluded that he was a man with some conscience after all and that he may not have forgotten her.

Jannat had landed herself on the horns of a strange dilemma. Her curiosity had led her onto a crossroad and she did not know which way to turn. She entertained the notion of confronting Yuba but then, she reasoned, to what avail. After all, they had been together barely a year or so and it had been 20 years or more since their separation. Yet having learned of his feelings of remorse, she could not help wondering if she continued to be a part of his conscience. After having accepted her fate unquestioningly and even having willingly forgiven Yuba long ago, she nevertheless entertained a hope of obtaining a fair quittance from the man who had transgressed her dignity. She wondered whether she could induce Yuba to accept his past even though she knew that reentering his life now could be a grave provocation. If just a hint of his past became public knowledge, it would humiliate him. It would almost certainly undermine his diligently acquired status in life and reduce to naught a lifetime of hard work that had led to such spectacular successes.

Such contradictory impulses created grave doubts about the future course of action and she was inclined to let it all be, to carry on with life the way she had been carrying on for so long. In the midst of this mental turmoil, Jannat reminded herself of the rumors of Ayub's generosity. She reckoned that if he was so generous to complete strangers, might he not be even more generous to ones who were in some ways still his kith and kin. Could she persuade him to assist the mother and daughter without revisiting the sordid past or reviving their obsolete relationship? Jannat had lived out her life in misery and had nothing to look forward to for herself. If she were to engage Ayub in this manner, it would only be for the sake of the girl, the sole reason of her will to continue with her life. Now that destiny seemed to offer her an opportunity to secure a more comfortable future for her girl, she would be a fool not to exploit it, she reasoned. That argument finally put to rest her doubts and the fickleness of her resolve gave way to a new determination. She decided to make her presence known to the man.

Jannat proceeded to put her plan in action. She would send a message to Ayub and Noor would be the messenger. She was a simple woman but never naïve and could very well imagine the effect on the man when he discovered the identity of the messenger. Nevertheless, she would have to tread carefully over what might turn out to be an embarrassing and wholly ill-conceived undertaking. As soon as Noor returned from work that day Jannat addressed her on the subject almost nonchalantly.

"How was the day, dear?"

"Good, Mother but this job is so exhausting. We had half a dozen different functions today and the demands of the guests were outrageous. You know when our guests hire the premises for the day, they act as if they are lords and masters and we, their lowly servants. Some of our guests are so boorish. They have such despicable attitudes."

"Well, that's the nature of your job and you will have to put up with it, at least for now."

Jannat then casually produced the photograph that was to form the main plank of her design, placed it in front of her daughter and proceeded to reveal her purpose in a falsely assumed matter-of-fact tone.

"By the way, do you remember this picture from the leather expo? You showed it to me a few days ago. I looked carefully at it and would you believe it, I seem to recognize the man whose name you said was Ayub Qureshi, the wealthy industrialist. He is a distant relative from the village. I only knew him in my youth and I knew him as Yuba the butcher but I am sure it is him."

Noor let out a chuckle, in total disbelief of her mother's insinuation.

"Mother, how could you recognize someone you only ever met in your youth and have not seen since? It must have been 20 years or more. You could be awfully mistaken."

Jannat's expression changed suddenly. A morose look covered her face as she spoke out somewhat bitterly.

"I am absolutely certain. I could never forget that look; the distinctive contours of the jaw, the ferocious eyes, the deep furrows on the forehead. How could I ever forget that impertinent grimace on his face and the fist that is forever clenched in such brazen determination?"

Noor was perplexed at the change in her mother's demeanor though naturally she could not gauge the bitterness in her reaction. She was quite innocent of her mother's past or else she might have understood why Jannat could never forget Yuba's face. Jannat calmed down immediately to unfold the plan in hand and to enlist her daughter's participation in its implementation.

"You know I have lost touch with my village all these years but I have a desire to learn of my relatives before my life ends. Perhaps, this man could help me in that regard. I, therefore, wish to renew his acquaintance."

Noor protested, though she did so somewhat faintly and without conviction.

"Now, really, Mother! Our status being what it is, he might not wish to associate with us in any manner."

"Exactly, which is why I would like you to visit him and convey my message. It might be imprudent for me to approach him in person."

It was an artful plea for a simple woman to put together. Noor was confounded at her mother's strange wish.

"Frankly, Mother, I cannot understand the need to rekindle a tenuous relationship which might have existed in the distant past. It would be too embarrassing for me if he spurns me."

However, Noor could sense her mother's resolve and decided to go along with the scheme even though it could put her in a disconcerting situation. The dilemma having thus been resolved, the mother and daughter decided that Noor would carry a note to Ayub and if he should acknowledge them and agree to see Jannat, a meeting could then ensue in an appropriate manner.

CHAPTER 16

The association between Ayub and Shahzaib grew stronger with each passing day. Ayub developed a personal liking, perhaps even a fondness, for Shahzaib. The two met away from the office whenever the harrowing pace of their schedule permitted them to do so, often dining together at the older man's mansion. A strong familial relationship had begun to develop between the two and each man savored each other's company. Yet, it seemed they could never get away from their single-minded obsession with their trade and their conversation usually revolved around the subject. Themes of more general interest would occasionally come up for discussion but it was rare for either man to open up unreservedly or to share his innermost personal feelings with the other. Shahzaib was quite surprised when Ayub sought to probe his private life one evening. Ayub pointedly inquired of Shahzaib if he had ever loved a woman. Shahzaib ventured to mumble that he had not had the good fortune thus far. Ayub, however, seemed to be in a wistful mood and not particularly interested in Shahzaib's answer, offering his own account instead.

"I have never loved a woman. In fact, I have never held intimate feelings for any other person, man or woman. That emotion is alien to me. I am, it seems, incapable of loving anyone, though today I have found a companion, a friend and a confidante in you for the first time in my wretched life."

Ayub's characterization of his life as wretched shocked Shahzaib though he was under no illusion about its great allure. Ayub slumped in his leather chair with his eyes now half-closed and a distraught look on his face. It seemed as if a dissolute force had possessed him and was goading him on to an entirely unpredicted homily. Shahzaib was at a loss to understand the thrust of Ayub's conversation as Ayub continued.

"You must have heard people say that I came to town a bachelor and never married. That is not true. I was married once and even had a baby girl. Twenty years ago I committed a grave injustice and my wife left with the baby."

Ayub suddenly went silent, sensing the attention with which the young man was listening to him. It seemed as if he expected Shahzaib to prod him on but the young man chose to maintain a respectable detachment. He said nothing. After a few awkward moments, Ayub continued.

"At the time I was but a degenerate drunkard. I committed a despicable act under the influence one evening. I woke up the next morning to a reprehensible reality; I had lost my wife and child forever because of my rancorous wantonness. The disgrace was unbearable. I swore in the aftermath of the incident that I would not partake of any intoxicant for as long as I lived but that pledge was too little too late. My action had caused an irreparable damage to three lives, those of my wife and child and, indeed, my own. I am destined to carry the burden of the guilt and dishonor for the rest of my life. I must live on with the distressing knowledge that my brazen action might have jeopardized innocent lives."

Ayub was careful not to reveal the exact incident, even insinuating dishonestly that his wife might have left of her own volition though admitting his culpability indirectly, that she might have done so because of a monumental indiscretion on his part. He just felt utterly disgraced at the mere mention of the incident. Yet, after years of bottling up his turmoil inside him, he felt the need to lighten his burden by opening up to his young friend, the only person he had ever trusted enough to do so. He continued with his vague disclosure.

"I became saddled with a family at an early age though I had no desire to marry. I was a victim of circumstances. My wife was not to blame naturally. She was but a child and she too was a victim of the very same circumstances, perhaps even more so than I was. As I recall her now, she was not particularly beautiful or intelligent, being from a peasant stock, just as I am too. Nor was she educated or accomplished but then I was barely better on that count myself. I must admit, though, that she was gentle, decent and kind. Dare I say also that she was a forgiving soul for she had not only forgiven but also forgotten many of the wrong doings that my family committed against her. Alas, I expect never to find out if she has forgiven me for the sin that I committed against her at our parting. I wish fervently to atone for my monumental mistake but I was never to set eyes on my wife and child again, despite my best efforts to locate them. I do not even know how they might have fared in life. Despite that, I seek their return even to this day, though I suppose only a miracle can make that happen. I have placed my trust entirely on divine intervention."

Ayub went silent once again, agony writ large on his face. His eyes, now moist, seemed ready to burst into a rain of tears but Ayub was made of sterner stuff. He had the will to suppress his feelings, or perhaps he wished not to waste fresh tears over an old grief lest he had no tears left for a new grief. He composed himself and even allowed a slight smile to appear on his face as he continued.

"I was left alone in the world to put up with my shame as best I could, to bottle up my feelings within myself. Yes, it is true that I have not thus far taken another woman. How could I, since I awaited my wife's return. Alas! There seems no possibility of that any longer."

Ayub's revelations stunned the young man. Shahzaib could not possibly extend approval to such an unusual past but he listened to the older man's story with diplomatic silence, not once interrupting nor acting brash enough to ask for elaborations. He reasoned that it was not for him to judge the actions of another. In any case, the moral issue of Ayub's past never really bothered him. He reckoned that the penitence shown by the man was punishment enough. The confessional had revealed a side of Ayub that Shahzaib could never have imagined even in the depths of a profound introspection over his subject. He could see a cavernous pit of remorse as he peered into the eyes of his mentor. If eyes are a window to a man's soul, then Ayub's eyes revealed much, in fact too much—sadness, anguish, anxiety, and shame—all on account of a single disgraceful act perpetrated by him so many years earlier.

Ayub had broken his silence for the first time in twenty years in an attempt to emerge from the darkness of his past. He had finally found the courage to confront the demons that had tormented him for so long. He had been careful, though, not to face his shame squarely. Perhaps, the time was not opportune for a tryst with destiny just yet. For the moment at least, his conceit had won the day.

More to the point, though, the revelation had a method to it. In fact, Ayub might have been recalling the past as prologue for the future. Opening up to his young friend, taking a load off his chest, must certainly have been therapeutic. It might also have meant to be a rationalization for change. He might have been suggesting that he had borne enough punishment; that he had gone through sufficient suffering for his sins. He might have finally felt that there was no point in pretending to be in perpetual penitence and that he was entitled to live out a normal life. He might have wanted to free himself from the restraint he had imposed on himself and end his loneliness. The fact that he saw no possibility of the return of his wife was tantamount to suggesting that that was sufficient reason to take another.

CHAPTER 17

The private life of Ayub was an abiding mystery and had been the subject of much speculation in business and social circles. No one seemed to know him or his circumstances sufficiently well to make any meaningful observation on it, except that he was an immensely wealthy person with neither a woman in tow nor any heirs in sight. Indeed, no one had known Ayub to have had a meaningful relationship with a woman. In that respect at least, he was a rarity in a society where the first order of the day for the rich and powerful is to covet the favors of women; and, of course, the more the merrier. It was not beyond speculation, therefore, that he could be living a secret life, though no one could imagine the necessity for maintaining such a secret.

The truth of the matter was the one that Ayub had chosen to disclose to his young friend, albeit scantily. All through his years in ascent, he had never courted any woman. The reason for that was straightforward. He could not think of taking up another woman after what he had done to Jannat.

In fact, in some ways he still felt committed to her. Thus, he had continued to abstain from a relationship. If Ayub had indulged in casual encounters purely because of carnal needs, he must have been extremely discreet. There was really no hint of any scandal in his life. He seemed to have no life beyond his work.

Ayub was a lonely man but with advancing years, the loneliness was becoming unbearable. So, with the resolve of his youth now waning, he had of late become less averse to finding a partner. He was not nearly an old man and was still quite vigorous, though he knew he was not likely to remain so for long. If he did not seek companionship now, he could remain deprived of the pleasure for the rest of his life. With his guard finally down, it was only a matter of time before an encounter ensued, and so it did. He had formed a relationship with a young lady, which was a secret as closely guarded as the incident of his youth. Ayub had disclosed the affair to no one, not even Shahzaib, which was perhaps well enough, since his life did not always follow his plans.

During the course of his business travels in Europe, Ayub had chanced upon a young woman by the name of Myra. She was of decent parentage, the only child of a prosperous businessman of native origin who had settled in Europe many years earlier and had married a local woman. Myra's mother had unfortunately passed on while she was not yet in her teens. Growing up bereft of her mother was never easy on young Myra. She spent her adolescent years mostly under the tutelage of her European grandmother, who was at once her most intimate companion and her eyes and ears. Myra relied on her guidance for all matters, especially those of a personal nature. Myra did occasionally visit her father's homeland where she still had an extended family and had become somewhat acquainted with the local language and culture.

Ayub had had extensive business dealings with Myra's father over the years and his was a familiar presence in that household whenever he was in town. He had first come across Myra when she was just a little girl. She soon grew into impressive womanhood, handsome, quite well educated and cultured, one who had the makings of a woman of substance. For the present though, she was lively and frolicsome and somewhat flighty and flirtatious, a charming presence in any situation. Her sassiness infected the men around her and Ayub was no exception. However, if he did have an inappropriate inclination towards her, he managed to restrain it sufficiently, at least for now.

It was during this blithe period of Myra's life that a horrendous accident took the life of her father and she was left to fend for herself, with only her grandmother's emotional support to tide her over. Her father had left enough of a bequest for her so that she could have lived comfortably on the annuity for the rest of her life. However, the life of a woman of leisure did not suit her disposition. Though carefree and devoid of intense cogitation, she was never frivolous. Her grandmother had indoctrinated her with sound European values, a sense of responsibility and an ingrained loyalty to her father's vision for her. She now stood behind her at this critical juncture to have her take up the challenges thrust upon her because of her father's absence, as he might have willed her to do. By all accounts, she acquitted herself well in her trial.

With Myra now running her late father's business, Ayub naturally came into even closer contact with her. He now looked at her differently. She was no longer the little girl he had known earlier but an attractive young woman.

The compelling charms of the young woman were clearly beginning to beguile Ayub. The reticent older man's amorous interest in a much younger woman was quite inexplicable and Ayub was in fact perplexed at his own behavior. He was initially uncomfortable in his advances towards the child of a man who had been his friend but he finally made a hesitant overture. If Myra had similar qualms about Ayub's friendship with her late father, she made no exhibition of it. To his great surprise, not to mention heartening delight, Myra responded to Ayub's overtures amply. However, at that embryonic stage of their association, neither the older man nor the young woman was prepared to cross the bounds of civility. The courtship of Myra by Ayub endured over an extended period and in time the budding romance transformed itself into an intimate relationship. Ayub made up his mind to seek Myra in marriage in spite of his reservations over their compatibility on some counts, though those were obviously not of sufficient gravity to deter him.

Myra had known men of her own age and standing but a mature, successful man like Ayub best tempered her own confident and headstrong ways. She had fallen for the authoritarian manner of the older man despite her youth and her liberal instincts. Her infatuation with a powerful father figure, could well have been the result of having been left without a dominant influence early in life. However, Myra's grandmother was convinced that Ayub was not a suitable match for her grandchild, not just for reasons of age but on more substantive concerns—the difference in temperament, in attitude towards life and in the social background of each. Though she did not know Ayub well, she knew her grandchild like the palm of her hand. Her grandmother's objections gave Myra pause and she did hesitate briefly but, for the first time in her life, Myra overruled her grandmother and consented to be Ayub's wife.

An important corollary of their decision to marry was the need for one of them to move in order for them to be together. Myra had spent her entire life in Europe but readily agreed to upend her settled life to be with Ayub. The whole-heartedness of her resolve overshadowed even the enormity of her impending move. Her only regret was that she would be without her grandmother's caring presence. However, both consoled each other on Myra's promise of frequent visits to Europe. She then proceeded forthwith to close down her business, liquidate its assets and conclude the exercise by selling off her personal belongings. All said and done, she would be worth a large fortune. Myra started readying herself for the big leap though it would be some time before it materialized.

CHAPTER 18

Noor set off for Ayub's office early the next day, having taken off from work. Upon entering the office premises, she asked to see Ayub. The receptionist told her he had not come in yet. As she sat in the reception area, Shahzaib came out of his office to meet with people who had apparently been waiting for him. After having dispensed with them, he turned his attention briefly towards the young woman. He asked her if he could help her in any way but she informed him that she had come to see Ayub for a private purpose. He then sauntered off without displaying further curiosity. Shahzaib obviously failed to recognize Noor from their brief encounter at the hotel. Ayub arrived shortly thereafter and Noor approached him with the request to see him privately. The man turned indifferently towards her and addressed her blandly.

"What is it that you wish to see me for?"

"I am not here on business, sir but to speak to you on behalf of someone else."

The man looked at her a bit more quizzically now.

"Yes, and what is it?"

Noor started to address Ayub rather artlessly, quite innocent of the import of her mission.

"I have been sent by an old acquaintance of yours, a woman named Jannat. She is in town and wishes to see you. She has sent me to enquire whether you will see her."

At first Noor's nervous utterance did not quite register. He was not sure if he had heard her right. Soon he became alert to the significance of the name uttered by her.

"Did you say Jannat? And who might she be?"

"She is a widow who once lived in the same village as you, perhaps a distant relative of yours whom you have not met since your youth. She seems to recall you distinctly as Yuba."

Noor's elaboration shook Ayub as her words resonated in his head. He was obviously alarmed at the implication; that the girl was in fact speaking of Jannat, the woman he had disgraced so many years earlier. He muttered a few words under his breath with a great deal of difficulty, turning away from the young woman. He asked her a rhetorical question but just as quickly answered it himself in a gesture of supreme mental confusion.

"Is she alive? By God, she must still be alive!"

Ayub struggled to remain composed as he turned once more to Noor who was by now a bit baffled at his behavior.

"And who are you?"

"I am her daughter."

"And what is your name, your given name?"

"Noor, Noor is my name."

The name was enough to send Ayub in a spin. He needed no further confirmation about the identity of the woman who had sent the message or that of the messenger.

He imagined he was standing face-to-face with the baby he had so callously abandoned. A vivid image of the disgraceful spring evening flashed in the eye of his mind. He was mesmerized. Could it be true, or was he dreaming? Many thoughts converged on him as he contemplated Jannat's reappearance but the one that held sway was whether she had revealed the events of that fateful night to her daughter. For now, he had no way of telling but he felt a great deal of anxiety while he awaited an answer.

"Do come into my chamber, I want to hear more."

He led her hurriedly through a corridor passing by the open door of another chamber where Shahzaib was poring over some papers at his desk. They entered Ayub's lavishly furnished chamber.

"Sit down, Noor. Sit down."

Noor's name parted from Ayub's lips quite spontaneously but it so rattled him that he suddenly started trembling. He barely managed to sit down, moving immediately to the edge of his chair and began his query with the thought that was uppermost in his mind. Everything else would have to wait for now.

"What did your mother tell you about me? What did she say our relationship was? Did she relate any incident by which I might identify her?

"She told me nothing other than what I mentioned outside; that she is from the same village as you and that she might be related to you in some way."

Noor's words were a source of some relief. Jannat had not betrayed him to the child he had abandoned along with her. She had obviously behaved most respectfully towards him in spite of his crime. He felt more comfortable now that he had cast his doubts aside. He then went on to more mundane queries, mundane only in relation to his previous query though still of considerable consequence to him.

"Your mother, is she well?"

"Mother doesn't keep too well. She has never quite been in robust health but her condition has worsened since the death of my father."

The mention of her father's death alerted Ayub to a new reality. He had all these years formed a belief that the stranger who had paid for her might have married her. He assumed, therefore, that the girl was now referring to the death of that man. Evidently, she took her mother's husband as her father, he thought.

"When did her husband die?"

"Father died a few years ago. I was 15 years old or so when he died."

"And where are you staying?"

"We live in a small flat in the city."

By such conversation, the man was able to glean bits and pieces of the circumstances that might have befallen his wife and daughter. The full denouement of the past would have to await his meeting with his former wife. He nevertheless continued with another rhetorical question, as if pinching himself to make sure he was not dreaming.

"And you are her daughter?"

Noor might have answered his query but Ayub paid no perceptible attention to it. In fact, he was quite convinced of her identity so that the query was largely emblematic. Ayub continued to stare at his ostensible daughter through a few moments of shattering silence that seemed like an eternity; to the girl's obvious discomfiture. Ayub's eyes were now moist and he suddenly turned his face away from her gaze. He continued to address her, more purposefully now.

"I want you to take a note to your mother. I should like to see her."

As he started writing the note, he eyed Noor's clothes. They were of somewhat inferior quality though neat and clean.

"Your mother has not been left very well off by her late husband, has she?"

Ayub had meant to take a measure of the state of the mother and daughter by his observation but Noor obviously took it as an affront. She answered Ayub's remark defiantly, as if resenting his insinuation about her father's goodwill towards them and even went on to defend her mother's efforts.

"Father took good care of us while he was alive. We may not be very well off but we manage to get by. My mother has done all she could for me and brought me up very well after Father's death."

Ayub said nothing and meanwhile wrote a few lines on a writing pad. He then stood up, walked to a safe in the corner of the room and took out a wrapped packet of currency notes. He stuffed the currency and the paper from the pad in an envelope and handed it to Noor.

"Please deliver it to your mother personally."

Noor stood up to face Ayub while receiving the envelope. Then without saying a word, Ayub took Noor's hand and held it briefly. The man's gesture was plainly inappropriate and it might have offended the young woman but the warmth of his hand overpowered her. Noor felt a strange emotion. She was confused at the manner in which the man reacted to her and at the way she responded to his reaction. Both were so sorely out of place. After all, according to her mother, he was merely a distant relative. As for Noor, he was but a total stranger to her. In fact, the whole episode with Ayub frightened her somewhat. Noor stood standing as Ayub made his way back to his chair. She then turned around to leave, observing the man keenly. Ayub's distraught state of mind showed itself more distinctly as he sat gaping, his eyes fixed on the departing figure of the young woman. The ghosts from his past had finally come home to roost. Still he could not be sure of anything until he set his eyes once again on Jannat. He had arranged for them to meet that very evening. The rendezvous with his shame could not wait. Something about Noor, though, had touched his instincts and he felt no doubt that she was his daughter. Somehow, it was the prospect of a reunion with his long-lost daughter that beckoned Ayub more than the idea of getting back with his former wife.

For a moment, the enormity of the occasion eclipsed Ayub's interest even in Shahzaib. When the younger man dropped by his chamber a little later, his demeanor took him aback. He was suddenly so distant. The young man soon realized what some knew better, that Ayub was prone to sudden and tortuous swings of mood.

CHAPTER 19

Noor returned to her house only to find her mother waiting expectantly, almost on an edge. Jannat rushed towards the door as soon as she heard it open and started inquiring about the meeting in desperate anticipation.

"How was the meeting? How did he receive you? Was he rude or insolent? Did he chide you for the imprudent approach?"

"Relax, Mother. He did nothing of that sort. Not only was he polite but he was oddly emotional. He even held my hand briefly. I must admit, I too felt an emotion. Are you sure you have told me the whole truth? I think there is more to your relationship with him than you have chosen to divulge. You must tell me the whole truth, I insist."

Jannat only looked at her daughter blankly. Noor handed over Ayub's envelope to her and ambled away, sensing that her mother would not humor her. Though barely literate, Jannat sought no help from her daughter in reading the letter. The message was hers and hers alone to digest. She read the note haltingly.

"Meet me at the Central Park at 8 p.m. this evening. I will be at the gate by the main road. I can say no more now except that the discovery has overwhelmed me. The girl seems to know nothing of the past. Keep it that way till I have met you."

The note mentioned nothing about the currency he had enclosed; there was no need for it. Though the money was now nearly worthless, it was not without significance. It was what remained of the sale consideration after Yuba had treated the degenerate company to a few rounds of Sheeda's concoction. Ayub had never used any of that money even at the depth of his penury and returned it now to impress upon his victim that he had obviously suffered deep regret over the incident. Jannat was restless for the remainder of the day. She told her daughter only that the man had asked her to meet her that evening and that she was going to meet him alone. Of course, she did not disclose the fact that their meeting had an air of intrigue.

Ayub drove to the park a little before eight. At first thought the choice of the park as the venue of the rendezvous was an odd one. On closer examination, however, it was a well-thought-out place for a prominent man to meet his long-lost ex-wife. It would be virtually impossible to single out one couple amongst the many that assembled there in the dark, each keen on its own privacy. Besides, the park was easily accessible from all parts of the city. Ayub left his car some distance away, walked towards the gate of the park and stood there waiting for Jannat to arrive. Jannat soon reached the venue of the meeting. Ayub could discern the approaching figure of the woman in the dark and as she came closer, there was no mistaking her identity. Soon they stood face-to-face once more, 20 years from the last such moment. At first, there was a painful silence as neither spoke. More than once the frail woman seemed on the verge of falling in a faint but managed to stand firm. Oddly, there was no display of raw emotions. One might have thought that the unusual circumstances of their parting and the long interlude of separation would touch a raw nerve in both. At last, Ayub spoke. Any other man placed in such circumstance might have begun his amends with a profuse apology but Ayub's first words were not an apology.

"I do not drink. I have never had a drink since that night."

He had arranged his words both to put his disgraceful behavior in perspective and to serve as an assurance for his future conduct. The woman merely bowed her head as if in understanding. After a moment of further silence, he spoke again.

"I looked all over for you. I took all possible steps to locate you and Noor. I found no trace of you anywhere. Why did you keep silent all these years?"

There was still no apology. Ayub continued to reiterate the efforts he had made to make amends for his action that night. He knew very well that she could not have known where he had drifted to or what became of him. Her silence was, therefore, no mystery. Yet he seemed to reproach her on a supposed lapse on her part rather than on his own. Jannat finally started to speak, addressing Ayub by a name that he himself had almost forgotten.

"Oh, Yuba, you disgraced me in public with such vile invectives. You gave me away to another man in exchange for money, money that you have preserved to this day. You divorced me in front of a crowd. You knowingly pushed your baby and me in harm's way."

Jannat spoke those words in a soft, controlled tone of voice even though she could have been excused if she were shrill but she soon became emotionally charged.

"How can you now ask me why I had been silent all these years? You are treating my helplessness as an offence, as if I had planned a great escape from you. I have suffered enormously all my life because of your action."

Jannat's emotional outburst did not surprise Ayub even though he had not really expected it from the soft-spoken woman. True to his nature, even her emotions could not provoke him into admitting his folly. He was relentless in his defense.

"You walked off with a total stranger in the middle of the night with a child in your arms. How could you take a drunken man so seriously? How could you be so simple? I had never meant it to be that way and you should have known that. Did you ever even think that I too might have suffered because of the incident? Look, I never spent a cent of that money beyond that night. I lived the life of a vagrant while carrying an enormous sum of money."

The weight of the emotional moment was too much for Jannat and she finally broke down in a heap of demonstrative torment. She even became somewhat apologetic.

"I don't know. I was sure you have had enough of me. You blamed me for everything. Why did you speak the dreaded words of the divorce when I begged you to stop? The divorce made it so conclusive, so unalterable."

Ayub's demeanor changed slightly as he took a measure of the present instead of dwelling on the past.

"Yes, yes, you are right. It only makes me feel you are an innocent woman. But why do you lead me into this now?"

Jannat was startled at Ayub's assertion. He seemed to be accusing her of an ulterior motive. She responded with a loud exclamation, as if alarmed at the suggestion. In fact, she feigned her reaction to ward off the insinuation of having planned to rope him into her life, though that was indeed her plan.

"What, Yuba! Are you accusing me of attempting to re-enter your life for a gain? I met and married a kind man and I owed him faithfulness to the end of one of our lives. I could not desert him after what he did for my child and for me. I meet you now only as his widow. Had he not died, I would never have come to you, never. Of that, you may be sure. I have no claim on you. I have come only for the sake of Noor."

Jannat was quite succinct in her response. There was really no reason for her to disclose the manner in which she had spent her life beyond what was relevant to her mission. In any case, she was not sure where this assignation would lead her. She could not even be sure whether Ayub would admit the intrusion of the mother and daughter into his now sanctified surroundings. She need not have worried though.

"No, no, don't get me wrong. I am not accusing you of an improper approach. In fact, I am grateful to you for your initiative. It is just that I am fearful of the fallout of the secret of our past, should it become known. What will Noor think of me when she finds out about the bizarre event that connects us? She would despise me bitterly. I could not bear that. That would be rubbing salt on my wounds; wounds that have refused to heal even after all these years."

The conversation was beginning to perplex Jannat. She was unable to ascertain the direction of Ayub's dialogue. She nevertheless continued with the advocacy of her cause.

"That is why I brought Noor up in total ignorance of your existence. I could not bear it either. Don't forget my wounds are even deeper than yours."

Jannat's claim that she had brought up Noor in ignorance of Ayub and the incident because she might have been concerned about the fallout, was obviously not true. At the time of the separation, she had no way of knowing that she would ever confront her past in this manner. The eventuality of the two meeting again would have receded into near impossibility with the passage of more than twenty years. Her improbable encounter with Ayub had simply awoken her to an opportunity and she was determined to exploit it.

"You have no doubt heard that I am a big businessman. I am also politically and socially important."

"Yes, I know."

"My position in society and the dread of Noor discovering our disgrace makes it necessary to act with extreme caution."

"I think we mother and daughter will stay away from you or even go away at once to another town, if you wish. I mustered the courage to contact you only for the sake of my daughter and her future. As for me, I want nothing from you. I have lived out my life for better or for worse."

"No, no, you mistake me. I want to do right by you and Noor. I committed a sin against you so many years ago and ever since my emotions have waged a war within me. I seek penitence for that sin so that perhaps my soul may rest in peace after I pass on. I have borne my burden with patience, waiting for the day when I might be able to lighten it. Now that that day may finally have dawned, please do not deny me a just requital."

Jannat remained silent, touched by the genuine sadness in Ayub's expression, convinced of his sincerity. Ayub paused in contemplation for a few moments and then continued.

"I have just thought of a plan if you should go along."

"Oh, Yuba, I will go along if it is the right thing for Noor."

"Very well, then! You and Noor will put up in town in a decent house as Mrs., whatever his name was, as his widow, you know. I will court you and marry you again though nobody need know that this is our second marriage, not even Noor. She can live with us as my stepdaughter. This way I will have the pleasure of seeing my only child under my roof once again and my disgraceful past too will remain unopened. The secret will be just yours and mine."

Ayub's words took Jannat aback. She was truly shocked that he would even entertain the thought of reviving an association with her, much less marrying her again. She was quite unprepared for such a far-fetched eventuality. She had only tried to conjure up an opportunity to lift Noor out of her constrained circumstances. Regaining her composure, she immediately grasped the consequence of her ex-husband's proposition and decided to seize the moment.

"I trust you to do the right thing, Yuba. I came to you for the sake of Noor. For myself, if you tell me to leave this very moment and never come back, I shall be quite content to go away."

"I don't want to hear that. You will not leave again. I will give you enough money to set you up as a genteel widow. The girl must not know of our shame. That is what makes me most anxious."

"She is unlikely to dream the truth. How could she suppose that what you did could ever come to pass in this day and age?"

"Yes, I suppose so."

Jannat displayed a glum satisfaction at the outcome of her carefully thought-out scheme. It had succeeded beyond her expectation. Though it was all for the sake of her girl, it was not without a fair measure of redemption for her own cause. Jannat's manner seemed to take on a triumphant air as she declared her approval of Ayub's scheme.

"I quite like the idea of repeating our marriage. It seems the right course. Now I must go back to Noor and tell her that you, our relative from the village, have promised to extend us your help."

"Very well, I will drop you."

"No, no. Do not run any risk. Please let me go alone."

"Right but just one more matter. Do you forgive me, Jannat?"

Jannat murmured something under her breath but Ayub could not have possibly made out her words. He could not have ascertained from her response whether she had forgiven him for his monumental transgression. In any case, without waiting for a clear answer, Ayub spoke on.

"Judge me by my future and not my past."

Jannat took his leave and stepped back onto the street to catch a bus. Ayub walked to his car and slipped in. He sat silently in the dark of the night for a few moments and heaved a sigh of disbelief before driving off.

Chapter 20

Once back in his house, Ayub slumped in a sofa in his study, as he was wont to do in his moments of overbearing anxiety. It had been a harrowing night. He could not stop wondering why fate had brought Jannat back into his life after such a prolonged absence. He had ostensibly come to the city to search for her and the baby in the aftermath of the incident but had failed to find them despite his best efforts. Shame, overwhelming guilt and a lack of self-esteem had prevented him from ever going back to his village though ultimately, it was his presumptuous self-will that had made him stay on in the city. His decision not to go back to the village had transformed his life radically but it was obvious that he was in this way fated to re-unite with Jannat. He paused to think of what he had just committed to her. He had a faint feeling that by promising to remarry her, he would be embarking on yet another ominous escapade. He reminded himself of the solemn pledge he had taken at the shrine of the saint and concluded that the burden of his avowal was too great to evade. He was damned if he did and damned if he did not. There in, perhaps, lay the seeds of his tragedy.

His thoughts soon wandered off to Myra and the promises he had made to her, promises that were now on the verge of being shattered. She had been there when he needed her and had given herself to him wholeheartedly. She had extricated him from the periodic fits of doom and gloom that he suffered on account of his loneliness, when his world sometimes seemed to have the blackness of hell, when he cursed the day he was born. He had asked her to uproot herself from her comfortable surroundings and she had complied unquestioningly. How could he now abandon her? Might he not incite the fury of a scorned woman? Paradoxically, he would be doing right by a wronged woman only by inflicting a wrong on an innocent woman. He was leaving one woman for another under a peculiar compulsion of his own making, yet ironically, he had never been a philanderer. It was impossible for a man of his sort to go through life without making more blunders, or so it seemed.

There was no point in pondering over the quandary any further; he had to carry out what he had committed to Jannat. He had left himself no escape hatch. Nevertheless, he owed it to Myra to at least inform her of his plan in as appropriate and timely a manner as he could, so that perhaps the impact of the devastating indignity that he was about to inflict on her would lessen somewhat. He sat down to frame a letter to her, explaining his predicament in as much detail as he thought feasible for the purpose at hand and with all sincerity at his command.

Dear Myra,

I cannot explain cogently the compulsion with which I write this letter. I know well that you will regard it with a lot of anger and, perhaps, some sadness. I caused you to uproot yourself on my promise to marry you. Indeed, I yearned desperately for companionship after years of a barren and lonely existence and you responded so warmly, so tenderly. Yet today circumstances compel me to shatter the trust you placed in me so selflessly and to renege on my promise of marriage.

I failed in my entreaties of fond feelings for you to disclose the fact that I was once married to a woman who bore me a baby girl. A grave accident caused us to part and thereafter I had no way of knowing whether the mother and daughter were still alive. It was under such circumstances that I had the good fortune of meeting you. Now my wife and child have made their presence known to me just as suddenly as they parted. I am constrained, chiefly for the sake of my daughter, to admit them both into my life again. I wish to inform you, therefore, that I plan to marry my former wife and mother of my child as soon as we can arrange to do so.

Do forgive me if you can find forgiveness within you. I can assure you that I had neither deceit nor dishonesty in my purposeful overtures to you. My act of omission of the details of my life that I have now revealed was entirely because of my fear of losing your affections. My present action too is borne of a compelling sense of propriety, not least to extricate you from any future social complication.

I trust that you will not divulge the facts I have outlined above to anyone as I have disclosed my past to no one but you.

Ayub

Ayub felt emotionally drained as he wrote the gut-wrenching plea, after which he sat through the night contemplating his complication, wondering what else life had in store for him.

"Can it be that it will go off so easily? Forgive me, Myra but I have to make amends to Jannat."

However, even his contrition could not conceal the fact that he had conceived his actions carefully enough. The man who, as a mere boy of 17, had participated in the murder of his sister at the whiff of an improbable scandal was willing to take back a woman after 20 years of separation, not knowing where she had been or what she had been doing during that time, not knowing whether she too had been scandalized. He had taken her back without hesitation or second thought, all because of a supposedly solemn oath he had taken at the shrine of his patron saint.

CHAPTER 21

The letter from Ayub arrived just as Myra had almost completed winding up her business and was ready to head for what she thought would be her new and permanent home with him. She was dumbstruck by the suddenness of the reversal. The reasons proffered by him galled her more than the act itself. Ayub had never once mentioned the fact of a wife and child. He had been less than truthful with her on that count and, she imagined, he might have been so on other counts as well. Myra had never really thought of investigating Ayub's circumstances during her acquaintance with him; there was no reason for her to do so. She had not come by even a hint of an unusual past from any source.

Myra did not just feel let down, she felt utterly humiliated. Ayub had forsaken her at a time when she was feeling alone and without another friend in the world. She was desperately in need of intimate company. She would have continued with her business, for better or for worse, if it were not for Ayub. She was a thoroughly modern woman, unfazed by challenges. Yet she had welcomed the opportunity to share her life with one she thought she could respect. She was mindful, of course, of the man's wealth but that was never the reason for her assent to his proposal of marriage. She was quite well off in her own right, having inherited considerable assets and cash balances from her father. Besides, the business that her father had left behind was doing quite well. Her inheritance would have permitted her to live in great comfort if not in grand opulence.

As Myra contemplated her future, two thoughts clearly bore heavily on her mind. Her first and for now her foremost concern was the fact that she had practically uprooted herself from her familiar moorings, having sold her business and her house in preparation for a future with Ayub. She entertained the thought that she might try to reverse the deals she had carried out but that, she concluded, would be impractical. She had readied herself for the journey to her father's homeland and decided that she would undertake it anyway. The fact that she had family there who, she knew, would go out of their way to help her settle down, comforted her enormously. Besides, she could set up a business similar to the one she was presently running in Europe, trading in leather and leather made-ups. She snapped out of her despair as she evaluated her prospects. She was not at all worried about her future.

Another thought though caused Myra more disquiet, the thought that she had committed many indiscretions in her relationship with Ayub, which could at some point come back to haunt her. She did not think Ayub was the kind of person who would inflict any indecencies on her by revealing salacious details of their relationship. Nevertheless, she thought it prudent to extricate herself completely from her past with him. She sat down to write a note to him mainly on that count. The note she wrote was not a groveling complaint but a purposeful entreaty. It bore an unusually civil tone, in spite of having been cast aside so heartlessly.

Ayub,

I suppose that your marriage would have taken place even as I write this letter and I can imagine that it would be quite impossible for any future communication between us. You do realize no doubt that you have landed me in a dilemma from which I must now try to extricate myself as best I can. I will not demand any further explanation from you, noting as I do that, perhaps, the circumstances sketched by you left you with no option but the present one. I do appreciate that you at least had the graciousness to inform me immediately. I thus look at this as a misfortune of mine and absolve you entirely of the consequences that I may possibly suffer as a result.

I must ask you, however, to protect my reputation at all cost. I would desire for the sake of both of us that we should keep a secret of our lives together. I pestered you with intimate letters day after day in the heat of my feelings for you. I see now how indiscreet those contacts were and ask you to ensure that they remain confidential. To this end, may I request you to return to me any such material that you may have in your possession, particularly the letters written in the heat of passion and the intimate photographs that I created so thoughtlessly.

Myra

After having dispatched the letter, Myra became preoccupied with her thoughts. However, instead of contemplating her future, she found herself engrossed in reminiscing the past. Instead of planning around the new reality to formulate a course of action, she found herself reliving her life with Ayub. While she knew that she would have to get on with her life, with or without Ayub, she knew also that the episode with him would be hard to put behind. For now, she waited to receive her mementos back from her former lover. Oddly enough for a woman of such extraordinary attributes, Ayub had been the only real love of her life.

CHAPTER 22

The relationship between Ayub and Shahzaib continued to flourish for now. Yet one could not help wondering how long their understanding would endure in the same vein. The personalities and characters of the two men were in such stark contrast to each other that one could not rule out a clash on that count alone. Shahzaib was always calm and collected, never excitable. He had a balanced approach, in life generally as in business. Ayub, on the other hand, was prone to great swings in mood and the swings were even more marked in times of distress. He had of late come under some stress because of his personal circumstances and had begun displaying a rashness that had hitherto remained subdued. However, since the association of the two men was rooted in the conduct of business, a rift between the two could likely come about because of their dissimilar styles of conducting business. Ayub had after all hired Shahzaib for that purpose alone, even though subsequently their personal relationship had developed quite endearingly.

Ayub had always conducted business as a tribal chieftain would conduct the affairs of his tribe. He was the lord and master of his establishment and ran it rather whimsically. Being nearly uneducated, he operated his business informally. He understood the essence of business management simply as the art of buying and selling. He could recall his transactions with remarkable accuracy, never needing to look up the written record. Ledgers and logbooks, files and folders were never of much use to him. Accounts were a simple arithmetic of that which was receivable and that which was payable. He left it to his staff to create a paper trail. Unsurprisingly therefore, the quality of the office record was poor, disorganized and barely discernible to outsiders, not that it bothered him a great deal. He would often remind his business associates that written records or even contracts and agreements were not nearly as sacrosanct as a man's word of honor. Those were not vacuous words either. In his business dealings, his reputation was immaculate and his word unfailing.

Shahzaib, on the other hand, was a manager, conducting business as a maestro would conduct a philharmonic. He was a man who had directed his entire working life by the book. Besides being a trained leather technician, he had also had some formal education in business administration. He was concerned over the disorderly manner in which Ayub handled his transactions. Therefore, when Shahzaib moved to the main office as the general manager he took upon himself the task of putting Ayub's haphazard office record in order. In the process, Shahzaib discovered the magnitude of mismanagement. Ayub's business had grown tremendously in the past decade or so but its organizational structure had remained unchanged and its operations informal and personalized. Shahzaib set about making subtle changes in the manner in which business was conducted at Ayub's establishment.

Ayub was quite satisfied with the results since Shahzaib's induction as the general manager but privately he could not help pity the man who, by his reckoning, was so finicky. He did not really appreciate the changes that Shahzaib sought to carry out. Ayub was often at a loss to navigate through the processes that his young protégé had instituted in place of his rough and ready ways, often resenting his inability to do so. There began to arise points of disagreement between the two, with increasing frequency as time went by. The unthinkable could happen sooner than one could anticipate.

CHAPTER 23

Ayub set Jannat up in a comfortable house in an affluent neighborhood with all appropriate furnishings. As soon as the mother and daughter settled down, he started visiting them and often stayed for dinner. Soon these visits became so regular that the gossipmongers perceived the event as an affair in the offing. A rumor spread stealthily all over town that Ayub, once so indifferent to the opposite sex, was enamored of the genteel widow. His choice, though, seemed inexplicable. A man of his status, wealth, and power who still sported fairly handsome and firm features should have been in a position to choose well, yet he chose a widow who was gaunt and showed visible signs of decrepitude. Besides, she was the mother of a grown-up girl who was living with her. Naturally, many suspected that the union was an affair from the past. Shahzaib too was quite surprised at the apparent fixation of his mentor with the woman. Ayub, of course, had no need to offer any explanation to anyone and so it was unlikely that Shahzaib would have connected the mother and daughter to the account that Ayub had given him of his wife and daughter.

Little did anyone know that there were no great fires of passion burning between the two except for the man's resolve to make amends to the woman he had wronged, to provide a home for his daughter and not least, to castigate himself on his shame. In due course, Ayub and Jannat married—or should we say remarried—as planned. Mother and daughter moved in with Ayub and became a permanent part of his respectable social orbit. As if to reinforce a semblance of change in his life, Ayub had the whole house renovated and refurbished.

It was a triumphant moment for Noor. She left her job as soon as the mother and daughter moved into their new dwellings. She did so on her mother's insistence, who was no doubt acting more out of circumspection than because of the good fortune brought about by their new circumstances. The freedom that Noor experienced and the indulgence with which everyone treated her was beyond her expectations. The easy, affluent life to which her mother's marriage introduced her was, in truth, the beginning of a great change in her. Yet, she was judicious and comported herself with quiet dignity that belied her former lowly status. None of the modulations of moods that characterize sudden changes in one's station in life afflicted her in any way. Like all people who have known bad times, frivolity seemed to her too irrational and inconsequential. She would display brief moments of recklessness but refrained from bursting out like a water lily in spring. Although far from glamorous, she had transformed herself into a statuesque presence, carrying herself with an air of quiet serenity. She was not yet sophisticated in the ways of her new environment but there was perceptiveness in her character that would hold her in good stead with the passage of time.

As their familiarity grew, Ayub became quite fond of Noor. He was eager to do all he could for his daughter, though the girl supposed him to be her stepfather. He was, in fact, proud of Noor and wanted the whole world to see her in all the fineries becoming of a daughter of a wealthy man. Noor in turn found herself spending more time with her stepfather than with her mother. That is how it had always been with her. Paternal love came easily and readily. She had always taken her mother's presence for granted but had only had a fleeting episode with a father.

One day as the threesome sat at the breakfast table, Ayub looked silently at the girl. Soon husband and wife were alone as Noor got up and left, having finished her breakfast and announcing some chore. Ayub suddenly addressed his wife with an unexpected and perplexing query.

"I thought Noor's hair was jet black when she was a baby. She also had dark eyes, piercing dark eyes like mine, did she not? Both her hair and eyes are of a different hue and her complexion too is a shade lighter than I can recall."

Jannat was slightly startled.

"Was it? I do not see how you could remember such details after the passage of such a long time. Even I don't particularly remember."

"What I meant was that the girl's hair looked as if it would eventually turn out much darker than what it is now."

"The color of a baby's hair changes all the time and the color of the eyes can sometimes change too, you know."

"True. But both usually turn darker not lighter, isn't it?"

The expression on Jannat's face betrayed an uneasiness that was somehow meaningful. She knew from her past association with Ayub that he viewed even minor observations with suspicion. Ayub might have been trying to ascertain the paternity of the girl, trying to determine whether the girl was indeed his flesh and blood. But then again, she thought, it might have been an honest observation or even an attempt to impress upon her the fact that after all these years he had not forgotten even the faintest details. In any case, the uneasiness soon passed as Ayub continued without really pressing for an answer.

"Well, never mind. She looks perfectly fine. Now, I did want to talk to you about Noor taking my name as her legal family name though. It is not right for my own flesh and blood to bear the name of another man."

"No, no. But ………. I mean ………. it might be painful for the girl to be asked to erase the memory of the man whom she had called father as far back as she can now remember."

Jannat stammered and fumbled through a straightforward proposition, giving the impression that she was quite reluctant to have her daughter change her surname.

"Surely, if she is willing, you would want it too."

"Oh, yes. If she agrees, I'll ask her right away."

As soon as mother and daughter were alone, Jannat told Noor of her father's wish to have her change her family name. Then before Noor could even respond, Jannat acted in an uncharacteristically emotional manner. She seemingly implored her daughter to desist from an affirmation.

"Can you agree? I mean ……… would it not be a slight on the man you have called father ever since you could say the word. Now that he is dead and gone, could you so completely banish his memory?"

In spite of her mother's disconcerting tone, Noor reflected calmly for a moment and replied rather complacently that she would think about it. Noor saw Ayub later in the day and at once addressed the matter in a manner that expressed her mother's concern.

"Do you wish this change of name very much, Father?"

"Wish it! Come now, I merely proposed it. If you feel comfortable, do it. Don't go out of the way simply to please me."

Ayub may still have harbored a desire to pursue the subject but he dropped it for now; its importance paled before the enormity of his changed state of affairs. Yet the conversation was one of great significance, especially in view of Jannat's emotional outburst. As time went by, Ayub's life became more tranquil. His hitherto barren personal circumstances seemed to acquire more meaning. His quest for redemption had finally come to fruition, or so he thought in his high-spirited satisfaction. However, Ayub's desire for redemption may not have been without forfeit. He might even have exchanged a past agony for a present sorrow, for there is no getting away from the fate of a condemned man. It would be hazardous to predict what else fate had in store for this unfortunate man.

CHAPTER 24

Ayub showered an extraordinary amount of fatherly love on Noor but he also continued to show great affection for Shahzaib. Noor was quite aware of the cordial or even cozy relationship between Shahzaib and her stepfather. She had quietly observed the strong bond between the two men. On her part, she had looked at Shahzaib with some interest. After all, every now and then, he was a welcome guest at the house. A familiarity had set in between the two because of their frequent encounters though neither made any romantic overtures to the other and their relationship remained correct and rather formal. Noor was quite mindful of the fact that her earlier encounter with Shahzaib at the hotel had left no impression on him. Indeed, he never really recalled having met her there. Now that she was Ayub's daughter, he obviously saw her in a different light. In any case, they had never chanced to meet alone and so neither had had the opportunity to take a measure of the other, to gauge their suitability for each other.

It was a Sunday afternoon and Noor was lounging around lazily after a late breakfast, trying to settle down with a book. Both her father and mother had gone out for the day on a rare visit to some friends. In the midst of her leisurely sojourn, a servant entered to announce the arrival of Shahzaib. Noor was surprised. She had absolutely no idea about the purpose of his visit on a Sunday and especially in the absence of Ayub. He may have some urgent business, she thought, and may not have known of Ayub's absence. She changed quickly and went down to receive him. After exchanging pleasantries, the two sat down on adjacent sofas in the living room. Noor ventured to explain her father's absence.

"I am sorry Father is not here and he is not likely to be here for the rest of the day."

Shahzaib seemed a bit perplexed at Noor's answer and looked embarrassed.

"But I received a message on my cell phone asking me to come to the mansion for lunch."

Noor was surprised and somewhat nettled. Her mother had told her nothing about the lunch or the guest. It was now her turn to be uncomfortable.

"Is that so? I have no idea. In that case, I am sure my father and mother will return soon. Let me call them to find out what their plans are."

Noor went out of the room to try to get in touch with her father. She tried repeatedly but her father's phone was off. She then tried her mother and her phone was off too. The strange situation was now beginning to confound her. She did not know how to handle the embarrassment. Someone had created a misunderstanding and put its onus, knowingly or unknowingly, on her. She went to the kitchen and inquired from the cook of any plans for the afternoon.

He informed her that he had indeed prepared lunch for some guests. She could not imagine her father making such a faux pas. Ayub was always meticulous in matters of engagements and schedules. The present situation was beyond her comprehension. She went back to the living room to redress the awkward situation, concerned at the same time over what might have happened to her mother and father. Nevertheless, she managed to remain composed in the presence of Shahzaib.

"I am sorry but I was unable to get my father on the phone. I am a bit intrigued though, because you were apparently expected. The cook was instructed to prepare lunch for some guests."

"No, no! I might have mistaken the day. I think I will take your leave now."

"What! And let that sumptuous meal go to waste. Absolutely not! You will not leave without lunch. Besides, Father may yet remember and come back sooner than you would expect."

Noor was concerned that Shahzaib might get the notion that she had created an opportunity for the liaison. Explanations ensued and then both agreed that there had been a terrible mistake. It was an uncomfortable situation, though the discomfort formed a mercifully short interlude. Each made light of their embarrassment and soon the two were engaged in lighthearted banter, the conversation assuming an easy informality as they moved from the lunch table to the living room for a cup of coffee. Shahzaib thanked Noor for her hospitality and took leave with a promise to call her the next day. Noor stood on the porch transfixed as she watched Shahzaib depart, both waving at each other warmly.

It is amazing how trivial happenings can sometimes lead to events of greater magnitude. Noor was thrilled with this contrived encounter. Shahzaib's advances became more serious and Noor reciprocated abundantly. She had never before experienced a relationship with a man and felt exhilarated. As Noor settled down somewhat more comfortably in her routine as part of Ayub's household, her involvement with Shahzaib too started to blossom, although it was not quite passionate yet. Nevertheless, the stage was set for the next level, if no unforeseen event derailed it in the meanwhile. Ayub should have been pleased at the prospect of a union between his daughter and Shahzaib. In the scheme of things, it would have been the most desired outcome for all concerned. Yet one could take nothing for granted in any matter involving Ayub.

CHAPTER 25

The diversions that had of late entered Ayub's life had caused him to become detached from his business. He began to absent himself from the office quite often and left important matters unattended. Shahzaib had assumed the general management of the company and was making most day-to-day decisions but many extraordinary matters were beyond his purview. Ayub controlled the company's finances and Shahzaib had never been privy to the books of accounts. Now with Ayub's apathy in the matter, Shahzaib had to take it upon himself to ensure that pending payments to suppliers and others were cleared so as not to cause a disruption of the company's normal operations. This unusual responsibility necessitated delving into the company's accounts and as Shahzaib examined the books, he immediately perceived a financial disorder in the business. Shahzaib was alerted to a reality he had not known prior to his foray into the company's finances.

Ayub had been running his business in an almost casual manner, with lax controls and superficial appraisal of the results. The manner of the conduct of his business provided him with very little insight into the actual state. In fact, the business was in some disarray but Ayub was blissfully unaware of it. As Shahzaib dug deeper into the company finances, more out of concern than curiosity, he discovered its true state. The company was incurring losses continually but the apparently falsified accounts indicated otherwise. There were large receivables, which were obviously unrecoverable and should have been written off. Yet they continued to appear as part of income. As a result, the negative cash flow—the disparity between current income and expenditure—was not being reflected in the books. Actually, the gap was being bridged by rising levels of debt, which too was being availed on false premises. The book value of the company's assets had been greatly inflated and compared favorably with its liabilities, which then enabled the company to avail further debt. That debt was being utilized to service previous debt, in the manner of an inverse pyramid. The company was drowning in a vicious circle of debt and was afloat only by the grace of God and creative accounting.

Ayub had made his fortune in simpler times, when his business was small and the market was strong. He had continued with his wayward ways even as his business expanded manifold during his ascent. Ayub's style of management had clearly become unsuitable for addressing the complexities associated with size. He was able to carry on with his relaxed ways only because his cronies in the banks were willing to keep the cash flow going. Banks often continue to facilitate large businesses with increasing amounts of loans long after it has become imprudent to do so. Market creditors, however, know better than to go down with a sinking ship and jump out at the first sign of a leak. In the case of Ayub's business too, the market creditors were now beginning to pull out discreetly. There came a time when Shahzaib was no longer able to manage the jugglery required to keep the operations going. He had streamlined the manufacturing process but he had to reckon with the problem of cash flow that was becoming increasingly acute. Market creditors were now hesitant to extend credit facilities in the same liberal manner that they did before, causing shortages of raw material, disrupting scheduled production and delaying export shipments. Foreign buyers observed a stringent timeline keeping in mind their own imperatives and declined to accept late shipments. Those goods then found their way into foreign warehouses with no easy way of disposing them.

Shahzaib realized that the music was likely to stop soon. The severity of the entropy would remain concealed as long as the market was vibrant but a downturn would expose the weak financial position of the company instantly. Once it did, the floodgates would open. It would then be impossible to contain the onslaught. Banks and market debtors alike would descend on the carcass, like vultures. It could even lead the company into bankruptcy. It had become absolutely necessary to take immediate corrective measures. The company would have to streamline its management, restructure its debts and reorganize production and sales to increase efficiency and profitability.

Shahzaib could not naturally make such significant moves without Ayub's permission. Ayub was the owner and absolute boss of the establishment. However, Ayub had become so preoccupied with his personal affairs that he would brush off Shahzaib's attempts to engage him. The delay in implementing long overdue measures was only hastening the inevitable and so Shahzaib decided to confront the challenge immediately. The decision was injudicious but it was made with all sincerity, in the interest of the company and in Ayub's interest.

Shahzaib went about his task methodically. He took stringent austerity measures to bolster the company's finances, taking on the labor union loath to give up privileges so generously accorded by Ayub. As a first step, he got rid of the excessive flab in the shape of an army of parasitical hangers-on. He then set about rationalizing the business plan and decided to retain only the most profitable core. The company would henceforth restrict its operation to finished leather of superior quality. It would no longer manufacture and export made-ups such as leather jackets and other leather garments. These made-ups involved a longer gestation cycle and hurt the cash flow badly.

The changes brought about by Shahzaib were so profound and so plainly palpable that they could not escape Ayub's eventual notice. Ayub did not take too kindly to many of the measures that Shahzaib had instituted, though he did not question his sincerity or honesty. Ayub was particularly rankled by Shahzaib's activities in the factory. Shahzaib found himself spending a good deal of time there, trying to cope with the shortage of raw material. Imports of hides and skins were becoming difficult to arrange because the company could not discharge letters of credit on time and so Shahzaib had to procure most of the raw material from local suppliers. The local trade in hides and skins was of a personal nature and Shahzaib took it upon himself to deal personally with the now increasingly reluctant suppliers. He started cutting deals and settling contracts with them on his own cognizance. Ayub's authorization was no longer necessary in the matter. His writ was dissipating. In many ways Ayub was becoming an outsider in his own establishment.

The two men now engaged in arguments on every matter and these encounters were becoming all too frequent. Their attitude towards each other sometimes bordered on animosity, though both men continued to tolerate each other for the present. The exuberant warmth that not very long ago was the hallmark of their relationship was now beginning to fade away. Ayub started acting rather formal towards Shahzaib. He was courteous, too courteous, in fact. He seldom or never again put his arm on Shahzaib's shoulder the way he did in the balmy days of their ardent friendship. Matters were coming to a head between the two men and something would have to give, sooner rather than later.

CHAPTER 26

Jannat's health had taken a turn for the worse and she was now too unwell to look after herself. Ayub provided her with the best of care that money could buy. She was admitted to the finest hospital with the ablest doctors and nursing care in attendance but she continued to deteriorate. Noor was constantly by her mother's bedside, as she grew progressively worse. A few days went by thus and the caring daughter was with her mother all day and all night. Jannat woke up suddenly one night and addressed her daughter eagerly. She was barely audible.

"Do you remember the Sunday lunch at the villa where you and Shahzaib ended up alone? You asked me for an explanation but I was rather evasive. That made you quite angry, did it not?'

Noor was somewhat startled not only at the subject of her mother's concern but the resolve with which she addressed her at such an ill-appointed hour.

"Yes, Mother I do remember but why are you reminding me of it? I assure you I took no offence to it."

"Well, I hope not. I contrived the whole situation. I arranged the lunch and the invitation to Shahzaib and I kept your father away from it. I turned off both our phones because I knew you would call as soon as Shahzaib arrived. I wanted you two to get together, to get an opportunity to meet each other alone and to get to know each other better."

"But why, Mother and why do you bring up this matter with such urgency in the middle of the night?"

"I wanted you to be married while I was still alive. There was a reason why I wished so, beyond my desire to see you settled in life. I cannot explain my dilemma but you will surely find out in time. I thought of Shahzaib as the perfect match for you and I did entertain the hope that you would one day marry him."

She let out a deep sigh of despondency and continued with some difficulty.

"Alas, that is not to be. I may not live long enough. In any case, Yuba will never permit Shahzaib to court you anymore. He fancies him much less now than he did earlier. I know his intractable ways. I know him well."

"Please, Mother, do not despair. You will be better soon. I do not think Father and Shahzaib are so far apart. They will perhaps be good friends again someday. Fate alone will decide how my life turns out. It can be no worse than the trials and tribulations we have faced together."

"I don't know, I don't know."

Jannat was quite listless as she muttered those words. A vacant look appeared on her face. She slumped onto the pillow, closed her eyes and a few minutes after the conversation, she was dead. With Jannat's death died a thousand rancid secrets, or so one might have supposed.

CHAPTER 27

Jannat's death had left father and daughter in each other's exclusive company. Now that the two were alone, Ayub had greater opportunity to communicate with his daughter but it was never easy for the two to engage in any meaningful exchange. Their relationship never permitted a facile dialogue in spite of the apparent affection between the two. Ayub persisted in probing the innermost feelings of Noor and he did so without caution or prudence. His constant inquiring caused a great deal of discomfort, not to mention some embarrassment, for the poor girl. Ayub, however, had an overwhelming need to reconcile his own feelings with that of his daughter, to establish a true father-daughter relationship now that it was unhindered by the presence of her mother. He was relentless.

"Noor, did your mother talk much about me? I mean, did she tell you who I am and what our relationship was before we got married?"

"Not much except that you were a distant relative from the village, a second or third cousin, perhaps."

Ayub winced at her reply.

"And you were never curious how the marriage came about so suddenly?"

"I suppose I was but I had no reason to press for an explanation. I have no need for answers to mother's personal life."

"Your dead father, do you think often about him? I mean, do you even think of him as a father, I mean, ahead of me?"

It was a puzzling query and took Noor by surprise. She had no idea where the conversation was headed and was now becoming a bit exasperated. She thought Ayub might be trying to reaffirm a relationship that her mother's death had torn asunder. As far as she was concerned, the only basis of her relationship with Ayub was the marriage of her mother to him and with the death of her mother, the relationship stood terminated, at least legally it did. Instead of laying bare the insinuation it seemed to contain, she replied calmly but rather forcefully, even addressing Ayub as father to allay his misgivings.

"My father is dead but please don't call him my dead father. I do think of him every single day and I do think of him as my father. How could it be otherwise? You are my stepfather but I wish very much to continue to think of you as a father, if that is what you wish too and if you permit me, Father."

Ayub had meant to lead Noor on, to prod her to place him ahead of the other man she had known as her father. It was obvious from such conversations that he was constantly seeking reassurances from his daughter. The thought that his daughter was ignorant of her paternity annoyed him, even though he had instructed Jannat not to reveal their earlier separation to the girl. He was concerned over the tenuous nature of their relationship and so it would remain as long as Noor was unaware that he was her real father. As he continued to confront the dilemma, he also became obsessively concerned with the possibility of losing Noor. Ayub could never rein in his impulses even when he knew that his impulsiveness would consume him. At last, he could no longer suppress his fear and one day he divulged the true status of their relationship to Noor. Ayub was never good with words and his sharp tongue had a rather blunt edge to it. He addressed Noor on this sensitive subject with his characteristic bluntness.

"Your mother should have told you more about me. It would have made it easier for me to stand before you today. Noor, I am your real father and not the other man you have always thought of as a father. Your mother and I were man and wife when we were young and you were our only child from the wedlock. I even chose your name. What you saw by way of our marriage was actually our remarriage. Shame alone prevented your mother from telling you the truth. I am telling you everything because I'd rather that you should hate me bitterly for my disgraceful past or even despise my presence in your life than to be ignorant of our ties of blood."

He then went on to disclose the manner of their separation, though suitably avoiding the more sordid details of the incident. At first Noor had no idea what Ayub was talking about. The deeply emotional manner of his address reinforced her confusion. However, the thrust of Ayub's crudely delivered verbiage soon became apparent. Noor stood ashen-faced. She could not decide whether to believe his story to be true but she became greatly agitated. Her knees weakened and she dropped on to the chair, weeping inconsolably, cupping her face in her hands. She wanted to confront Ayub but her nerves failed her. Suddenly, she seemed oddly troubled by his presence. Ayub too could discern her awkwardness plainly. He did not even attempt to defend the reprehensible action of his past. He exerted himself only to secure his present position in a passionate effort to evoke sympathy or even pity.

"Don't cry, don't cry. I cannot bear it. I am your father; why should you cry. Is it because I revealed a bitter truth? Am I so dreadful because I chose to shake you out of your complacent ignorance? I admit I treated your mother roughly but I will be kinder to you than your supposed father ever was. I'll do anything if you would only look upon me as your father."

He then departed from her presence abruptly and left her alone for the evening, to her great relief. She sat down and wept, not for her mother now but for the man she had known as a father for much of her life, agitated by the thought that she would be desecrating his memory by accepting Ayub as a father.

In the days ahead, Ayub and Noor became more comfortable in each other's company though. The emotions displayed by Ayub had quite convinced Noor that he was indeed her father. She had come to know him sufficiently well to conclude that he could not be feigning such emotions. He was simply incapable of hypocrisy. Even otherwise, for practical consideration, she saw no reason to dissociate herself from Ayub. Noor had always been a practical person, thinking through problems with her mind rather than accessing her heart for solutions. She, therefore, set about becoming the true woman of the house.

The subject of changing her family name now became more pertinent and she readily agreed to her father's precept. She rationalized that she would not be showing any disrespect for the man she had supposed as her father by taking on the name of her real father. The next morning as Noor announced breakfast, both father and daughter were in good cheer. For the first time, Ayub bent down and kissed his daughter on her forehead.

CHAPTER 28

It was natural that the state of affairs between Ayub and Shahzaib should become a point of gossip within the trade. There even arose rumors that Ayub was planning to part with his young protégé. He could now barely tolerate Shahzaib anymore. He had started reasserting himself in the position that he had abdicated and reversed many of the decisions that Shahzaib had taken earlier. Ayub's newfound assertiveness had placed Shahzaib in an untenable position and he had started distancing himself from the affairs of the company. The tug-of-war between the two men was having an adverse effect on the business that was already in some disarray. There came a final breaking point and Ayub dismissed Shahzaib from his employment.

The news of Shahzaib's dismissal spread like wildfire and there was intense speculation as to what the younger man would do next. Most thought he would go back to his hometown and take up a job there, perhaps even reclaim his old job. The thought that he might go away saddened many of his acquaintances. The leather trade in the city had come to admire him for his knowledge of the craft and even appreciated his business acumen. Besides, everyone knew that he was loyal to Ayub and that his dealings were clean and above board. The general opinion was that Ayub had caused himself a grievous loss and that Shahzaib's departure was a misfortune for his boss.

Soon the news reached Noor. She had quietly observed the changed attitude of each man towards the other of late and that had made her anxious. She thought that if Ayub severed his relationship with Shahzaib, he would probably leave town. The anticipation of Shahzaib's future with Ayub had continued to weigh heavily on her though there was nothing she could do about it. She could broach the subject neither with her father nor with Shahzaib. Now that Ayub had finally parted with Shahzaib, she worried over his imminent departure. Noor decided to see Shahzaib and find out for herself. They met and took a walk along the street. Shahzaib opened the conversation, as usual.

"I have been looking for you. I wanted to tell you that I might be leaving town soon."

"But why would you leave?"

She faltered in her speech, anxious to seek hurried answers to a most unsettling question that was bedeviling her.

"I fear I have offended your father irretrievably, as a mere matter of business of course, nothing more, nothing personal. Yet I cannot see how we can continue our personal relationship anymore."

Noor breathed a melancholy sigh as Shahzaib continued.

"I wish I were richer and your father had not been offended by me, I would have asked you to . . ."

He trailed off without finishing his thought but continued with the insinuation.

"But that's not for me now."

What he would have asked her to do remained unstated, at least for now. She did not press him either, remaining incompetently mute.

"By the way, I am to this day curious about that lunch at the mansion. Did you ever find out who or what was behind it? I still think it was meant to allow us to meet alone though I do know for sure that the situation was not of your making."

Shahzaib gave out a chuckle, as if to make sure Noor understood that his remarks were in jest and did not interpret his words to imply that she had a particular interest in him. Noor, however, took no note of it and went on to answer him quite blandly.

"Yes, I did, it was Mother."

"I wonder why?"

"I am not sure."

Noor's reply was not quite honest. She knew well that there was no point to it now. There followed a long silence before Shahzaib continued the conversation wistfully.

"I wonder if the folks around here will remember me when I am gone."

"Nobody will forget you, I am sure of that. I wish you would not go away at all though. Do think it over again."

Noor spoke those words with deeply felt sadness.

"I will, but I see no reason to stay on. I must take your leave now. I will go my way alone and not accompany you to your home, lest word of our liaison reaches your father."

They both walked their separate ways, at least for now.

Ayub was aware of the developing relationship between Shahzaib and Noor. The courtship of his daughter by Shahzaib would have been a source of great delight for him only a few months earlier but it was beginning to cause him anguish now. Noor reached home only to find her father pacing the floor of the foyer, waiting for her. As soon as she entered, he turned around to address her and she stopped dead in her stride. There was something in his tone and general demeanor that foretold the contents of the speech about to emanate from him. She appeared alarmed.

"I have been hearing from people that you and Shahzaib have been cavorting all over town. You were with him just now, were you not?"

"Yes, Father, I was."

"I just want to caution you. You are my daughter and I do expect that you will always act in a most dignified manner. I am not blaming you, you understand, but I hope you haven't promised him anything, or gone beyond casual conversation."

"No. I have promised him nothing."

"Good. I particularly wish you not to see him again."

Noor was astounded at her father's words. It was, in many ways, an audacious demand coming from a person who had until recently been a total stranger. She had yet to get accustomed to Ayub as her real father and did not desire to confront him, much less defy him. In any case, she had always been compliant by nature, not at all aggressive. Her response would not have surprised her mother at all.

"Very well, Father, if it means so much to you."

Noor delivered her assurance quite meekly but it was clearly without conviction. In fact, she was hurt at her father's lack of compassion.

"Yes, it means a great deal to me. He is now a hazard to our business interests and an enemy of our family."

Ayub confirmed his stance curtly to leave no room for ambiguity. In an instant, he had declared his erstwhile favored friend an enemy, not only of his business but also of his family, a family that had not even existed when Shahzaib became a necessary cog in his life. Upon hearing her father's irrational edict, Noor left abruptly for her room upstairs. Ayub entered his study, sat down on his desk and started writing a note. The object of his communication was to convey to Shahzaib what he had already instructed his daughter, a pithy note devoid of any reference to their past relationship.

Shahzaib,

> *I am writing this note to tell you that in future you may not meet or speak with my daughter. She, on her part, has promised not to contact you under any circumstance. I expect you will not force yourself upon her.*

Ayub

To someone unfamiliar with the dark underside of Ayub's personality, such conduct would have seemed strange. Yet it was so becoming of his character that that was, perhaps, the only way he was capable of responding to the latest vexation in his life. Any other person so convinced of the man's utility would have encouraged him to marry his daughter but such a scheme for buying over a potential rival was alien to Ayub's headstrong faculties. Such finesse and diplomacy was not the stuff his ego could forbear easily. The only emotions he ever experienced lay in the extremes of love and hatred.

CHAPTER 29

Over the next few days, the course of action that Shahzaib had chosen became quite clear. He decided to set up his own business in town and rented a small tannery that would serve as a base for his operations. If he were fortunate enough to garner work beyond the capacity of that tannery, he could get it done on contract at other establishments. Though he was starting out with precious little capital, he had the one thing that could tide him over initially, his good will within the local trade.

As he went about setting up his business, Shahzaib was mindful of the fact that he was able to do so only because Ayub had provided him the opportunity to cut his teeth in the trade locally. His elevated standing in the market was due only to the fact that he was a representative of a large and well-known business house, though he had subsequently earned the respect and trust of the trade because of his extraordinary acumen. The trade received the news that he was setting himself up in the business with a measure of anticipation and equanimity, even demonstrative alacrity. Yet the fickleness of the trade that Shahzaib was entering now as an independent agent was a well-known fact. Newcomers, big and small, had entered and departed with regularity. Despite such odds, many in the trade wished to see him succeed, not least because of their own antagonism to Ayub. Some though were simply eager to see how he would fare when he finally moved out of Ayub's shadow.

Shahzaib had established his creditworthiness in the market, buying and selling for Ayub independently of his oversight. He had cemented his personal credibility by somehow making certain that the contracts he negotiated never defaulted, even when Ayub's business began floundering. He was now in a position to parley the same contracts to his own account. Suppliers of hides and skins were willing to extend credit facilities though they were appropriately cautious. He had dealt with many foreign buyers on behalf of Ayub. Some of them willingly switched over to Shahzaib as an alternative to Ayub's failing business, foremost amongst whom was Ayub's linchpin in Europe, his longtime agent. The trade reposed such confidence in Shahzaib in so short a period that even those who had profited from their dealings with Ayub during his long and steady ascent had no qualms about dealing with him. There was no doubt within the community of those who dealt in leather or leather goods that Shahzaib was a rising star. Indeed, many recalled Ayub's own exploits in the trade and were quick to make comparisons, comparisons that were obviously inappropriate given the divergent circumstances of each.

The news that Shahzaib had set himself up independently soon reached Ayub and as could be expected, he did not take to it too kindly. His unthinking reaction was that Shahzaib had set himself up in competition with him. He was at a loss to understand why, when he had been so kind and generous to him, would Shahzaib pit himself against his benefactor. Ayub was convinced that Shahzaib was intent on causing his business harm. The more he thought of it, the more incensed he became with the young man. Years of self-control had brought him much success but his tone and manner once again started exhibiting the unruly volcanic stuff of his past. The mere mention of Shahzaib brought out the worst in him.

"Well, he has been a friend of mine. If I have not been a friend of his, who has? Did I not keep him with me and treat him as a son? Did I not lavish money on him and give him whatever he needed? I liked him so much that I would have shared my last crust with him. Now he has defied me. Well, damn it! I will have a tussle with him. If I cannot compete with an upstart, I have no business being here. I'll show him that I can run my business better than he can run his."

Meanwhile, Shahzaib had none of the animosity towards his former employer and friend and had no notion of competing with him. The trade was large enough for everyone who wished to try his luck and he intended to keep clear of Ayub. He was so eager to show an absence of antagonism towards his erstwhile mentor that he discouraged Ayub's old customers from ditching him in his, Shahzaib's, favor.

"He was once my friend and it is not for me to take business from him. I am sorry to disappoint you but I cannot hurt the business of a man who has been kind to me."

Shahzaib was a good man and such entreaties for the good of his former employer made him even more credible. His business increased by the day and nothing he did could go wrong. Whether it was his tremendous energy or sheer luck, he seemed to be on the right track more often than not. Luck, of course, is an inescapable part of any success story, as indeed it had been for Ayub. In the case of Shahzaib, it manifested itself most prominently in the fact that after years of downturn the leather industry picked up just as he entered it. The trade in leather was mostly an export trade and as Europe emerged from a recession, there was a great upsurge in demand internationally. Shahzaib just happened to arrive in the midst of this boom. A year earlier, he would have found it hard to survive in the depressed market. He was therefore lucky to be in the right place at the right time.

Luck, however, is not the whole story; character is fate. Ayub was essentially a person of gloomy disposition who tended to look at the dark side of the picture. It would not be inapt to describe him as a man who had quit his vulgar ways but had failed to find a light to guide him on a better path. Ayub viewed life as a mortal battle and failure was simply not an option. Shahzaib was just the opposite, a glowing personality who generally tended to be optimistic, a straightforward man with no kinks in his character, a man who strove for success but took failure in his stride.

A time came when Shahzaib could no longer avoid collision with his former friend. Try as he might he was compelled, in sheer self-defense, to retaliate against the fierce attacks of his former boss. The battle between the two was of great interest to the trade. Few could actually guess the end. Ayub was using up his already scarce resources against an enemy who had nothing to lose. It was in his character to put everything at stake to feed his immense ego. Shahzaib had become an enemy in essence, for henceforth the identity of Ayub's existence was the essential enmity of Shahzaib. He paid no heed to the consequences of his adventures. His personality knew no compromises.

The two men often encountered each other in the course of business. Shahzaib was always ready, even anxious to say a few friendly words but Ayub invariably gazed scornfully past him in the manner of one who had trusted and lost on account of a friend and could not find it within him to forgive the wrong. Since their now-storied estrangement, they had barely spoken a civil word to each other. Ayub watched Shahzaib's business grow with a certain bitterness even as his own began to wane. Indeed, the sullenness of his mind was as much to account for his rash decisions, as did the faults in his stars. In his bitterness, he was drinking poison hoping that it would kill the one who was the cause of that bitterness. In less time than could be imagined, two or three years at most, Shahzaib had established his name within the trade. Ayub, on the other hand, had started faltering. The trade soon began to note Ayub's increasingly impulsive and reckless manner in business. He started defaulting on his commitments and there were now fewer and fewer merchants ready to engage him or extend him further credit.

Ayub's success in the leather trade had given him more than just riches. He had been a resolute presence in the politics of his trade association and had twice served as its chair. He was subsequently elected as the president of the chamber of commerce and industry, the highest forum of the country's trade bodies. With his term at the chamber approaching its end, he had hinted to his friends that he would be interested in running for the chair of his trade association again. This time around, though, it would not be an easy proposition. With his business now faltering badly, his influence within the leather trade too was waning. Ayub could no longer commandeer the will of his fellow members as easily as he used to do in the past. He had inevitably stepped on many toes and those toes had never stopped hurting. There were many within the leather trade who took vicarious pleasure at his predicament. Now, what better way to humiliate a man then to have him put down by his own underling, one who owed his good fortune to his generosity? It would add insult to injury. Those who had previously lacked the courage to confront Ayub were now setting up the stage for his ultimate humiliation. Indeed, the thought of Shahzaib as 'the enemy of my enemy and hence my friend' was quite alluring.

CHAPTER 30

The news that Shahzaib had decided to settle down and start an independent business in town was a source of great relief for Noor. Nevertheless, she did apprehend that Shahzaib might have further endangered his interest in her by setting up a business in competition with her father. His move would no doubt only earn him more of Ayub's wrath. She hoped it was a passing impulse that had led her father to speak to her so harshly on the subject of her involvement with Shahzaib.

In the meanwhile, Shahzaib had received Ayub's request to discontinue any relationship that he might have had with Noor. His meetings with her were almost certainly devoid of passion or intimacy, so that the request was superfluous. Yet both had felt a certain romantic interest in each other that could have materialized in something more meaningful if pursued further. After some reflection, Shahzaib decided it would be prudent to let go of the relationship, for the girl's sake no less than his own.

Thereafter, Shahzaib and Noor had few if any opportunities to meet. On occasions that they did encounter each other, though neither contrived any, the exchange between them was always formal. The encounters were devoid of the lively banter that had begun to take place between them before Ayub's admonishment. Neither Shahzaib nor Noor was of the type who wore their passion on their shirtsleeves. Nor was either of them in any particular hurry to be involved in a serious relationship just yet and so, the incipient love was stifled in its tread. Shahzaib may have had some regrets on that count but it saddened Noor considerably more as the episode had promised to brighten up her lonely and almost dreary existence. In any case, both accepted the situation without too much remorse.

CHAPTER 31

In the meantime, Myra had disengaged herself from her business, her home, and friends in Europe and could not now avoid making the move. Her decision was motivated less by a desire to be close to Ayub—although one could not discount that factor completely—than by the fact that the measures she had taken in preparation for her move had rendered her virtually rootless. She would in any case have to start her life over again and she thought of making a new beginning in a new land.

The support of her relatives helped in easing her transition and in acclimatizing her to unfamiliar surroundings. With the passage of time, she set herself up independently. She bought a decent townhouse and furnished it in her own elegant style. She then set up a small office and soon thereafter commenced business as a buying house of leather products, attending to her business with a serious intent. In due course, she began hiring some staff and advertised her requirement in the local newspapers. The job situation in the country was such that a huge number of applicants responded to her advertisement for the handful of positions she was offering. Out of curiosity, or perhaps to gauge the quality of the available human resources, she decided to invite all applicants for an interview even though some may not have merited the call otherwise. She then got ready for the onslaught.

CHAPTER 32

Noor had convinced herself that Ayub was her real father but she had of late begun to feel less and less comfortable in the mansion. After the death of her mother, she was alone for the most part and her loneliness was becoming unbearable. She had not been brought up in the mansion and never really felt it belonged to her or she to it. She now felt a desperate need to occupy herself outside the house. Noor had been a working girl as far back as she cared to recall and had not been able to reconcile with her idleness. She predicated her decision as much on her need to maintain her sanity as on the expectation of earning some money. The money would rid her of her occasional supplications to her father and reduce her dependence on him. She was aware of her father's intransigent feelings towards working women but that did not dampen her enthusiasm for a change in her routine. She thought she would confront her father over the issue at a fitting time.

Noor scoured the local newspapers for job opportunities but came upon few, if any, that fit the profile of a young woman of her background and experience. She was so eager that she sent applications without too much concern for the qualifications for the job. She had made up her mind to accept the first offer that came her way. The moment finally arrived and Noor received a call for an interview. She had very little information about the nature of the job that she was being called for but that was a trivial concern.

Noor arrived at the office and took a measure of the premises, not that it mattered much. Nevertheless, she found the place quite agreeable and at once reckoned that she would not mind working there. She informed the receptionist of her purpose and was soon escorted to a chamber. On entering, she was pleasantly surprised that the person who was to interview her was a woman. The woman introduced herself as Myra. As Myra poured over Noor's application, she was alerted to her father's name. It read Ayub Qureishi. Qureishi was a common last name in those parts, as was the first name Ayub. It was hardly worthy of attention to come across an Ayub Qureishi at random. Yet Myra could not help wondering whether the applicant was the daughter of the man who had walked out on her.

The interview began as all job interviews do. After the usual pleasantries, there followed the stock questions and answers about qualifications, experience, salary, and so on. However, Myra could not contain her curiosity and started asking questions of a personal nature. She queried Noor about her father's antecedents. She wanted to know who he was, what he did for a living and where he lived etc. In an instance, she knew that the applicant's father was the man who had abandoned her for a supposedly higher calling and that the girl now sitting before her was the substance of that calling. She nevertheless continued probing Noor; the discovery had suddenly heightened her interest in the girl. Myra inquired whether mother and daughter both lived with the father. Noor was perplexed at the uncalled for query in the context of the job interview but informed her anyway that her mother had died sometime earlier. The news took Myra by surprise. It was not that she was saddened at the death of the poor girl's mother. She was, in fact, a bit shocked that Ayub had not bothered to communicate his new situation to her. Myra decided to offer the girl a position as her special assistant, a position that spelt out no specific job details but paid a good salary. She wanted the young woman to stay by her side for a good reason.

CHAPTER 33

Noor was a bit confused at the manner in which the interview had been conducted and the abrupt and immediate job offer. She had no idea what prompted the woman to offer her the position though she had a feeling that the personal questions had somehow led to it, perhaps, because of who her father was. She could not have imagined that the death of her mother might have been the more important factor. Nevertheless, she was, delighted to have obtained the job and immediately gave her willingness to come to work with the nascent company.

Noor had not expected to find a job so soon. She had planned to inform her father of her intention in due course and, perhaps, convince him to allow her to work outside the house. She would now have to inform him that she already had an offer for a job. She was certain he would upbraid her for having the temerity to take such a step without discussing it with him first and so she braced herself for his reaction. When her father returned home later that evening, she sat down with him to apprise him of the job offer. His first reaction was one of great surprise. He was surprised that someone would offer a job to his daughter that paid so well. Yet, he displayed no curiosity at all about the nature of the job or the identity of the company. It was now Noor's turn to be surprised. She had expected her father to react in a most sullen manner; she had expected anger, even rage. In the event, he displayed something worse, absolute indifference.

"Well, make the best of it and I hope the office teaches you a bit more than you learned in my house."

"You don't object?"

"No, I don't object at all. I want you to be independent."

Having thus obtained her father's permission in an unexpectedly facile manner, Noor started working at the office. She found the routine most pleasant and the kindness with which Myra treated her was overwhelming. She often dreaded leaving the office to return home and was quite content to work long hours. Working at the office was a learning experience. Above all, Myra introduced her to the ways of the genteel society, guidance that Ayub was ill equipped to provide. In time, Myra became a friend and a teacher to Noor. Noor, of course, had no idea of what lay hidden in Myra's past. In retrospect, she should have at least felt uneasy with Myra's continued interest in her personal affairs, such as when Myra asked her if she had shared any details of her workplace with her father. Noor, of course, had not done anything of that sort, chiefly because she knew her father would not care to know anyway. Noor just took Myra's queries in her stride, mistaking them for a show of concern for a new employee.

CHAPTER 34

Myra did entertain the thought of entering Ayub's life again when she learnt of the death of his wife, though the fact that he had not informed her of his new circumstances had riled her. The thought had crossed her mind merely as a protective mechanism. She no longer had the same feelings for him but for strong social reasons, she felt she could still marry him. She had employed Noor to facilitate a renewal of her acquaintance with Ayub or at least to make her presence known to him. She found out soon enough that Noor would not serve as a conduit to her father; there was obviously a complete lack of communication between the father and daughter. Under the circumstances, she felt compelled to contact him directly using the pretext of securing her artifacts. She thought of calling him on her phone but on second thought, she decided to write a note instead, to allow him time to contemplate her presence in town.

Ayub,

> *This note will no doubt surprise you. Yes, I have set myself up in town. What could I have done? I had already uprooted myself on your instructions and I had communicated the fact of our impending marriage to all my friends and relatives. It would have been demeaning to inform everyone that you had called off the marriage, that you had forsaken me for another woman. I do understand that you acted on the call of your conscience but others may have misconstrued your action. Even if I had somehow managed to retrieve my possessions, I could never have stayed on there.*
>
> *I would not have had the courage or the audacity to communicate with you directly if I had since not been made aware of the death of your wife. Even then, I am writing only because you have neglected my request to return my personal mementos. I wish very fervently to have them back. Since we now find ourselves in the same city, you may deliver those to me personally at my office. It will be quite appropriate for you to visit my office as I have in my employ your daughter and you can pretend to be visiting her.*

Myra

Ayub received Myra's letter in the midst of a great turmoil in his personal circumstances. He was leading a life of quiet desperation, immersed in enormous problems and deprived of a sincere friend. After the death of his wife and his estrangement from Shahzaib, he had no one he could turn to for moral support. The presence of Noor did give him some comfort but he could not unburden himself with her. He had all but erased the memory of Myra and had no idea about her new life or how she might be faring.

Now, as he went through Myra's letter, his eyes lit up and his heartbeat quickened with each line he read. He became excited at the possibility of renewing the relationship but his excitement subsided as he contemplated the motive behind Myra's letter. She was really only asking for her mementos and had done so in a previous communication too. Yet, he wondered if she had another object. He was hoping that the affection she once harbored for him had lingered on. He had to find out for himself. Ayub was so excited that he would have immediately set out to see Myra but there were far too many distractions to contend with, far too many issues competing for his attention just then.

CHAPTER 35

Ayub's business continued to wither due at least in part to a lack of adequate attention to its affairs. He had hired another manager after Shahzaib's estrangement but the man was the very antithesis of his predecessor. Not only was he incompetent, he was dishonest to boot. Ayub saw the need to replace him at once and lost no time in firing him. He was now once again in search of a new manager. Shahzaib had imparted a semblance of stability to Ayub's business but all those efforts were now truly in tatters. To make matters worse, the business had acquired the reputation of a sinking ship. Ayub's own reputation as an irrational, erratic and abusive boss was gaining currency and did not help him in his efforts to seek competent and honest men to his fold. In any case, his search for a manager had acquired a sense of urgency and he could not delay it any longer.

At that crucial moment, Alam Mirza re-entered Ayub's life in a chance encounter. Since his dismissal from Ayub's service, Alam Mirza had scraped by on odd jobs. He was in a bad way financially and scarcely able to take care of his family. As soon as he saw Ayub, Alam Mirza greeted him in a most supine manner. Without really meaning to offer him the job, Ayub made it known to him that he was looking for a manager.

"I heard that, sir. I heard Shahzaib was most ungrateful."

Alam Mirza was obviously trying to seize the opportunity to win over his old boss by vain remarks. In a moment of extreme thoughtlessness, Ayub blurted out a vacuous offer to him.

"Do you want your old job back?"

"Why certainly, sir!"

"When can you start?"

"I can start this very moment, sir. To be honest with you, I haven't had much luck since I left you."

"Very well, come by tomorrow morning and get on with the job."

Ayub had known Alam Mirza for a considerable period. He was aware of his character thoroughly. Yet so distracted was he from reality that he seemed not to remember the disgraceful manner in which he had treated Alam Mirza before dismissing him callously. Might he not now recall the harshness with which Ayub had dealt with him? Might he not recollect the deprivation that Ayub's conceit had made him suffer? Might he not evoke the anguish he suffered on account of his humiliation? Alam Mirza was a scarred man, a man of flawed character. It did not occur to Ayub that a man's character tends to deteriorate even more in times of great deprivation. Ayub had evidently begun to lose touch with reality. He was reliving his past without a shred of concern for the future. Delusional fantasies of power and inflated self-esteem seemed to overshadow his once vaunted pragmatism.

"You know I am still the biggest name in the leather trade in these parts and I aim to retain my position. Shahzaib has been making great strides but we must cut him down to size. Do you hear that? We two cannot exist side by side, that is clear. One of us must pass completely from existence. I have faced hardships all my life and even the worst vagaries of my existence have not been able to vanquish my will. Nor will I allow my own protégée to overwhelm me now."

"I, sir, have been a witness to your bold spirit. I cannot see how a mere pretender can usurp the exalted position that you have come to occupy by the dint of your hard work and the grace of God. You, sir, have divine sanction for worldly success."

Even Alam Mirza's abundant skills of sycophancy could barely disguise his false disposition, both of which had been his hallmark throughout his life. It was amazing then that a perceptive man like Ayub failed to penetrate the thin veneer of sincerity that Alam Mirza draped around him. Ayub chose not to look at the dark side of Alam Mirza's character because he was more comfortable with familiar faces, irrespective of their quality. It was one of his more enduring traits, though Shahzaib was a sterling exception.

"By God, I shall dispatch this upstart to his rightful destination. I mean, we will annihilate him by fair competition, of course, by hard, keen and unflinching competition. I want to grind him into the ground. I have the capital, mind you, and I can do it."

Alam Mirza was quick to enlist himself in furthering Ayub's plans.

"I know exactly what you want and I know how to do it."

Alam Mirza disliked Shahzaib because he had displaced him and deprived him of a decent living, though that was not strictly true. This made him a willing tool against him but it also made him at the same time a hazardous choice. Alam Mirza listened to Ayub with feigned enthusiasm as he continued with his barely coherent diatribe.

"I sometimes think Shahzaib has some kind of a divining glass which shows him the future. His success is beyond the comprehension of all those who carry on their trade honestly. But we must beat him at his own game and snuff out his pretensions."

The re-hiring of Alam Mirza was yet another monumental indiscretion of Ayub, at par, perhaps, with the re-induction of Jannat in his life.

CHAPTER 36

It was once again the time of the year when the faithful slaughtered a large number of animals as a ritual sacrifice because of which enormous quantities of hides and skins flooded the market. This year though, the market was chock-full of sellers and few buyers and so prices were at a near all-time low. Nevertheless, the market did anticipate an eventual upsurge in time for the next production cycle. By all indications, it seemed like an opportune time to stock up. Moreover, itinerant traders laden with large stocks were prepared to settle for easy credit terms. Ayub had designs that suited the traders.

Ayub had made his fortune under similar conditions many years earlier, buying recklessly in a weak market. This time too he decided to mop up the market, though not necessarily for sound commercial reasons. In fact, he had designed his move to pre-empt Shahzaib from stocking up. Even though Ayub had been faltering on his payments, he was still in a position to lift large quantities of goods on his word alone. Besides, the traders too egged him on in his recklessness because they could off load their stocks at a higher price on credit. Easy availability of credit is often the cause of ruin as it leads to lax financial controls. Unfortunately, this time around, Ayub had no one by his side who could make him aware of his follies and so he was defenseless.

Shahzaib had also been eager to stock up but he was more cautious. He had with him old hands, once fiercely loyal to Ayub, who restrained him and advised him to be selective in his purchases. His lack of opportunities no doubt also tempered his ambition. He had not yet cultivated the banks sufficiently to enable him easy access to funds. The traders too were cautious in dealing with him, in spite of his impressive credentials. They had not really dealt with him extensively in his own capacity and did not want to take an excessive risk. What Shahzaib might have imagined as his weakness, though, would turn out to be his strength.

Ayub managed to corner the market but he racked up millions in debt in the process. In the midst of his heedless adventure, prices suddenly started crashing further instead of surging. It was a freak phenomenon. An unusually mild winter in a neighboring country and a sudden abatement in the civil war there encouraged herdsman and merchants to dump their wares and to store up on food and other commodities. Ayub now held huge stocks that continued to lose value but he would not heed the advice of the market punters. Instead, he would bellow fiercely at anyone who tried to remind him of the harsh reality.

"It's nothing serious, my friend, nothing serious! These things happen, do they not? I know people are going around saying that I am a bit tight these days but is that anything rare in a large business such as mine. A man who is scared of the common hazards of trade has no reason to be in the market."

Ayub soon started faltering on his payments, his defaults acquiring a more distressful dimension each passing day. His dealings had been so extensive that he had exposed himself even more extravagantly than he had planned. In the ensuing turmoil that engulfed the market, Alam Mirza could no longer deal with the situation effectively. Ayub had to step in personally to confront the mess. A time came when he could no longer postpone a settlement with the traders. Tempers were now beginning to fray. Ayub had to endure long harangues of his trading partners with a constrained bearing. He had never been through such humiliating sessions with the traders before. As Ayub came out of one such session, Alam Mirza walked up to him and uttered a few words of sympathy. His words were like a detonator to a keg of dynamite and Ayub flew into a volcanic rage immediately.

"If it hadn't been for your blasted advice, I would not be standing here in this position. How could you fail to read the market? Why did you let me go on buying when a word of doubt from you would have made me think twice?"

The words emanating from Ayub were vintage Ayub. He was passing on the burden of his rashness on one who was a weak link in the chain and was trying to extricate himself from the damning onus. Alam Mirza had nothing to lose, of course. Ayub would be the one to suffer the consequences and so Alam Mirza continued to engage Ayub, now in scathing terms.

"I did inform you sir, that the market was turning volatile and my advice was to do what you thought best under the circumstances."

"A useful bit of advice that was and the sooner you stop providing me with your inane advice the better it will be for me. So take your wares elsewhere and be done with me."

The conversation continued in that vein until it ended in Alam Mirza's sacking. Ayub dismissed Alam Mirza for the second time but his humiliation by him had been a perpetual feature of their long relationship. Ayub's had a proclivity to humiliate constantly supine and servile individuals such as Alam Mirza. Yet, he could continue an association with such people. It was usual too for a person of Alam Mirza's ilk to keep bearing Ayub's humiliation with such shamelessness yet continue to harbor expectations from him. Ayub had the knack of never learning from his mistakes but Alam Mirza was a quick learner. Ayub turned around and left whereupon Alam Mirza gazed at him spitefully, muttering a warning under his breath.

"You will be sorry for this, Ayub, sorry as a man can be."

If Ayub thought he knew Alam Mirza well, he had no idea of his evil capacity. People of Alam Mirza's disposition could create unimaginably grave circumstances when their fury is aroused. An ant can cause grave damage to an elephant merely by entering its ear.

CHAPTER 37

Noor had started feeling more content with her life now than she had been in a long time. The atmosphere at the office and the companionship of her boss was imparting a very positive impact on her personality. She was now more self-assured and assertive and no longer fretted over her father's odd moods or heeded the many restrictions imposed by him. In her newfound confidence, she even managed to summon the courage to telephone Shahzaib. Shahzaib had taken Ayub's admonishment seriously and had kept clear of Noor since. He had no burning passion for the girl anyway and wished not to create a situation with her father. Now when Noor informed Shahzaib of her new circumstances— that she was on her way to becoming independent—he was curious. He promised to visit her at the office as soon as he could. Noor waited for his visit expectantly.

Myra too had entertained certain expectations; she had expected Ayub to call on her immediately on receiving her note. She knew his impetuous nature well and could readily anticipate his reaction. She was therefore unable to figure out why he had not called on her forthwith. Myra had no way of knowing Ayub's preoccupations in other matters just then. She could not inquire from Noor either. She at once concluded that his arrogance had kept him away, or else he would have at least informed her of the delay. Her thoughts were now castigating her for the naivety of her presumptions. Perhaps, she had made a mistake by inviting him in the first place. It was obvious, she thought, that he had no further interest in her and she too lost whatever zest she might still have had for him up until then. Still, there was the matter of the mementos that Ayub had yet to return despite her request. It had become even more imperative now to retrieve them from his possession. She wrote a second note, taking care this time to neither address it directly to him nor attribute it to herself. It was, of course, unnecessary to do either.

> *I am sadly disappointed that you have not come to see me at my invitation. I can hardly suppress my anxiety over the possibility that a careless or inadvertent move might reveal our past. It concerns me even more now that I have set myself up in the same city. The coincidence of our nearness can highlight our relationship even more prominently before society. I would appreciate it very much if you could return my letters and photographs forthwith. You may come to my office on Monday morning and announce yourself as a business associate. I had thought that your daughter's presence in my office would present a convenient excuse for you to visit but it may have been the cause of your neglect. I will send her away for the morning so that I shall be quite alone to receive my possessions.*

As soon as Myra reached her office on Monday, she instructed her staff at the reception about the impending visit of a business associate, without actually naming the man. She then waited anxiously for Ayub. Presently, there was a knock on the door and a man entered her office. The man was many years younger than Ayub and somewhat pleasant looking, though not particularly handsome. He wore a smartly cut suit, quite in contrast to the constant drabness with which Ayub draped himself. It was Shahzaib and he had come to visit Noor. The receptionist had directed Shahzaib to Myra without even inquiring of his purpose, mistaking him as the business associate expected by her. The sudden appearance of the man caught Myra unawares, putting her in an awkward situation. Shahzaib tried to redress the uncomfortable situation as he attempted to explain his position.

"I am sorry. I came for Noor and your receptionist showed me in here. I would not have caught you in such an unmannerly way if I had known."

"I was actually expecting somebody and I thought you were the person."

"I might have come to the wrong office."

"Oh, no, you are in the right office but the wrong chamber. Noor will be back shortly. You may wait for her, if you wish,"

Myra had obviously forgotten that she had sent Noor off for the entire morning in anticipation of Ayub's visit. In any case, she had meant for Shahzaib to wait at the reception. Shahzaib mistook her expression as an invitation to occupy the vacant chair in her own chamber. He hesitated, looked at the chair and the seemingly innocuous offer and sat down. Myra was uncomfortable in the presence of the stranger particularly since she was expecting Ayub but she thought it would be an unbecoming gesture if she were to ask him to leave her chamber now that he had taken a seat. Shahzaib too was not particularly comfortable and sat clumsily. After a short interlude of embarrassing silence, Myra ventured to rid the moment of its awkwardness.

"By the way, I am Myra. If you are here on business, I may be able to help you."

"Oh no, I am not! I am not even aware of the business conducted in this office. Actually, Noor invited me to come by. It is a personal visit."

"Have you known Noor long?"

"Yes and no. I met her a while back but was properly acquainted with her only recently. Noor told me that this office was only just set up. Are you the moving spirit behind the venture?"

"You are making me self-conscious, really. Yes, I did set it up but referring to me as a moving spirit would surely be an absurdity."

"You are being modest. It takes a lot of courage and perseverance to set up a new business. But what, may I ask, is the nature of your business?"

"I am in the leather trade. I am a buying agent for finished leather and leather made-ups for clients in Europe."

"Oh, really, now that is interesting. I am a manufacturer of precisely the type of goods that you buy. I did not introduce myself, did I? My name is Shahzaib."

Shahzaib fished out a visiting card from his pocket and handed it over to Myra. Myra reciprocated with her card. She had no idea of the man's connection with the guest she was expecting or else she would have been desperately anxious to rid her office of his presence before Ayub's expected arrival. On the contrary, she was beginning to feel comfortable with the young man's attendance. Something about his comportment, which had awakened the interest of Ayub, Noor and the people he worked with had made his unexpected presence attractive to Myra. The pleasantness of finding that they had common business interests and that the business of one in some ways complemented that of the other, contributed to further their attentiveness in each other. As they continued their conversation, uneasy though it was at first, their manner became more relaxed as Myra threw the first volley of lighthearted wit.

"Well, congratulations. I have just anointed you as my first client. You know how it works in these parts. The first client is always entitled to a discount and you qualify for it."

Myra chuckled and gestured in a manner that seemed to announce that the proposition was none too serious. Her repartee set the ball in motion and Shahzaib too was not above a little adroit verbiage of his own.

"So you do think I qualify for such consideration? It seems my visit may yet turn out to be a blessing in disguise. Now seriously, my company is new and even though I am quite experienced in the trade, I am quite concerned for my business prospects. I wonder if you feel the same way."

"Not really. I too have worked in this trade for a few years in Europe, first with my father and then on my own. I don't see how it could be any different here."

"Ah but you fail to take into account the nature of our society and, more importantly, the peculiar nature of this trade. Our society is male-dominated and the leather trade even more so. Worse still, it is not exactly a gentlemen's club. It is a rough trade and education and genteel manners may even be a disqualification. You are probably the only woman associated with it. Anyway, I wish you luck and if you should need any help, I would be happy to assist you. I can imagine you must be quite alone."

The reference to her being alone was obviously not an earnest inquiry of her personal situation but an allusion to

Myra's single-handed effort. Yet it did have the effect of a double entendre, as an inquiry of her single status, perhaps, and threw Myra off guard for a moment. That, of course, was not Shahzaib's object at all. Be that as it may, Myra was quite competent to deal with it. She flung her hair back, smiled faintly and offered a rather meaningful riposte.

"I don't know that I am alone but I am certainly lonely."

Shahzaib was not nearly as quick-witted as Myra and he continued with his inept conversation.

"But you are rich, are you not? Wealth can buy you any kind of company you desire."

His assessment of her riches was no doubt superficial and carried out in the same awkward vein but Myra was never at a loss of words except in the company of Ayub. In fact, one could at times misconstrue her forthright manner as leading men on.

"If that is so, I don't know how to enjoy my riches. I came to this city thinking I should like to live here. But I wonder if I shall?"

"Where did you come from, madam?"

"My father was actually born in this city but I was born in Europe and have lived there all my life. I have visited this city many times over the years, though, and I do have relatives here."

"I am not from the city either though mercifully I have not had to travel as far as you have. It is better to stay at home but a man must go wherever his work takes him. It is a great pity to be compelled to leave your native land. Yet I can have no complaints. I have done very well here."

Myra regarded him with a critical interest. He was somehow different from the men she had met since she arrived in the city. During the course of the conversation, Shahzaib deliberately avoided looking at Myra fixedly, exchanging only occasional glances. At last, their eyes met in an evocative exchange. Both seemed transfixed for a moment. Shahzaib was the first to blink, muttering an uneasy and entirely unnecessary apology.

"I am boring you now."

"Oh no, not at all. On the contrary, I would say you are rather interesting."

Shahzaib was beginning to show signs discomfiture. One could now discern a slight blush on his face.

"I must leave now. I have taken too much of your time."

He got up to leave. Myra continued to sit in her chair as she held out her hand towards the man. Shahzaib leaned forward to reach out to her. Their hands lingered on in an embrace for a few moments before he made his way towards the door and stepped out. Myra's action in holding out her hand was instinctive, as was to be expected from a woman rooted in European cultural traditions. Shahzaib's reaction though might have been one of awkward acquiescence. In his social milieu, men and women did not shake hands. Yet, the moment had its magic. Interestingly, Myra too was exhilarated with her own seemingly innocuous gesture. As she sat watching him depart, an embarrassing thought crossed her mind.

"My god! Was I flirting with this complete stranger? I hope he did not take too much notice of my responses. I hope he didn't misconstrue my conduct."

Curiously, no mention of Noor came up in the course of the conversation beyond Shahzaib's statement of the purpose of his visit. She, after all, was the reason for Shahzaib's visit and not Myra. The mention of Ayub too eluded their exchange. He, after all, was the object of Myra's anticipation and not Shahzaib.

More importantly, the four had converged in a single space though not necessarily of their own volition. None of them was a native of the city but the city had enticed each of them in turn, though the presence of each was a result of circumstances unique to him or her. Surely, they could not all have come together as an improbable accident of no consequence.

CHAPTER 38

The unintended encounter between Myra and Shahzaib is worthy of further introspection, not least because of its unusual characteristics. From merely affording Myra a new form of idleness—idle conversation on which she never wasted her time—Shahzaib had gone on to awaken her curiosity. In turn, Myra seemed to enkindle the young man's enthusiasm until he was brimming with awkward sentiment. In the days that followed, Shahzaib sought opportunity to both call and visit Myra, pretending at first to be making business inquiries. The fact that both were engaged in complementary trades gave credence to his pretense of a professional interest in her. Soon he dropped all pretenses and started visiting her in her own right. Myra too reciprocated amply, receiving Shahzaib with enthusiasm on each visit. Their demeanor could barely mask the true nature of their interest in each other. Yet the two conducted their relationship in an extremely guarded manner. One could evidence the indecision between their desire not to separate and the need for circumspection.

Noor was naturally privy to at least some of Shahzaib's visits to the office. She was not naive, of course. She had observed enough to lead her to conclude that there was more to their encounters than met the eye. Myra's obvious inclination towards Shahzaib and his undisguised excitement in her company offered more than tell-tale signs. Soon it became impossible for Noor to overlook their growing relationship though her feelings in that regard were quite ambiguous. After all, there had been no deep involvement between Shahzaib and her, nor any firm commitment for the future. She did recall her warm feelings for him, though not quite passionate yet but she rationalized that it was, perhaps, her insecurity that had attracted her to the man in the first place and that eventually it might have turned to naught anyway. Under the circumstances, Noor thought that it would be best if she stepped out of the way of the budding romance. For the present though, Myra persisted in dragging her into the circle, more for maintaining a decorous appearance than for any purposeful engagement. Conventionally speaking, Shahzaib would converse with both Myra and Noor but it was plainly evident that the object of his interest was Myra. He appeared to see right through Noor as though she were invisible. He answered even her occasional quip with civilly indifferent remarks. Noor was more like an awkward fifth wheel that had no immediate relevance but that could be of great utility in times of need. At first Noor managed to bear Shahzaib's frosty treatment with equanimity but she later thought it best to remove herself completely from the inharmonious situation in which she found herself. In any case, he hardly seemed the same person who had almost courted her not so long ago. Her contrivance to detach herself from the amorous duo proved unnecessary as Shahzaib and Myra moved into the next phase of their intimacy.

CHAPTER 39

Ayub received Myra's second note and at once decided to meet her on that fateful Monday. However, his ongoing problems distracted him and he failed to keep the appointment yet again. Subsequently, he attempted to meet her several times but she was unavailable on each occasion. His constant inability to see Myra perturbed him. He became convinced that it was no accident, that perhaps she was being inaccessible because she might have perceived his lack of response as a snub. In any case, he did visit the office again but this time he did not bother with the receptionist and virtually barged into Myra's chamber. Myra was sitting at her desk and stood up as Ayub entered, more out of surprise than as a gesture of high regard. He greeted her casually in the manner of a routine get-together even though the two had parted under unnatural circumstances and had not met since. Ayub was acting as if nothing had transpired in the interregnum but Myra was not amused at all. Her passion for Ayub had lasted well enough until a new love usurped it. She did not even reciprocate his greeting and instead reproached him for his sloth.

"Why do you come now when so many days have passed since I invited you to visit me?"

Ayub shrank back a little at the unexpectedly harsh tone employed by Myra and became almost deferential.

"Why, I called before, on the first opportunity that my business affairs permitted me to but you were not available. I am here now and I cannot tell you how happy I am to see you again. I hope you understood the compulsion under which I had to call off our marriage. The woman for whose sake I was forced to sever my ties with you is dead. Please give me another chance and I will make it up to you. I promise you."

Ayub had evidently assumed that Myra's overture was a call for resuming their relationship at the point where he had severed it, a continuation of the balmy old days. He made no effort to gauge her changed circumstances since he met her last and was of a mind to treat her as he usually did. It did not surprise Myra at all.

"Why do you assume that I am ready to resume our relationship? You never even informed me of your wife's death. I learnt of it from your daughter. Did you expect me to grovel before you, to beg you to take me back? I invited you only for the purpose of retrieving my letters and I can tell that you have come without them."

Myra could see that her forceful reproach had had the desired effect. Ayub just stared at her blankly, unable to read the nature of the situation in which he had landed. Myra moderated her tone as a measure of caution and continued with an evasive response designed to placate Ayub somewhat. Ayub was always capable of reacting in a most vile and maladroit fashion.

"Besides, I am not prepared for a relationship just yet. I need time to settle down in my new life before I commit myself for the future."

"Yes, yes, I suppose it is early. I can see your changed state. You are an independent businesswoman now, even more so than the hesitant young woman who took charge of her father's business reluctantly. The fact is that it is a bit awkward to direct attention towards you in your present situation."

"And why is that so?"

"Well, there's nobody in the world I would have wished such success more than you and nobody becomes it more. I can only say that I am proud of you."

Myra felt visibly embarrassed at the warm feelings of admiration exuded by Ayub. It was so off character for him to heap such profuse praise that she flinched at it. She gathered her wits about her and immediately composed herself.

"I am greatly obliged to you for those sentiments."

Her patronizing manner upset Ayub and he suddenly took on an altogether different attitude, one that was more in conformity with his character.

"You may or may not be obliged and what I am saying may not have quite the polish you are accustomed to. But my sentiments are real and they are for the woman I knew in her past."

"That's a rather rude way of speaking to me."

Ayub at once toned down, feeling the bite in her speech. Both Ayub and Myra were waxing hot and cold, unable to gauge accurately the thrust of each other's response. They were, it seemed, taking a measure of each other's attitudes like boxers in the opening round of a new matchup.

"I do not wish to quarrel with you. I have come as you desired and I have come to make good on my promise to you, to safeguard your past. On my previous visit, I had brought along your letters and other articles but I was unable to deliver those."

The mention of her past by Ayub seemed almost as if he was threatening her. She was certain that he knew nothing of her newfound interest in Shahzaib but it was not difficult to predict how he would react when he did find out. She wanted to ward him off somehow and once again assumed a deliberately aggressive posture.

"How can you speak to me with such brutish vulgarity? Was my crime that I indulged foolishly in a young girl's passion with too little regard for propriety? You made me suffer at a most worrisome time. If I am a little independent now, surely the privilege is not unmerited."

"Yes, you are right. It is certainly not unmerited. Unfortunately, society will judge you not by reality but by perception, not by substance but by appearance. I, therefore, think you ought not to be carried away with quaint notions of independence. You should accept me for the sake of your own good name. What is known abroad may get known here."

Myra was flabbergasted at Ayub's insinuation. She had never been at the receiving end of such uncivil language from him in the past. She was certainly unprepared for it, especially at the first meeting after an interlude for which he alone was to blame. She might have understood if she had known about the setbacks he was faced with and that these setbacks were beginning to unhinge him emotionally, causing his real character to emerge stealthily. In reality, he was hardly the same person she had known in his previous circumstances. At any rate, anxiety suddenly overcast Myra and she thought it best to deflect Ayub's unsavory parries with gentility. She did not want matters to come to a head, at least not yet. She could not be sure just yet where her tryst with Shahzaib would lead to.

"For the present, let things be. Time will …"

She trailed off but there was no need really to complete the sentence. Ayub was relentless. He now asserted what he had previously assumed in his own mind, that Myra's missive was in fact an invitation for reviving their relationship.

"You came here entirely on my account but now you refuse to respond to my offer. You are being so unnatural. I can perceive a falseness of character that I did not know existed in you. For your own sake, I wish you would reconsider your stance at once or else …"

"Or else what?"

Myra's inquiry was in earnest and she delivered it in a tone that betrayed intense concern. Ayub's threatening harangue had left little to the imagination. He suddenly got up and left without bothering to answer her query.

As soon as he was gone, Myra slumped in her chair in deep despondence. Then just as suddenly, she jumped up and started pacing the floor in angry desperation. She was passionate in her resolve.

"I won't be a slave to my past. It would be madness to bind myself to him. I will love whomever I want."

CHAPTER 40

Having thus decided to break away from Ayub, one might have supposed that Myra was capable of aiming higher than Shahzaib. She was beautiful, well-groomed and well turned out, a highly desirable woman. The fact that she was rich, educated and talented served to further enhance her aura. Shahzaib could match none of Myra's attributes. He was of medium height or even shorter, pleasant-looking but by no means handsome. His background was modest, his education minimal and his social graces emerged essentially from his training in Ayub's nursery, which is not saying much. As a matter of fact, if one were to evaluate the two men presently in Myra's life, Shahzaib would compare rather unfavorably with Ayub on many counts. Ayub had a remarkably handsome visage with a physique to go with it, both of which lent him a towering personality. Besides, he was rich and powerful, which fact merits no further elaboration.

It is unlikely that Myra would have carried out any such comparison but nevertheless her inclination towards Shahzaib was calculated. He had qualities that complemented her own and he was desirable on that count alone. His steady, though drab, persona suited her at this stage of her life more than the flamboyance of Ayub. Myra felt none of the burning passion for Shahzaib that she had had for Ayub. Instead, she felt she could come to respect him, at least in relation to the lack of respect she had of late begun to nourish for Ayub. Beyond that, there were practical considerations. For Myra, it was a simple proposition. She had reached an age and a station in life where she could no longer be without a reliable companion. She was part of a society now that was skeptical of single women trying to make it on their own. She had to have a man by her side for the sake of propriety in both business and social situations. Myra had concluded after honest reflection that she needed Shahzaib. Once she made up her mind, Myra reasoned nothing more. Nature had endowed her with a natural lightness of heart and she took kindly to whatever fate had to offer, *que sera*. She had not yet experienced life in all its fullness but she knew enough to understand that providence will not always grant her what she might desire and she might be fated to accept that which she may not necessarily desire. She had perhaps hit a middle road with Shahzaib.

Myra's decision did indeed represent something of a compromise but it was not at all unusual for one of her bearing. It is sometimes the case with women of eminent qualities that they tend to be attracted to one of lower accomplishments or of a lower social status, even one who does not quite match their faculties or their physical attributes. There is in such cases an attraction of opposites or a polarization that somehow stimulates the senses. More importantly, she felt that marriage with Shahzaib would be free of the rigors of an intense relationship at home or competition in their professional pursuits, which is often the case when two high-powered personalities vie for each other's attention. With Shahzaib she could continue to live life on her own terms. She would be dependent on him for nothing more than companionship. In fact, she entertained a distinct notion that he would be at her beck and call constantly.

CHAPTER 41

Ayub had his own deep reflections to make. Myra's bearing was troubling him. She had received him rather indifferently or even diffidently. Her attitude was callous, even while granting her due deference to her present situation and her newfound independence. He became convinced that no ordinary fancy possessed her now or else she would never have comported herself in such an uncivil way in his presence. He was a man who relied on his instincts and he concluded instinctively that there was rivalry in her heart by another. He could feel it in the air around her, see it in the glint in her eyes. An antagonistic force was agitating her. In her presence, it seemed he was standing in the midst of a tidal wave. The intensity of the tide increased as he waded in deeper. Neither reason nor rational thought would sway him anymore. He was riding an emotional roller coaster. The wronged wife for whom he had sacrificed the love of another was dead. The daughter that he supposed was his flesh and blood would not acknowledge his paternity unequivocally.

The man he had nurtured almost as a son was now a rival in both business and love, though he was yet blissfully unaware of the latter. Now, the woman whose love he sacrificed in order to compensate his wronged wife was acting truly as a woman scorned.

One adversity engenders another, or so it seems, until adversities converge on a man with the intensity of a hound in a hunt. It is not because the stars are cross but because adversities enfeeble even the strongest mind, bringing one's character to a sullen pass. The true measure of a man is his response to hardship and Ayub could not measure well. He could no longer restrain the falseness of his emotions. He was fast losing the capacity for sound judgment. Everything he would do henceforth would only take him deeper into the abyss of ignominy. Whom the gods would destroy, they first make mad.

In the midst of his personal turmoil, Ayub had to deal with another pressing matter; the affairs of his business had taken a turn for the worse. He had earlier managed to square off the market debt from his imprudent adventure but his impatience and ego had put him in a bind. He had sold off his accumulated stocks at a ridiculously low price to pay off the market in its entirety even though at least a part of those stocks had been purchased through bank loans. That had left him bereft of both raw material and cash flow, resulting in a complete halt of production. A more prudent businessman would have tried to bide his time so that if he had waited long enough to sell, he could have at least minimized his maximum loss while ensuring continued production. Ayub could have easily warded off market pressure for a considerably longer period. The market looked upon him alternately with grand deference and great consternation, respecting and fearing him in equal measure.

However, market debts are personal in nature unlike debts owed to financial institutions and Ayub could never grovel before his debtors. He would rather default on loans owed to banks than those owed to the market.

In the bargain, he now had a bigger problem with which to contend. The company had been drowning in bank debts even before his imprudent adventure. The situation had become worse subsequently. The banks were pressing hard for a settlement and were even threatening legal action. For the first time in years, Ayub had to visit the boardrooms of banks when once senior bank officers would come running to him at his faintest beckoning. The trade was buzzing with the rumor that the banks were in the process of foreclosing on their debts. They could immediately obtain court orders to take over his factories and the remaining stocks of goods belonging to his companies. If that happened, Ayub could be dispossessed of everything he owned in an instant.

CHAPTER 42

The thought of rekindling a relationship with Ayub was receding from Myra's heart in direct proportion to the great attention that Shahzaib was lavishing upon her. The regular visits at the office soon led to romantic late-night phone calls at home and the inevitable rendezvous at secluded places. Finally, Shahzaib picked up the courage to speak his mind, though he was careful with his words. He chose to disclose his purpose to Myra in the seclusion of his car and did so with the unmistakable inflection of a man in love.

"Myra, I must admit I am always at a loss for words in your presence, though in truth I am really not a man of many words anyway. I am sure men seek you out for your position, wealth, talents and beauty and frankly, I do not know why you are alone thus far. I do not know if you are one of those women who revel in the thought of having many admirers. I wish though that you could now be content with one."

"Oh, really? And who would that be?"

Myra started laughing while Shahzaib looked on with some embarrassment. Before he could gather his wits and add to the awkwardness of the moment, Myra turned serious as she pondered over his question.

"You are proposing to me, are you not?"

"Yes, indeed I am. Will you be my wife?"

"Are you sure you are not the jealous type?"

Those words made no immediate impression on Shahzaib though there was an air of mystery about them. Myra's enigmatic words had an import that he could not possibly have understood just yet. Shahzaib said nothing. He held her hands in his as if assuring her of his complete faith in her. It was now Myra's turn to take the proposition forward and she again did it in a manner that only created another riddle.

"I love no other person or else I would not lead you on. Yet if I were to consent to your proposal, I should wish to have my own way in some things."

"In everything you wish! What special thing did you mean?"

"If I should want to leave this city for whatever reasons, would you then accompany me?"

Shahzaib could do no better than to mouth a set of conventional homilies. He assured her that he would follow her to the end of the world, so smitten was he of her wily charms; and so on and so forth. Myra took his great protestations of love rather seriously.

CHAPTER 43

Ayub happened to be driving by late one night when he thought he saw a familiar face in a parked car. He turned his car around and looked again at the occupants. Sure enough, it was Myra; he could see her face clearly in the blinking neon lights. Then as he closed in, he immediately identified the obscure silhouette of the man. It was Shahzaib. He could not believe his eyes. The sight of Myra with Shahzaib in a decidedly romantic posture was like a red rag to a bull. Their purpose was abundantly clear to him. He had of late formed a view that Myra had developed an interest in another man. It was beyond Ayub's capacity to bear with such rivalry in matters of intimacy with a woman but he had never until now known for sure. At first, he thought of taking Shahzaib on right away but better sense prevailed. He thought it more appropriate to confront Myra instead.

Ayub kept in wait at a discrete distance and as they were about to leave, he hurried on to Myra's house. He kept sitting in his car in the darkness of the night, waiting for her. He did not have to wait long. Shahzaib dropped her at the gate of the townhouse and drove off. Ayub quietly got out of his car and moved towards the gate. Myra entered the premises and as she turned around to lock the gate, she saw the figure of a man approaching her. She let out a stifled cry, her voice choking in terror. She recognized Ayub as he came face-to-face with her and she let out a worried exclamation, questioning at once his motives, her face pale with fright.

"How can you frighten me in such a dastardly manner, and what in hell are you doing here? It is past midnight and you have no right to surprise me here at such an odd hour."

"I don't know whether I have a right but I do know that I have an excuse. Yes, it is well past midnight and you are not in Europe, in case you have forgotten. You should know better than to carry on in such a disgraceful manner. What were you doing with that upstart? How can you seek the company of another man when you are committed to me?"

Myra was now getting wary of the continued standoff and wished not to engage in any further discourse. She sidestepped Ayub's ranting and tried to appeal to his sense of decorum.

"Please, can we talk about it another time, perhaps in the morning? It is too late in the night for propriety. What will my neighbors think?"

"I don't care. This is no time for manners and customs. It is strange that you should talk of propriety after the indecency you have perpetrated in public. I came by earlier in the evening and you would not see me even though I knew you were at home. You are doing wrong by me. You cannot toss me aside at will. I have a little matter to remind you of, one that you seem to have forgotten."

Myra was compelled to ask Ayub in, knowing well that he was quite capable of creating a scene. It could jeopardize her relationship with Shahzaib, now on the cusp of consummation. Once inside she sank into a sofa, dreading the outcome of the encounter. Ayub began a crude narration of the way they were, reminding her of their balmy days in Europe. His startlingly direct allusion to those days took her aback. She cupped her face in her hands and cried out in anguished.

"I do not want to hear it! I do not want to hear it! It is sheer vulgarity on your part to even bring it up."

"But you ought to hear it."

"It came to nothing and all because of you, not because of me. You dumped me without a second thought for what you considered a higher duty, to marry your long-lost wife. Then why do you not leave me alone and leave me to the freedom I gained with such sorrow. Had I thought that you wanted to honor a commitment, I might have felt bound now but you have planned it out of charity, almost as an unpleasant duty, because I had given myself to you and compromised myself and you think you have a duty to protect my honor. Yet even your sense of duty is so fragile that you failed to inform me of the death of the woman in whose favor you sacrificed my love."

"Why did you come here then and why did you contact me?"

She was silent for a few moments. She had at first nurtured a faint hope of getting back with Ayub but her involvement with Shahzaib had sealed the outcome. She ventured a plea, hoping it would fall on receptive ears.

"My circumstances have altered since you left me. I am hardly the same person that was betrothed to you and you too are not the same person that I had known before. Our new circumstances warrant a fresh appraisal for the sake of both of us. I beg you to leave me alone for now"

Ayub retorted vehemently to her explanation, adding a strange defense to boost his case.

"That is not true at all. You are the one that is pretending to have changed while I am still willing to keep my end of the bargain. Your argument has nothing in it because you simply wish to replace me and that is not right. Besides, the man you are thinking of is not at all a suitable replacement."

Myra made another passionate plea, hoping this time to shame Ayub into backing off.

"If you were as good as he, you will leave me alone!"

But Ayub ignored her ministrations and persisted with his demand now with brazen vulgarity. He was obviously in no mood to comfort her.

"You cannot in honor refuse me and unless you give me a promise to be my wife this very moment, I'll reveal our intimacy in common fairness to other men, including Shahzaib, even though I should not care if he were to romp with a slut or a whore."

Then, he continued in a further display of uncouth sarcasm.

"Do you see how fair I am? I am fair even to my rival, one who will contrive to possess even my soul though, by God, I will never allow him to prevail."

Myra was disgusted with Ayub's crass diatribe. A look of resignation settled upon her and she broke down in torment. The defiance that she had conjured up in a brief moment of strength all but melted away with Ayub's persistent tirade. Now in her moment of extreme impuissance, she seemed ready to accept Ayub's immoral authority.

"Please don't dwell on it any further. Please leave me alone for now. I will do as you wish but please leave me alone. I don't feel well."

Ayub had reduced Myra to an emotional wreck. She started begging him to relent, muttering her plea under her breath rather feebly. Ayub felt the bitterness he had generated and had she chosen any man in the world other than Shahzaib, he would probably have had pity on her at that moment. However, the man who had superseded him in her favors was an upstart and an underling. Ayub could not bring himself to abdicate his superior entitlement in favor of such a man.

"I agree not to agitate our matter any further if you promise to be mine."

"I do, I do."

She uttered the thoughtless declaration under a most stressful coercion and bade him to leave yet again. Having thus extracted a promise from Myra on the pain of great humiliation, Ayub left abruptly without another spoken word. His spirited stride spoke volumes; it had a triumphant air to it.

CHAPTER 44

Myra did not go to the office the next day. Noor called her several times but she would not attend to her phone calls. It was uncharacteristic of Myra to absent herself without informing the office and even more so, to leave calls unanswered for the better part of the day. Noor was worried and decided to go to Myra's house to inquire personally. The front door was unlocked and as she entered the house, she looked around for Myra. Noor called out for her but when she failed to get a response, she went upstairs. She called out again. Myra emerged from her bedroom, pushing the door open. Noor was stunned at the sight of a man through the opening; it was Ayub. Ayub in Myra's bedroom? Noor was dumbfounded. She could not figure out what her father might be doing in her bedroom. She had no idea that the two were even acquainted, much less so informal that they would take up with each other in a bedroom, behind closed doors. Noor rushed in to confront her father about his little secret. For some odd reason she wanted to seek an elaboration from her father rather than Myra; perhaps, she knew instinctively that her father probably had a greater say in the matter. Before she could utter a word, her father took her by her hand and abruptly informed her of a future commitment between the two, without a word of explanation of the past.

"Noor, I want you to hear this. Myra has agreed to marry me. Isn't it so, Myra?"

Myra strained for the words that Ayub expected from her.

"If you . . . wish it, I must agree."

Noor was shocked at her father's announcement and her friend's acquiescence. She could readily discern from Myra's tone that all was not well, that she was clearly unhappy with the situation. It was immediately obvious to her that her father had extracted the promise forcibly but she could not naturally guess the burden of the compulsion, though she thought it to be of sufficiently grave nature. Noor sat down besides Myra at the edge of the bed and held her hand. She demanded a clarification from her father in a manner she had never dared to employ with him before.

"Father, what fear drives her to say this when it is so obviously painful to her? Do not compel her to do anything against her will. I know she cannot bear such intense harshness."

Ayub admonished Noor drily for exhibiting such simple-minded ignorance of the ways of the world.

"Don't be such a simpleton! This promise will leave him free for you, if you want him."

"Him? Who are you talking about, Father?"

Myra jumped up with a start and began shouting hysterically.

"Nobody, as far as I am concerned."

"Oh, well. Then it is my mistake but this business is between Myra and me. She agrees to be my wife."

"Ayub, please don't argue about us with your daughter anymore."

"I will not."

Ayub turned around and walked out of the room. Noor continued to sit by Myra's side, stupefied by the shocking demonstration of vulgarity she had just witnessed. She was fairly disgusted with her father's crass behavior. She thought she had seen enough of his dark underside but even that had not prepared her for the evil she saw him perpetrate. Be that as it may, she could not help wondering at Myra's own role in the conundrum. She realized that there had to be more to Myra's story than she had supposed in her reflexive reaction directed entirely towards her father.

"You called my father Ayub, as if you knew him well. How is it that he has this great power over you to force you to marry him against your will? Ah! You have many secrets from me."

"Perhaps you have some little secrets from me."

Myra murmured the barely audible words with closed eyes. She was actually unsuspecting of Noor's little secret, that she too had yearned for the same young man not too long ago. However, it was Ayub who was the subject of discussion presently and not Shahzaib and so, the two let go of that premise as Noor pressed on with her queries.

"I cannot understand how my father can command you so. I do not sympathize with him in this matter at all. I'll go at once and ask him to release you from the promise."

Myra was wary of permitting Noor to play any part in her personal affairs.

"No, no, let me deal with it the way I see it fit. You know nothing of my past, though it is not in any way unbecoming."

She then told Noor the whole story behind the incident, unpleasant as it was to recount. By the end of Myra's account, Noor had all but decided that the time had come to leave her father's house. She had not felt a single day of joy in the mansion since her mother's death. She could imagine too that she would no longer be welcome there anymore after the incident earlier in the day. Now, even as Noor contemplated leaving her father's house, she was unaware of an impending situation that would in any case lead to the same consequence and act as a further wedge in the tenuous relationship between the father and daughter.

CHAPTER 45

The dark clouds that hovered over the business affairs of Ayub led ironically to a deeper introspection of his life. There were many who had witnessed his rise to wealth and prominence in society and the story of his rags-to-riches journey was by now a fabled tale. Yet nobody had been unusually curious about the details of his life before he came to town. Tongues did sometimes wag and there were rumors of an uncommon if not a blemished past. The absence of a woman in his life was particularly intriguing. There were muted rumors that he had been married once, before he set foot in the city and that through some misfortune he had lost his wife, never to marry again. Ayub had confided the broad contours of that phase of his life to Shahzaib, Myra and Noor, each in turn to serve a particular or even peculiar purpose. However, the source of those rumors had never been ascertained sufficiently and so the story had remained unauthenticated. Curiosity about his antecedents had once again been re-awakened because it seemed that his legend was about to turn a full circle.

Now it so happened that a worker met with an accident on the production line of Ayub's factory and expired. A motley crowd gathered outside the factory out of curiosity though none of them had any cause to be there. They were joined continually by passersby with nothing more valuable in their possession than idle time. Word soon went around and laborers from adjacent factories joined in to protest the allegedly indifferent treatment meted out to one of their own ranks. The small gathering grew into an unruly horde and turned into an agitation over the incident. A manager informed Ayub of the assembled crowd. Ayub was quite unperturbed by the situation. He was not the kind to shirk away from charged crowds. He had always dealt with such unsettling matters personally, never hiding behind managers. Indeed, in the days before he crossed the fence from a working class man to an entrepreneur, he had himself taken part in such agitations on many occasions. He set out for the factory immediately. Ayub's staff had alerted the police, though in retrospect its presence there turned out to be a source of added irritation. By the time Ayub arrived, the crowd had grown substantially and was threatening to become violent. Some elements within the crowd blocked Ayub's car as he arrived at the scene. Ayub stepped out of the car and faced the crowd squarely. Someone started shouting obscenities at him. Those invectives would have unnerved a lesser person but Ayub remained calm.

"You are a blood-sucker. You have sucked the blood of your workers for years and today you have left one to die a horrible death. You have blood on your hands."

Ayub's aides tried to pacify the crowd by recounting the great contributions that he had made to their lives. The hostility of the crowd was beyond comprehension. Most had nothing to do with Ayub or his factory yet they were fierce in their recriminations. Ayub listened to their reproaches with a calm demeanor, waiting for an opportune moment to address the crowd; he knew he could ease the situation without further incident. However, before he could do so a hoary old man made his way through the crowd, hobbling on improvised crutches. He came close to Ayub and started a hysterical tirade. The crowd's attention turned towards him, not knowing the man or the purpose of his speech.

"Do you think that man cares one hoot for the blood of another human? Here he is pretending to be a respectable man when in reality he is an evil man with no respect for life. I know him well. Let me share with all of you an example of the evil that this man is capable of."

The old man kept his finger pointed towards Ayub as he spoke those introductory words. The crowd shifted its gaze towards Ayub once again, viewing him now with greater curiosity. Having thus established the focus of his diatribe, the old man continued with what promised to be a lengthy monologue.

"I used to run a joint that served liquor in a small town on the highway out of this city and the man you see next to that magnificent car of his was a regular client. It must have been twenty-two years ago or more that he entered my establishment one day, the last time he ever patronized it, and drunk himself into a stupor. His young wife came in to tell him that his father had thrown her out of his house along with the baby. You would think he would take steps to redress the situation. No sir! He had no concern for the wife or the infant she was carrying, his own daughter. Instead he resorted to disgracing his wife in public in the vilest manner that I have ever witnessed, and believe me I have witnessed some vile manners in my time."

The old man paused, as much to take in a breath or two as to whet the appetite of the crowd.

"Hear this now, he then offered to sell the poor woman to anyone willing to pay her price. And that is exactly what he did. He sold his wife to a complete stranger and pocketed a large sum of money against the sale. Our man here divorced his wife in front of the dozen or so men who were present there and handed her to the stranger together with the baby. He couldn't care less what happened to them."

The old man's harangue had begun to tantalize the crowd. The story of a man who sold his wife in a public transaction—and that too in an illicit liquor joint—riveted the crowd's attention as the old man continued with his strange tale.

"The poor woman protested desperately but he took no heed of her desperation. The man who sold his wife in such a crude and disgraceful manner is now posing as a good and caring man. He calls himself Ayub Qureishi but I know him better than that. He is Yuba Kasai, a lowly butcher."

The old man lifted his arm and once again pointed a finger at Ayub, all the while nodding his head. He then folded his arms defiantly, looking keenly at his quarry. Suddenly, there was a hushed silence in the crowd. All eyes turned towards Ayub in a searing focus. Ayub stood still, his face deathly pallid. A loyal aide tried to counter what he saw as a quizzical accusation, totally flabbergasted by the old man's tirade.

"How dare you make up such brazen lies about a respected and upright man like Mr. Ayub Qureishi! So hold your tongue or else!"

Before the crowd could react to the aide's words of defense, a gruff voice boomeranged in the air.

"No, it is true. It is as true as the light of the day."

The crowd's attention turned to the source of those words, gasping in utter disbelief as they realized that the declaration came from Ayub himself. There was now no need for any further verification of the old man's accusations. After years of keeping up a firm guard, Ayub had indescribably let it down in an improbable moment of squaring with the truth. Ayub always faced the truth unequivocally but his admission was unnecessary. He could have simply kept quiet and the public would have dismissed the old man's tirade as an absurdity. Instead, he turned to his accuser and to the great bemusement of the gathered crowd, addressed the man by his name.

"You are right, Sheeda. I am no better than you or anyone else."

From the moment Ayub set his eyes on the old man, there was no mistaking his identity. Ayub had almost killed Sheeda Pistaul at their last encounter, some twenty-two years earlier but Sheeda had lived to fight another day, as he had willed. The crowd was now truly perplexed as they realized that the accuser and the accused knew each other well. But, Sheeda was not done yet. He had more tantalizing details to disclose about Ayub's life and he was undeterred. He turned to the crowd again and sought their attention.

"That is not all my friends. Let me tell you what happened to Yuba's wife and daughter. The taxi driver who paid for them was a pimp who procured women from the countryside and sold them to brothels in the city. I know because I was his accomplice and assisted him whenever he sought my help. I know because I was his business partner and received a commission. I was the one who informed him of the mischief that was brewing inside my joint that night. The taxi driver took the mother and daughter to the city right away. The next morning, he sold them both to a madam."

Sheeda was completely heedless of the consequences of the grave accusations that he was hurling, this last without a shred of demonstrable authentication. He was obviously unconcerned with the power and privileges of Ayub. In any case, the old man seemed to be savoring every moment of Ayub's discomfiture as he lapsed into an irreverent commentary, as if it were an icing on the cake.

"Let me tell you also that our good man here married his prostitute ex-wife and even now has her daughter with him in the mansion. Now hear this, the woman who is living comfortably in the mansion is not his real daughter. His real daughter, the baby who came with her mother, Yuba's flesh and blood, is even today with the madam who bought her. She is a veteran in the trade, a prostitute in this very city."

The sensation caused by the revelations was so great that it left the surly crowd completely immobilized. The weight of the sensational disclosures submerged the real cause for which the crowd had congregated. As for Ayub, he was stunned. He did not know how to react to the latter part of Sheeda's account and chose not to respond. He simply waded through the crowd towards the factory gate. But that very instant, the life that Ayub had cobbled up so assiduously was shattered into a thousand pieces. Ayub, the highly regarded denizen of society, would henceforth be seen as just another low life. That calamitous instant would also cause further disarray in his business and severely damage the prospects of a recovery.

CHAPTER 46

Ayub entered his office in the factory and shut the door behind him. He needed to be alone to ponder over Sheeda's revelations. He could not understand the man's motive. Sheeda was an old man now, a spent-up thug with precious little to look forward to in life. It was unlikely that he had waited zealously all these years to get back to Ayub for a minor infraction. Besides, Sheeda might have known the details of Ayub's past but it was unlikely that he could have become aware of the good fortune of his later life. In any case, his status in life belied the magnitude of his undertaking. It was unlikely that Sheeda had acted on his own. It was obvious that someone had prevailed upon him to carry out the hatchet job.

Sheeda's motive, though, was not of much consequence and Ayub set that aside for now. It was the substance of the revelations that was a cause of greater concern for him. Ayub publicly admitted the facts of the incident to the extent of his involvement but he knew nothing of the fate of his wife and child after they left with the stranger. He had a wrenching feeling in his guts that there could well be a kernel of truth in Sheeda's account. Sheeda was definitely in a position to know what might have transpired subsequent to the incident. Ayub could only hope that Sheeda's account was not the unexaggerated truth.

Ayub reflected on the account that Jannat had rendered of her experience subsequent to the incident. He realized now that she had never really given him a forthright account and had tended to rely on ambiguous evocations. She had told him only what she wished him to know and he had been content with what she had told him, never prodding her for elaborations. He had been so keen to escape the divine wrath of his grotesque action so many years earlier that he had accepted the version of her previous circumstances unquestioningly. Jannat had, of course, told him about her marriage to another man and his subsequent death. But she had also led Ayub to believe through insinuation and inference that the girl she had brought up was Ayub's own long-lost daughter. Ayub was suddenly alive to the inconsistencies in Jannat's stance on some seemingly trivial issues. He recalled her strange defense on the color of Noor's hair. He remembered too her emotional outburst at his suggestion to change the girl's last name. He apprehended the worst; Jannat could well have woven an elaborate web of deceit around him.

Ayub became greatly agitated at the thought and could not now leave the matter unattended. He was determined to find out the whole truth no matter how noxious it turned out to be. The prime object of his concern, though, was not his late lamented wife but his daughter. Mercifully, he would not have to deal with his wife's immoral past, if indeed that was the case. Her death had closed the book on all her bygone acts. He only fretted over the identity of his daughter. He faced the possibility that the girl who was part of his household now may not be the one he had lost so many years earlier. Worse still, his lost daughter could well be servicing the banal sexual needs of strange men. Ayub was hoping for an outcome that might extricate him from a moral quagmire.

CHAPTER 47

Ayub was now desperate to seek out Sheeda for Sheeda alone had the answers to the riddle that confounded him. Ayub had noticed Alam Mirza in the crowd and that led him to somehow suspect his former manager's involvement in the mischief. He had dismissed Alam Mirza twice and disgraced him far too many times, which was a good enough reason for him to attempt to get even. Ayub, therefore, decided to confront him. For all his tenacious knavery, Alam Mirza was clay putty in Ayub's overarching presence. He confessed that he knew of the scheme the minute Ayub caught up with him but he would not confirm his own active involvement. On the contrary, he labored to give the impression that he had tried to convey the information to Ayub and had even tried to dissuade the perpetrators from carrying out the foul scheme.

Alam Mirza had apparently stumbled upon the story almost by accident. He was an occasional visitor to a brothel where he had become acquainted with Sheeda. Sheeda had been assisting the taxi driver in procuring young girls from the countryside for the establishment over the years, a fact he later acknowledged before the crowd. Now that he was an old man and no longer suited to the rigors of his trade in the field, he had retired to the city. The madam who operated the brothel permitted him to stay at her place, entertaining his gratuitous presence largely out of pity. Sheeda was fond of bragging of an eventful past, regaling his audience with the recollections of his bygone years, even those of an inglorious nature, as old men are prone to do. His personal favorite, one that he was fond of repeating often, was the bizarre story of a man named Yuba the butcher. He happened to relate the same to Alam Mirza on one of his occasional visits. When Alam Mirza heard the account, he knew immediately who the subject was. After all, he was one of the few who had witnessed the transformation of Yuba Kasai into Ayub Qureishi. Alam Mirza sought to exploit the situation as soon as he got wind of the improbable story. Far from sympathizing with Ayub, he saw it as an opportunity to supplement his meager and now dwindling resources. There were many who might have wished Ayub's humiliation and Alam Mirza readily found willing partners.

Alam Mirza's tacit confession, though couched in a denial, was not of much import for Ayub for the moment. He would no doubt have dealt with him quite harshly under different circumstances. But for the present, Ayub let him off the hook quietly, with only a mild admonishment. He had far more pressing concerns to take care of then to settle scores with a base scoundrel. Moreover, he needed Alam Mirza to lead him to Sheeda even though the account of how he, Alam Mirza, had come upon Sheeda in the first place served only to whet Ayub's apprehensions over whether Alam Mirza too knew the identity of his daughter.

Alam Mirza arranged a meeting between Ayub and Sheeda. Sheeda was naturally apprehensive of the consequences of an imprudent meeting with Ayub. He had been at the receiving end of Ayub's effrontery so many years earlier for lesser reasons. Now that he had made his indiscretions public and sullied the character of his wife and daughter, he feared the worst. Alam Mirza allayed his fears with the promise of a large sum of money. Ayub and Sheeda met at a secluded rendezvous without the presence of Alam Mirza. As soon as they were face-to-face for the first time in years, Sheeda lost no time in profuse apologies. His rambling explanations were delivered in a voice trembling as much out of old age as from fear.

"I am a poor man, disabled and completely distraught. I had no idea how you had fared in life, I swear. Mirza, put me up to it. He offered me a lot of money. I did it for money. I did it out of a great compulsion. Please forgive me."

Sheeda attempted to bend down to touch Ayub's feet in a show of extreme submission, seeking exoneration. Ayub stepped back hurriedly to avoid the sordid gesture of Sheeda's supplication.

"I am not asking you who set you up, at least not yet. I want to know what transpired with my wife and child after the stranger took them away. I want to know where my daughter is, if indeed my daughter is out there somewhere."

"As God is my witness, I had nothing to do with what happened to your wife and daughter. I lied in front of the crowd when I boasted of my involvement."

Ayub handed Sheeda some money, staring menacingly at him in silence. Sheeda at once hurried on to the revelation, knowing well the purpose of the payment. He confirmed what he had already disclosed in front of the crowd, speaking hesitatingly while all the time avoiding Ayub's morbid eye contact. Sheeda was mortified in Ayub's presence and dreaded his reaction on learning of his daughter's state. If it were not for the penury he was suffering, wild horses could not have dragged him into the meeting. He told Ayub about the brothel where his daughter had resided continuously since the day of the incident. She was known now not as Noor but as Bina. Ayub was visibly incensed as Sheeda continued with his distasteful disclosure. His facial muscles were in a fit of convulsive twitches and his hands trembled but he restrained his vicarious urges. When Sheeda concluded his account, Ayub warned him at the pain of severe reprisal not to disclose the details of their meeting to anyone, especially Alam Mirza. Sheeda confirmed in the first instance that Alam Mirza had no idea of the identity of his daughter and promised on the holy book that he would never disclose it to anyone. Ayub decided to pay a visit to the madam's establishment right away. He wanted Sheeda to accompany him but Sheeda begged off. Instead, he provided him the contact of a pimp who, he said, would lead him directly to his daughter.

CHAPTER 48

Ayub set forth for the search of his lost daughter rather gingerly. However, Ayub's motivations were not nearly as benign as were those of Yuba when he set out to search for his baby twenty-two years earlier. His mission then was to make amends for the sacrilege he had committed. His present odyssey was no longer a matter of making amends. It was now a question of defending his honor. He even entertained the hope that he would rather see his child dead than find her leading a dishonorable life. Ayub's thought would have given great pause to those around him if they had been able to penetrate his mind.

His conduit to his daughter, though, was ironical to say the least. The man of honor had to seek out a pimp in defense of his honor. The pimp responded to Ayub's call with a fair amount of caution but a reference to Sheeda set him at some ease. He assumed that Ayub was a prospective client seeking his services. The two drove to Ayub's tryst with another shocking encounter with reality. Ayub was relentless in his self-flagellation but he had to do what he had to do. During the drive, Ayub's odd behavior confused the pimp. The pimp, of course, had no idea of the Ayub's real purpose or else he would have backed off promptly. The madam too would have reacted unpleasantly and would have had him thrown out unceremoniously had she become privy to his purpose. But he did manage to disguise his purpose well. Ayub and the madam carried out the transaction after which the madam led him into a bedroom. The young woman of the evening known as Bina would soon join him there.

Ayub was beside himself with anxiety as he waited for Bina. All manner of thoughts invaded his mind. How could he possibly ascertain if the girl was indeed his daughter? How much could she tell him about herself, or would she even know anything at all? How will he reveal her paternity even if he did ascertain it? Indeed, should he reveal it at all? The dramatic moment soon arrived as the young woman entered the bedroom but there were no instant dramatics. Ayub simply stared at her, saying nothing. He was taking a measure of the young woman, looking for telltale signs of blood ties. In fact, he was trying to size her up in comparison with Noor, the ostensible daughter that Jannat had brought along with her. The two were probably about the same age though Bina appeared somewhat more mature than Noor. Bina's skin tone was a shade darker than that of Noor, as was the color of her hair. He could make out a faint resemblance of the girl to Jannat, both in her looks and the structure of her body but he saw nothing of his own self in her, or so he thought. Yet something about her seemed vaguely familiar. That alone ruled out an outright rejection. In truth, Ayub had forgotten what he looked like behind his beard or else he would have seen a similarity in the outline of the firm jaw that Bina displayed. He could not, naturally, be sure of anything yet.

The young woman was carrying out an evaluation of her own. She was used to all types of men but Ayub seemed frighteningly different. The intensity of his expression was almost forbidding. The impenetrable eyes and the inscrutable countenance of the middle-aged man scared her somewhat. Were it not for the wrath of the madam, she might have walked away from the job. A few moments of awkward silence accompanied Ayub's appraisal of the young woman and that of Ayub by her. The young woman, sensing an inept discomfort, made the first attempt to communicate, asking for Ayub's name. Ayub simply cut her off. He addressed her blandly without replying to her query.

"I am not here for the usual purpose. I just had to see you and ask you a few questions."

The young woman shrank back instantly. Her fears seemed to come alive. She sensed that the man had come to her for an unusual purpose. She was alarmed and wanted to get out of the peculiar situation.

"You can have your money back. I will ask Baji to return your money, referring to the madam with a reverential sobriquet used for an elder sister. Maybe you would rather spend the evening with someone else. I mean someone a little older."

Seeing the anxiety of the young woman, Ayub tried to pacify her.

"No, no! Please do not do that. Please do not be frightened. I just want to talk to you. I need to know something about you, about your background. I have no ulterior motive, I promise you, though I cannot explain my compulsion. I will pay you well but only if you are truthful."

He took out some money from the pocket of his tunic and offered it to her. She looked confused, not knowing whether to accept the man's largesse. He had already paid for her and clients offered more money only for special favors. She observed Ayub with a lot of curiosity and concluded that the man was just another weirdo doing his thing, whatever it was. He had paid for her time and was even supplementing it for his weirdness. There was no reason why she should not go for it. She had known them all and then some. In fact, she thought of it as an opportunity to fleece the middle-aged man and during the course of their conversation, she did manage to extract more money.

"OK, go ahead but you better be brief. I will not entertain you all evening."

At the outset, Ayub wanted to know who she was and how she had ended up with the madam. Bina preferred to tell him only about the manner in which she had spent her life.

"I have spent my entire life with Baji as a menial servant. Even as a young girl, I knew what I would be required to do as I grew up. I had seen other girls bearing the brunt of Baji's foul temper and the beatings of her thugs. I felt no urge to rebel. In any case, I had known no other home or life and knew nothing of the outside world. Where would I have gone if I had run away? Who would have taken me in? There was no one waiting for me on the outside."

Bina's voice seemed to choke as she recounted the story of her helplessness. There was a perceptible sadness in her expression in spite of the docile conciliation that she seemed to have carried out with her status. Ayub was evidently dissatisfied with Bina's nuanced articulation. He repeated his query with a greater sense of urgency and a somewhat harsher tone this time. He needed answers and he needed them right away.

"Do you know anything about your parents, who they were or where they lived? How did you end up with Baji? That is what I want to know."

"I have no knowledge of my parents or how I landed at this house. I have never bothered with such redundant questions."

"But surely, you must be curious about your father and mother even though you may not know their whereabouts or even whether they are still alive. You may never face the prospect of ever seeing your parents again but would you not want to know who they were, would you not?"

"Now look here old man. I have told you everything I know about my life. Your time is up. I am a working girl and I have other clients to service. Your flight into my past is a nonsensical exercise and I do not wish to waste any more of my time on you. You had better leave now or Baji will be here soon with her thugs. It will be bad for both of us."

"I cannot believe that you have absolutely no knowledge of your parents. You have been with Baji all your life but you are not her daughter or even related to her in any other way. You are a menial and surely you did not just materialize in her household; someone must have left you here. You might have gleaned something of your past from casual conversations. There must be meaningful signs of your childhood in this establishment. Even the walls have ears. Just tell me whatever you know, even rumors and innuendos about your origins."

Ayub was even more persistent with his query and told her that he would not leave without answers, while at the same time handing her some more money.

"Well, if you must know, I will tell you what I have heard around here. I naturally have no personal recollection but the story around here is that a taxi driver had sold my mother to Baji along with me. Baji put mother to work right away. Apparently, mother escaped by marrying a client but she left me behind in this hellhole and never returned. Mind you, I have heard nothing of that sort from Baji herself. Sheeda Pistaul will even go a step further. He will tell you that he helped the taxi driver procure my mother from the countryside when her drunken husband, my father, I suppose, sold her publically. The only thing I know for sure is that I was called Noor when I was growing up. When I was ready to be launched, Baji thought the name was too bland and unsuited to the vocation. She changed it to Bina, which is almost a generic name in the profession, and it has stuck ever since."

Ayub got up with a jerk and left the room in stunned suddenness to the young woman's great puzzlement. Bina had repeated Sheeda's version to the dot but it was still only Sheeda's version until she recollected her childhood name. Ayub was left with absolutely no doubt about the girl's identity. That is all he needed to know. Yuba's baby Noor had become Bina and Bina could never be Ayub's daughter. He knew at once that he would have to deal with the situation in the only way honorable men dealt with such cases. Suddenly, the deceit of his wronged wife overpowered his senses. If Jannat had only told him the details of her past, no matter how sordid, he might have taken steps to safeguard the honor of the mother and daughter, and his own too. However, the woman had remained deceitful until her death and had intended to be so even beyond. Nothing more could be added to the account of Jannat's supposed simplicity but who could blame her? She had felt no obligation to inform him of the antecedents she had acquired because of his crime. If she were still alive, she would no doubt have justified her charade to have been chiefly for the sake of Noor, her Noor not that of Yuba Kasai.

CHAPTER 49

Ayub could not have gathered the exact circumstances of Jannat's life from the bits and pieces that both Sheeda and her unfortunate daughter Bina had recited. Indeed, no one could. The burdens that Jannat had endured and the indignities that she had faced in her life stood secreted with her remains for eternity. They are well worth recounting though.

In the aftermath of the incident, Jannat accompanied the stranger who took her to the city the same night in his taxi. The taxi driver said nothing along the way that might have revealed his intent. In her naivety, she assumed that the man would marry her when circumstances permitted such a union; in that part of the world, men commonly purchased a bride. Anyway, they reached their destination on the outskirts of the city late in the night. Jannat had no idea where she was. She had never before left her village or its surroundings. They entered a rundown cottage and the taxi driver led her into a room with a bed. Her anxiety over the events of the day was so overwhelming that try as she might she could not fall asleep. She relived the horror and trauma of the evening repeatedly so that she barely even thought of the fate that awaited her.

The next morning a man unlocked the bolt on the outside and entered the room. It was the taxi driver but Jannat had no way of telling who he was. She had not really seen his face clearly the previous evening to be able to recognize him now. He was not alone. A middle-aged woman accompanied him. The woman greeted Jannat in an abrasive manner. After a few moments, during which the woman seemed to appraise Jannat, the man and the woman started conversing animatedly. The man addressed her as Baji. Both then left a confused and flustered Jannat alone again. A short while later, two men armed with deadly weapons entered the room and ordered her to come with them. Jannat protested only to be at the receiving end of a vicious slap. One of the men informed her beneath a menacing grin that Baji had bought her off the taxi driver and she would henceforth be Baji's property. Jannat did not really understand what the man was talking about but she had no choice save to accompany them. The men transported her to Baji's house, which was marginally better than the one in which Jannat had spent the previous night.

Jannat was now beginning to be both confused and frightened. As soon as she entered the house, Baji snatched the baby away from her and handed her over to another woman. Baji rebuked Jannat harshly when she protested. The poor woman cried her heart out for the baby but she could not have done much else. Baji told her that the baby was no longer hers to keep and so she would have to forget her forever. Soon she was on the receiving end of a brutal beating on every pretext and the more she protested, the greater was the level of violence. The wantonness of her present custodians was so fierce, the savagery so pronounced, that she was terrified even of soft breeze grazing her cheek. For all his vulgarity, Yuba seemed like a gentle soul compared to the present lot. Jannat was hapless as the beatings and torture continued all day, that first day. The next day a hulk of a man entered her room and started beating her up brutally for no particular reason. He then assaulted her sexually. He raped her repeatedly until she lost consciousness. The pain and degradation was excruciating. In an instant, her spirit was broken irretrievably, in the same manner as the spirit of a mustang is broken by vaqueros. In less than two days, she had been subdued. Jannat was now ready to be launched in the oldest profession in the world.

Baji was, of course, in the business of servicing the banal sexual needs of the moneyed class. She operated her establishment with impunity though everyone in the neighborhood knew her antecedents. She paid the lower echelons of the police very well but never permitted them to avail of her services. She serviced the upper echelons to their entire satisfaction, some of whom even paid for the services of her girls. In fact, Baji herself had had a long running affair with a senior officer who was her patron and protector. The girls in her establishment were mostly from the countryside and Baji took great care in grooming them to the standards of the class she catered. The likes of Sheeda Pistaul and the taxi driver procured the girls for the brothel using different modes of operation; some, such as abandoned children and orphans, were easy pickings, others were simply kidnapped but surprisingly, there were many who were victims of their husband's rancorous excesses, as was the case with Jannat. The girls were in a bond with the madam for the rest of their natural life. They could never escape their great misfortune.

Baji had paid a substantial amount of money for 16-year-old Jannat. She would henceforth be relentless in utilizing her newest asset. The routine was always the same, no matter who the client. She would ready herself for the evening with some help, usually from Baji herself. When requisitioned for the evening, the hulk who had broken her in would invariably escort her to her rendezvous. Interestingly, she would never again have an intimate liaison with the hulk; Baji had prohibited him from ever doing so. The hulk would wait outside while she serviced the client, sometimes for the better part of the night. He would then drive her back to the safety of the house. Oftentimes she would be engaged in a quick episode at the house, especially during the day, before a second and more enduring round at night. Baji merely fed and clothed her for all her troubles. Jannat soon resigned to her fate as she settled down in her routine.

CHAPTER 50

The apprenticeship of Jannat continued apace in this manner. Her clients were a diverse lot, of diverse ages and backgrounds. Many were repeat customers and all were men of some means. She eventually became quite astute in dealing with her clients in spite of her qualms over the incessant vulgarity. Though some mistreated her or treated her with a decided lack of respect, others were more tender, some almost loving. She was most comfortable with the older amongst them who tended to treat her more compassionately. Most of her clients were married men, usually with grown-up children. It is not of much vantage to discuss why men, who in other regard are responsible members of society and eager to pass themselves off as respectable family men, should engage in such activities. Yet the question is as old as humanity and begs an answer. The simple answer is that these men seek out thrills that are cogently absent in their intimacy with their partners though not necessarily because of an overwhelming carnal need. It is an amusing fact, though, that men who seek professional women to escape the monotony of the companionship of their wives, tend to visit the same woman every time. Some of the men even develop an emotional attachment with such women and fall into an irrational web of feelings. Love is not the sole preserve of the young and these middle-aged men lose their way in a thicket of passion whose shelf life should not extend beyond the night.

In any case, it was not difficult to form a feeling for Jannat. She was pleasant to be with, always tender and caring in a homely sort of a way. Moreover, she was never crass or crude. Now it so transpired that one man from amongst her clients became particularly enamored of her and requisitioned her services quite often. She even observed a tinge of distaste in him whenever she mentioned the fact that she was available to anyone who could pay for her. The man was of reasonable social and economic standing and as his feelings towards her became apparent, Jannat was not beyond taking advantage of his weakness. It was under those fortuitous circumstances that this older man proclaimed his desire to marry the young lady of the evening. Jannat was not at all unhappy at the prospect. It was an opportunity to rid her life of an awful taint, to erase her past and to regain some respectability in the bargain. After all, Jannat's instincts were honorable even though her circumstances had veered her into a dishonorable situation. She found the opportunity most harmonious and accepted the man's proposal without hesitation, although she may not really have had an overwhelming desire to enter into another uncertain episode of marriage.

Jannat's marriage proved to be an unexpectedly happy twist to her otherwise reprehensible existence. In the first instance, her new husband freed her from Baji's bondage, no doubt with a hefty pay-off. Then, after the marriage, he declared her as his wife for the entire world to know even though some friends or acquaintances may have known his wife's previous status. In the peculiar nature of this subculture, birds of a feather usually flocked together and so she may even have serviced some of his friends. However, once the husband declared the marriage, none of them would reveal the past, not for the sake of the now wedded couple but for the sake of their own reputations, naturally. There is a covenant amongst those who cheat on their wives serially and so they hold their peace forever. The public acknowledgement of his marriage to Jannat was indeed a brave move on the part of her husband and one that would stand her in good stead in society.

Jannat's husband gave her a monthly stipend which was not only adequate but from which she managed to save a little for herself. In fact, she extracted a little extra from him on different pretexts and stowed away the same. Yet none could grudge her the indulgence after what she had been through in life up until then; she yearned for security with such great vehemence. In due course, the husband even bought a small flat for her in a middle-class neighborhood. The husband was regular in his visits to the flat and spent as many nights with Jannat as he did with his other wife and children. It was by all account a reasonably happy family life. The manner in which her new husband treated her was in marked contrast to Yuba's indifference towards her during the brief episode of their marriage. Oddly, he rekindled Yuba's memory by comparison. Jannat's life was definitely more tranquil now than it had been in her living memory.

Jannat gained her freedom in this manner but her child remained in the clutches of the madam. Her husband was either unable or unwilling to make the hefty pay-off that the madam might have determined for the child. She did not attempt to persuade her husband with any degree of vehemence for fear of jeopardizing her own cause. She thought she could attempt to free her child later, whenever she was in a position to do so. In the meantime, she had a girl with her husband and as if to fill the void of her firstborn, she called her Noor. With the passage of time, Jannat realized the vagueness of the possibility of retrieving Yuba's daughter from her fate. Her responsibility towards the younger Noor soon distanced her memory from her older child and thereafter she never really knew her fate beyond a notion of what might have befallen her if she were still alive. But surely, Jannat must have carried the burden of the guilt of abandoning her child until her dying days.

The society that Jannat inhabited was a frequent venue of such crimes against humanity. Those on the lowest rung of society's ladder were naturally the victims. They were the wretched of the earth and the indignities to which society subjected them could not have been of much consequence for the rest. None of what happened to Jannat would have been a subject of such intense introspection were it not for the fact that Ayub had made it big in a milieu that was unforgiving of such exploits by an upstart. No one would have noticed the indiscretions of Yuba, the poor butcher but the higher you reach, the harder you fall. That apparently was the only lesson one could make of the renewed interest in Jannat's life.

CHAPTER 51

Ayub had remarried Jannat chiefly for the sake of his daughter but events had reduced the whole scheme to ashes. It turned out that the daughter he had supposed as his own was of another paternity while his real daughter was a captive in a brothel, leading an immoral life. He had never quarreled with fate for the affixations that had accompanied him throughout his life but now a reflection ran through his passionate head; that, perhaps, he deserved it all. It seemed he could not shake off the burden of his distressed existence. He was destined to live on with dust in his eyes and thorns in his mouth.

The events of the previous evening continued to occupy Ayub as he sat down to breakfast with Noor. He looked closely at her and for the first time he saw what he had hitherto chosen not to see; that the girl bore no resemblance to him at all. He thought hard at the turn of events and the more he thought of it the more aggravated he became. His attitude towards Noor began to change and she could sense it. His demeanor turned cold and aloof, displaying a palpable indifference to her presence. Noor, though, was wont to attribute the change to her mother's death and tended to ignore her father's intemperance. But the gulf continued to widen each passing day. They never met except at meals and the only conversation then tended to be a monologue by Ayub, chiding her for everything she did. Her language, unsophisticated as it was, suddenly found extreme disapproval. Her penchant for physical labor, doing things around the house meant for servants, and her softness towards the menials irked him. He had worked hard all his adult life to erase the lines of poverty and lowliness that had marked his birth. He had acquired a certain status in life and was not about to let this girl remind him of his origins. The extent of her father's displeasure was quite out of proportion to what the poor girl deserved and the language he used to convey it was at times shocking in its pithiness. The relationship was now devoid of even a modicum of the fatherly love that Ayub himself had so assiduously contrived at the onset of the relationship. Soon, Ayub started absenting himself from meals at home so that the two hardly saw each other anymore. The girl became more and more morose and reclusive.

Ayub was particularly upset at his haste. Jannat had led him to believe Noor to be his daughter only by allusion. Yet in his unwarranted exuberance, he had declared his paternity to Noor when it was unnecessary to do so. He was shocked at his own naivety. How he wished he had not revealed his past to the girl or imposed his paternity upon her. He had convinced her that he was her real father and he could not now backtrack from his position. It would not only throw the girl into turmoil but would also be humiliating for him. More to the point, Noor was blissfully ignorant of her mother's improbably immoral past. Ayub had given her an account of his divorce from her mother and she had never sought any elaboration from him on that count. The revelation of the manner of the divorce by Sheeda did not add to her knowledge. The rest of Sheeda's story was generally dismissed as implausible and no one really believed it. It was treated as a vicious attack on Ayub's person by his detractors, too numerous to be accounted for. By the same token Noor could not have known of the existence of a half-sister living in iniquitous circumstances. Ayub's reversal would inevitably lead to the disclosure of both facts and would almost certainly destruct Noor's hitherto harmonious existence, not to mention his own peace of mind.

Ayub struggled with such contradictions, unable to come to terms with his feelings. Was he not morally bound to inform Noor of the truth, now that he had found out that she was in fact not his real daughter, that her mother had falsely led him to infer that she was? The knowledge that Ayub was not her real father would naturally drive Noor away forever. The formal and legal relationship between the two stood terminated with the death of Jannat. He thought it would not be right for him to continue to pretend to be Noor's real father. Eventually it would all come out and then the bitterness would be insurmountable. How could Jannat be so deceitful and put all their lives in such turmoil, he thought.

In the end he concluded that he could not disturb the delicate balance of his life just yet. He decided he would let Noor continue to think of herself as his real daughter even though the pretense went against the grain of his character. In that way the identity of Bina too would remain undisclosed. His rendezvous with honor would have to await a more opportune time.

CHAPTER 52

It was only a matter of time before the revelation of Ayub's misdeed became a topic of general discussion in society, although the second and graver part of Sheeda's revelations seemed not to have gained much currency. Myra too became aware of Ayub's bizarre youthful odyssey. A gradual misery spread over her face as she tried to digest the story. In the account that Ayub had given her of the separation from his wife so many years earlier, of his belief in her death, and so on, he had never clearly explained the actual and immediate cause of that separation. She knew, of course, that the women at the heart of the mystery were once, and then once again, central characters in Ayub's life. Ayub had disclosed as much in his letter of regret. He had told her about their reappearance but he had not accounted for the sudden decision to re-marry his ex-wife. She thought of the promise that Ayub had forcibly extracted from her earlier. Myra could not imagine a worse station in life than for a woman to commit herself to such a man. She was determined to chart a future course for herself without Ayub in it.

Myra was a troubled woman and alarming thoughts had gathered in her head like dark clouds before a storm. She came into the office one morning and immediately announced that she would be going away for a few days, to get away from the city that she thought had gotten too gloomy for her disposition. Noor did observe that Myra looked pale and unhappy. She had a good notion of the cause of Myra's distress, of course. So she encouraged her to take the trip, thinking a change would afford her relief. Myra did not come back for almost a week, during which time she contacted no one at the office. No one really knew where Myra might have gone off to, not even Noor. Noor could understand, though, that Myra might have wanted to be alone for a while and read nothing into her conduct.

Ayub, on the other hand, was quite indignant. He did not know what to make of Myra's absence. He had been calling her repeatedly but had failed to get a response. Her continued absence was a source of great irritation. The cause of his restiveness, though, was not so much because he missed her but because he had an urgent need to see her on a matter unrelated to their private lives. When he finally found out that she had returned, he called on her at home the same evening. Ayub met Myra with exaggerated civility, the likes of which she had not seen in him throughout their association. He addressed her in a tone that betrayed great urgency.

"Myra, I have been very anxious to see you these past few days. Ever since I saw you last, I have thought over the way I got your promise of marriage that night. You said to me if I were a man I should not persist with my unreasonable demand. That bruised my ego and I realized that I was wrong in the manner in which I approached you. A matter of such sensitivity should be decided through sublime agreement not through confrontation. Therefore, I agree to an indefinite postponement of our betrothal so that you may ponder over it."

Myra remained in deep thought over Ayub's puzzling overture and said nothing as he continued.

"There is one thing I would like you to do in the meantime though, if you think it appropriate."

She merely nodded her head listlessly as he continued.

"You may have heard that I have been unlucky in the recent past. I speculated rashly and lost. That has put me in a straitjacket, a financial bind if you will."

The thought of what Ayub might be asking for and how she might benefit from such a demand jolted Myra out of her subdued state. Before he could spell out his notion, she interjected sharply.

"Do you wish me to advance you some money?"

Ayub reacted as if he was angry at her suggestion.

"No, no. I am not a man to sponge on a woman, even though she may be as nearly my own as you. No, Myra, what I wish you to do for me is simple but it could go a long way in reversing my fortunes. Businesses, as you know, often pledge their goods with banks as a collateral security for their debts. I too have pledged a large quantity of goods with my bank. Now the bank is in the process of selling those goods. If they do that, it will ruin my reputation. Just a month's respite will see me through the worst but the bank's president has refused my repeated requests to postpone the sale. I know that the president was a good friend of your father when he was looking after the bank's branches in Europe and you are still in touch with him."

"I can speak to him on your behalf."

"No, that will not be enough. I know the man well. He will never accede to an impersonal request but there is another way. If we let him know that we intend to get married soon, he will relent. We could go together to him and I will tell him that we are on course to marry. We will ask him to keep it a secret for now. No one else needs to know."

It was slightly dark in the room. Myra had not turned on the lights yet even as the sun continued to set or else, Ayub would have observed the effect of his words on her.

"If it were anything else, I would gladly do it but . . ."

She began faintly but failed to spell out her thought completely. The dryness of her lips seemed to embed itself in her vocal chords.

"But it is no big deal. It is not as though you would be faking it. Have we not, in any case, contemplated marriage and merely postponed it just now to allow you to settle your affairs. I could have told him as much myself but I thought it would be more effective if we were to do it together."

"It is not that I won't, it is because I absolutely can't."

She now spoke with rising distress. Ayub burst out in intolerable rage as his mood changed instantaneously.

"You are provoking me, woman. I could force you to carry out at once what you have promised. You have promised to be my wife. How would you overlook my simple request if we were man and wife? Your attitude is disrespectful and I will not tolerate it.

"I cannot do what you ask me to do."

"Why? Is it because I have just now released you temporarily from your promise?"

"No. I cannot because he was a witness."

"Witness? Witness to what?"

"I must tell you what you will eventually find out anyway, Ayub. Please don't, don't reproach me, I beg you. I did what I absolutely and unavoidably had to do."

"Well, let's hear what you mean."

"He was a witness to my marriage."

"Marriage? What nonsense are you talking? Have you taken leave of your senses, woman?"

Myra turned inexplicably calm. She composed herself and then, with a firmness of demeanor that belied the frailty of her constitution, she spoke out in a defiant tone.

"I married Shahzaib last week and the president served as an official witness to my marriage. I am now Shahzaib's wife."

Ayub was shell-shocked and stared past Myra with his mouth wide open. Myra was so alarmed at his expression that she murmured something about lending him enough money to tide him over his immediate problem. Ayub snapped back at her in disbelief.

"Married him? My god, woman, married him whilst bound to marry me?"

"It was like this. I fell in love with him and I thought you might reveal our past and that alarmed me. Then you made me promise to marry you by threatening to do just that. I could see no other way out of the dilemma. So I married Shahzaib before any misstep drove him away."

She tried to explain her dilemma to Ayub, as if he were possessed of reason and rationality. There were tears in her eyes and tremors in her voice but then in the next moment, she again assumed a more resolute bearing and denounced his conduct.

"How could I keep a promise extracted in such a sinister manner, especially after hearing of your past deeds? I learned of the rumor that you had actually sold your wife in a drunken frenzy and sent her off with a total stranger along with your child. What woman would commit to a man who had treated his wife and child in such an atrocious manner?"

She again pleaded with Ayub, now in a more conciliatory tone that betrayed acute desperation,

"I know you would have carried out your threat of telling him about our past, as long as there was a chance of keeping me for yourself. But you will not do so now, will you Ayub? It is too late to separate me from Shahzaib."

"So now it is 'his wife' that I have begged for assistance."

He growled at her, without a hint that he had taken cognizance of her words uttered in turn in sobbing self-pity, angry pertinence and earnest supplication. But Myra was no longer the subdued girl who had prostrated herself before Ayub's desires. She would have none of the nonsense that Ayub was now spewing out at her.

"May I request you to leave now? My husband could not accompany me on the return journey and was to take a later flight. He should be here any moment."

"You false woman, you promised me. I have a mind to punish you, as you deserve. One word to your dear husband and your happiness will be blown to pieces."

"Ayub, pity me and be generous."

"You don't deserve pity. You did but you don't anymore."

"I will help you pay off your debt."

"What! Are you suggesting that I become a pensioner of Shahzaib's wife? If I stay here any longer, woman, I will say something vulgar or even do something horrible."

The wrenching rift between Ayub and Shahzaib, so enduring in its intensity, had now reached its zenith. There could not be a more consummate act of revenge than marrying a rival's woman. That, of course, was no part of Shahzaib's design. He knew nothing about the past relationship of his wife with Ayub just yet. Ayub stormed out of Myra's presence without looking back. Myra stood motionless, staring behind him. Ayub was capable of destroying her reputation, and with it her marriage. She could yet become an embattled symbol of slandered virtue.

Shahzaib arrived the same night and went straight to Myra's house. She had urged him to keep their marriage a secret for a while and he had consented without even asking her the reason for the secrecy. After the events of the early evening, there was no need for her to continue with the charade. Indeed, the sooner they established that she and Shahzaib were man and wife, the less likely that Ayub could harm her, or so she reasoned. Myra moved into Shahzaib's house the very next day. The marriage of Shahzaib and Myra came to the public knowledge immediately and was naturally, a point of constant discussion. Oddly, of particular interest to the community was whether Shahzaib would gain further ascendency over Ayub in their business rivalry because of the wealth of his new wife.

CHAPTER 53

Noor had earlier concluded that she could no longer live under the same roof as her father. She now decided to confront him over the issue. She figured she had enough income from her job with Myra to be able to afford a small flat. She had, as yet, no knowledge of Myra's marriage to Shahzaib or else she might have restrained herself for now. She took up the subject with her father the very evening of his distressing encounter with Myra.

"Father, I've decided to move out and live on my own. I hope you have no objection."

Ayub addressed her indifferently, without really replying to her question. The state of his mind was not in the least conducive to thoughtful reflection.

"Well, it might do you a lot of good to be away from me and my dark moods."

"You don't object?"

231

"No, I don't object. Why would I object? Do I have any authority over you? Do I have any authority over anyone anymore?"

Noor shrank back as Ayub virtually growled at her. Then after a pause, he continued in a more conciliatory mode.

"But you won't have enough money to live comfortably. I do not know whether your job pays enough. If you like, I could fix an allowance for you."

Noor thanked him for the offer in an ambiguous tone, not quite refusing or accepting it. She was confused at her father's attitude. He granted his acquiescence so readily that it seemed he was eager to get rid of her. In reality, Ayub was quite pleased with the notion. He viewed Noor's proposal as a reprieve from his dilemma. If Noor were to move out of his house, he would have to make an inconvenient adjustment but at the same time, it would make it easier for him to carry on pretending to be her father without a constant reminder of her paternity.

CHAPTER 54

The morning after her unpleasant encounter with Ayub, Myra called Noor and asked her over to her house. Myra wondered if Ayub had talked to her about her marriage to Shahzaib. In any case, she wanted to be the one to tell Noor about the circumstances of her marriage. Myra received Noor downstairs and proceeded immediately with her revelation.

"Noor, I have news that I want to share with you. Shahzaib and I got married last week."

The abrupt disclosure took Noor by surprise. She managed to repeat Myra's declaration haltingly, almost in disbelief.

"You . . . married… Shahzaib!"

Noor was quite aware of the budding romance between the two but the unexpectedness of Myra's decision took her aback, especially since she had already consented to be Ayub's wife. She felt that Myra might not have given it enough thought. In truth, she might also have been mildly disappointed at Shahzaib's ready assent. She may have taken cognizance of Ayub's words, that his renewed liaison with Myra would leave Shahzaib free for her. The marriage between Myra and Shahzaib had finally dashed all expectations of the prospect.

"Well, I must tell you that the news has come as a great surprise to me. There was not a hint of it from you, not a sign of it when you went away last week. I must congratulate you though and wish you both the very best for your new life together."

"I didn't want it that way. I had always dreamt of a grand wedding, not a secret event. But I was so desperate, so afraid of being forced into a grotesque relationship by Ayub, so afraid of revelations that would turn Shahzaib away from me that I resolved to marry him immediately. I decided to take this huge step no matter what the consequences and buy at least a moment of happiness at any cost."

Noor reacted to Myra's explanation in a rather cool manner, nodding her head carelessly. She was in fact lost in perplexing thoughts of her own at the unexpected event. Myra could not have gauged Noor's emotions, for she had not the least suspicion of her feelings for Shahzaib. Anyway, Noor managed to bottle up her turmoil with admirable control. Myra did have concerns over the impact that her new status might have on her future relationship with Noor but on a different count. She thought Noor might not want to carry on with the office though she had no cogent cause for the supposition.

"Noor, I do hope you will continue with the office. I want you by my side, I really need you now more than I ever did."

Noor replied tersely to Myra's plea and took leave immediately.

"Let me think about it."

On reaching home Noor reflected calmly on the new circumstances. She convinced herself that Myra's marriage to Shahzaib was of no consequence for her own personal life. Its impact on her livelihood though could be substantial; she could lose her sustenance altogether. She was unsure whether Myra would continue to operate her business even though she had made a seemingly obligatory offer to her to continue at the office. Noor had already informed her father that she would move out and could not now linger on in the mansion. She reflected on her father's offer to subsidize her but concluded that it would not be enough if she were to lose her job with Myra. Moreover, even if Myra decided to continue to operate her business, she was wary of Shahzaib's role in any future dispensation. His presence would naturally result in awkward situations. In the end, she concluded it was highly unlikely that Myra would allow Shahzaib to interfere in her business if she did decide to continue with it.

Myra was back in the office the next day. She was glad to see Noor and made it a point to inform her at once that it was her intention to keep on operating her business independently of Shahzaib's establishment. Myra assured Noor that her marriage would change nothing at the office and asked her to continue in the same manner. Noor had no other plans and felt relieved that she could continue with Myra. She informed Myra that she had taken leave from her father to move out of the mansion, whereupon Myra offered Noor her now vacant house. That would also solve Myra's problem of arranging a caretaker. There could not have been a better proposition for Noor in her current circumstances and she gladly accepted the generous offer. She moved into Myra's house a few days later.

CHAPTER 55

Ayub's freakish behavior at the shack so many years earlier had received great publicity but the amends he had tried to make late in his life were lost sight of. The incident, bizarre as it was, might have faded from memory by now had it become known years earlier, as is often the case of a wild act of misguided youth. However, since its discovery was recent, the black spot of his youth took on the appearance of a fresh crime. And so, the public revelation of the incident took on ominous overtones, robbing Ayub of a moral bearing and foreclosing any sympathy for him.

The revelations of Ayub's past formed the pivot in the further decline of his fortunes. In that bewildering instant he passed into the ranks of the inglorious. Ayub was a man who would have willingly given up his wealth for his honor but now both his wealth and honor lay in tatters. From here on, he would experience nothing but opprobrium. He was slipping inexorably into the black hole of shame. It was strange how quickly he sank in the esteem of society, though that was hardly remarkable. The fact of the matter is that the world lends every attribute and surpassing merit to one it looks on with favor but when it turns its face away, it snatches even his own excellent achievements and denigrates his fame. Socially, Ayub had received a startling setback and having already lost commercial credibility, the velocity of his descent in both aspects became accelerated by the hour. He now gazed more at pavements than at house fronts, more at the feet and legs of men and less into the pupils of their eyes. His lowered vision could only perceive the spatter of mud on the ground below his feet; he could no longer look heavenward to envision the stars. The piercing look, which once made many a man shrink in awe, had dampened and dulled. A dazed look had embedded itself in its place.

From then on, there was no respite for Ayub. Relentless onslaught from creditors became the bane of his life; he could no longer keep them at bay. But the worst was yet to come. The banks had started legal proceedings to foreclose his assets. Ayub realized the futility of a long drawn out and expensive legal battle with the banks. He had no ground to stand on really and preferred to part with his assets voluntarily. As a first step, the courts ordered his assets to be attached, whereupon Ayub was required to hand over those assets in the custody of the court for subsequent auction.

During the court proceedings, Ayub startled the judge by enacting an amusing cameo. He took off his gold watch and took out his elegant leather wallet, cupped them in folded hands and in a dramatic fashion, handed them over to the court. To a distant onlooker, he seemed to be begging with folded hands, as beggars are wont to do. He was in fact begging, begging to be relieved of the last of the belongings still in his possession.

"Sir, you have legitimately and rightly dispossessed me of all my assets. I cannot escape the consequences of my actions; I must answer for every act. Why then do you leave these in my possession? These belong to my creditors too, just as everything else I own. That way my creditors will have all I had in the world and for their sake I wish I had more."

Ayub's unusual and irreverent outburst took the judge by surprise but he soon sensed the irony of his action. He then addressed him directly in a most gracious manner.

"Well, though the case is a desperate one, I am bound to admit that I have never seen a defaulter who has behaved more fairly and, indeed, more honestly. The rashness of the business transactions which has led to this unhappy situation is obvious enough but as far as I can see, there has been no wrongdoing."

The judge then willed him to retain his watch and his wallet, telling him that he had no desire to inflict such contemptuous affront on any debtor, least of all one who was until that moment such a respected pillar of society. When the court adjourned for the day, Ayub kept sitting alone, looking at his watch and his wallet. He was muttering beneath his breath.

"Why the devil did he not take these from me? I don't want what doesn't belong to me."

Ayub was now well and truly dispossessed. The emotions that he experienced were strangely subdued. He was somewhat ambivalent in his feelings towards the momentous event. He did not feel angry. He did not even feel sad. He just felt humiliated.

As Ayub stood thoroughly annihilated, there was a belated outpouring of sympathy towards him. The tragic outcome of the events that had caused such a steep fall from grace had evoked an introspection of his labors. Those who missed no opportunity to condemn him now seemed to see his whole career more objectively. They now saw how admirably he had used his sole resource, that of boundless energy, to create a position of great prosperity out of absolutely nothing. All he had when he came to town was a butcher's knife and the will to succeed. Belatedly some even regretted his fall. Alas! It was too little too late. Only a few have the strength of character to honor without envy a friend or colleague who has risen from the depths of privation and prospered in life.

The people who were carrying out this much-deferred introspection knew nothing of the demons that were driving Ayub towards the precipice, from where it would only take a gentle nudge to finally push him off the edge. All they could do was to wonder at his fate. Even Ayub was unaware of where the excursion of his life would finally lead him. Man journeys in darkness even as his destiny rides towards him.

CHAPTER 56

Ayub vacated his beloved mansion and moved elsewhere. He did so quietly and secretly, leaving with only a few personal articles in an old car he had bought some twenty years earlier and the only one left in his possession. He wanted no one to bear witness to his inglorious departure and might have left in the middle of the night. The household staff probably took his excursion as a normal occurrence and were shocked when they found out that he had relinquished the mansion and would not return anymore. At first no one knew exactly where he had gone to live. In fact, he had gone back in time, a time when his then fledgling success had only just begun to manifest itself.

Ayub had bought a small cottage in a middle-class neighborhood as soon as he was able to afford one. He must have sought permanence so anxiously; no doubt recalling the nights he spent on the pavements and in the parks. As his station in life rose, he moved to better dwellings until he finally made the mansion his home. However, he retained ownership of the cottage even though he had no need for it. A person who has surmounted extreme hardship is often reluctant to part with the vestiges of his past as a mere matter of insecurity and not necessarily for sentimental reasons. Thereafter, Ayub handed over the vacant cottage to Alam Mirza who resided in it along with his family and, in fact, continued to do so even after Ayub dispensed with his services. Now that Ayub needed the cottage for himself, he asked Alam Mirza to vacate the premises. Alam Mirza sent his wife and children away to his native town immediately but requested Ayub to allow him time to make alternate arrangement. Ayub needed a place right away and so he simply moved in alongside Alam Mirza. Thus, the two men came to be in each other's peculiar company exclusively. Ayub's life had always abounded in ironies but moving in with Alam Mirza had to be the supreme irony of his life. He now occupied a room in what was still essentially Alam Mirza's residence, a person he had previously abused, insulted, and humiliated. Ayub and Alam Mirza made for an odd couple and their lives together could well have been comical if it were not for the seriousness of the consequences. Alam Mirza had dredged Sheeda Pistaul from the depth of Ayub's past to reveal his sordid act and Ayub should have had ample cause to be cross with him on his ill-intentioned bid to defame him. Yet he chose to be in even closer proximity to him than hitherto, when a man of more judicious disposition would have shunned such company.

The redeeming feature of Ayub's decline was the fact that his rise to the high point of his life had been gradual and sustained, not meteoric. He had always been comfortable in whatever situation he found himself. Though he was stern and diffident, he was never haughty and had no airs about him. While he took to some of the trappings of wealth, he never flaunted it. Indeed, his lifestyle even in his mansion was a bit ascetic. Ayub had never forgotten his humble origins and even though others might have seen him as a wealthy entrepreneur, he was at heart a working-class man. Moving back to his humble cottage was not as traumatic as it might have been for a man of fickle disposition.

Ayub was reserved and unsocial at the best of times. He had now become almost reclusive. He would admit no one in his presence. After his move to the cottage, the sighting of Ayub in public was a rare event. In fact, he might even have wished that the world would forget him altogether so that the incident with his wife and child could also recede in public memory. However, the world was not prepared to forget him, at least not yet, though not many may have bothered about where he had gone to live.

CHAPTER 57

Noor found out about Ayub's misfortune and was quite concerned for his well-being in spite of their soured relations. It would have simply gone against the grain of her character to leave him alone in the hour of his greatest ordeal. Ayub had convinced her that he was her father and she continued to think of him as such. Besides, he had embraced her as a daughter at a time of quiet desperation in her life and it was because of him that she enjoyed the somewhat exalted status. It was, of course, true that he had treated her quite roughly late in their relationship but she was ready to forget the unpleasantness of that episode. She still believed in him as nobody else did and wanted very much to stand by him. She was confident that Ayub would bounce back again from his misfortune and regain his pre-eminent position.

Noor had no idea where Ayub might have gone after he left the mansion. She looked for him desperately. She even pondered over the notion that when she did locate him, she might ask him to come and live with her, though she had a very good idea of how he would react to the absurd offer of taking up residence in Myra's house. However, try as she might, she was unable to locate him. She finally found out that he had taken up residence in his old cottage, of which she did have a faint idea. Ayub had once recounted for her the manner in which he had come to buy his own house for the first time. He had talked fondly about his uncomplicated life in that neighborhood and was always clear that if he ever had to move back, he would have no qualms about it. He would be neither uncomfortable nor ashamed. In hindsight, his feeling seemed suspiciously like a premonition, as if he expected to move back into the cottage one day or, perhaps, even wished to be back there. Noor decided to visit her father without further postponement.

Noor arrived at the cottage only to be greeted by an impertinent Ayub, hiding behind closed doors. He told her that he wished to see no one, not even his daughter. She tried to persuade him but Ayub was adamant. Noor was unyielding in her desire to see her father though for now she decided not to press the issue further. The knowledge of where her father was residing had at least relieved her of her curiosity. She left without seeing him but vowed to return soon. And so she did. This time though she was determined not to be denied admission. She barged into the house as soon as Ayub opened a crack in the door. Ayub was incensed. He resented her intrusion and chided her forcefully.

"Go away, go away. I don't want to see you."

"But, Father."

"I do not want to see you! I said I do not want to see you!"

However, Noor was steadfast in her resolve and finally prevailed upon him. She was aghast at the manner in which he was living; articles of dirty clothing strewn all over the dust-laden room, furnished with nothing more than a bed and an old chair. She immediately took upon herself to create a more conducive environment for his living. She cleaned up the room and did what little she could to make the living quarters more comfortable. She brought him food and groceries, and cooked and cleaned for him every day. Ayub became reconciled to his daughter in due course and even looked forward to her daily visit. The effect of her presence and her ministrations perked up his dreary existence and brought him out of his depression somewhat. However, despite such compassionate overtures and the empathetic feeling it engendered, Ayub could never again think of Noor with the same fondness he had felt for her when he thought she was his real daughter.

CHAPTER 58

In the meantime, the auctioning of Ayub's assets proceeded as ordered by the courts. There were many bidders and Shahzaib was amongst the more enthusiastic. Some read an element of indecent haste in Shahzaib's untimely bid. Others saw it in bad taste, as an act of disloyalty. The general opinion was that Shahzaib ought to have aided Ayub to recover his assets instead of trying to appropriate them for himself. The more observant amongst the onlookers even questioned Shahzaib's ability to underwrite his quest for Ayub's assets; he personally was not known to have the wherewithal to carry such a large financial burden. The considered view was that Myra might have egged on Shahzaib to participate in the bidding and that the intended purchase was to be financed by her. Be that as it may, Shahzaib did out bid the others and soon took over both Ayub's factory and office building, the two assets being bracketed together as the insolvent company's property.

Soon the factory which had remained paralyzed during Ayub's long ordeal with his creditors, was buzzing with activity. Ayub too might have wished to see the revival of his factory even though it had now passed into the hands of another. It would not be an exaggeration to state that for Ayub the factory represented a labor of love, the most cherished work of his life, a life that in many other ways had been misspent. He could never have been averse to the renewed glory of his life's work. But the real import of the takeover was expressed by the employees, some of whom might have been saddened by the ironical turn of events but were nevertheless satisfied with the outcome for pragmatic reasons.

"Mr. Shahzaib has bought the factories. It is better for us now than it was before. We work harder but at least we are not scared now. No bursting out in rage, no slamming of doors, and though we are paid less now, we have more of what really counts, peace of mind."

In time, Shahzaib purchased Ayub's mansion also. Thus, it seemed that the takeover by Shahzaib of the most treasured of Ayub's possessions, beginning with Myra, was now complete. The irony of the usurpation at the hands of an upstart was not lost on the wagging tongues. After all, Ayub had persuaded Shahzaib to join him, even prevailing over the young man's initial reluctance. Yet, Shahzaib was nothing but an unwitting instrument in Ayub's misfortune. In truth, his dispossession came about of his own follies, committed under an overwhelming emotional burden of the two women in his life. The presence of each was a passing phase yet each had somehow been consequential in his downfall, forming dark shadows over a brightly lit vista.

CHAPTER 59

Ayub and Alam Mirza made strange bedfellows. Alam Mirza had the irritating habit of giving Ayub a glimpse of the day's news and offering his views on it. In fact, he was the only contact Ayub had with the outside world. Ayub was usually indifferent to Alam Mirza's opinion but Alam Mirza never failed to offer it anyway. Ayub had no choice but to hear him out.

"Mr. and Mrs. Shahzaib have bought a new house."

"Oh, and which house is that."

"Your mansion."

Alam Mirza's retort betrayed a distinctly taunting manner. Ayub was obviously stung by the news.

"My mansion? So he has bought my house, out of the thousands that he could have purchased in this town?"

"Well since you couldn't retain it, someone had to buy it. There is no harm if Shahzaib bought it. I imagine he got a good bargain in the auction though. Of course, his gain is your loss, is it not?"

Alam Mirza was relentless with his taunts, savoring every second of Ayub's discomfiture. Ayub had felt no emotional upheaval when Shahzaib bought his factories and his office building but the thought of him taking up residence in his old house, and that too with Myra, galled him indescribably.

"Surely he'll buy my body and soul likewise."

"There is no saying he won't, if you are willing to sell."

Having planted these wounds in the heart of his once imperious master, Alam Mirza left Ayub alone to ponder over his latest supersession. Ayub merely stared at the emptiness, which was all his eyes could behold now.

CHAPTER 60

A lot of time went by thus as Ayub continued with his isolated life. He rarely left the cottage during this time and was beginning to feel claustrophobic. The confinement was quite contrary to his ingrained country disposition. But more to the point, having worked so strenuously throughout his life he could not bear being idle. He had enough money to last him a while though he knew well that he would not be able to live on it forever.

There was, of course, no reason why Ayub could not make a fresh start in a business he knew as well as anyone around. The knowledge and understanding of the leather trade that he had acquired over the years had placed him in a better position than the one he was in when he first started out. He was in the prime of his life and far more sophisticated in the ways of the world than the crude and unlettered Yuba. But, his was not a simple business failure whence he could pick up the pieces and move on. His spirit had been wrenched out, leaving him bereft of the will to survive. On the very day that he was exposed, he had acquired the seeds of self-destruction. From then on, his dire circumstances were of his own making, of his fervent wish to annihilate himself. In any case, it was too late now. Ayub had no wish to return to the experiences of his youth lest he made the same mistakes again and suffered even worse consequences. He had no wish to become a scapegrace all over again.

At last, he could no longer accept his uselessness and so, he went out into the world once again, sensing that an honest day's work was not something of which he should be ashamed. As he went around to some old acquaintances, he chanced to pass by Shahzaib who immediately stopped to greet his former friend and patron. Shahzaib knew of Ayub's distressed condition and wished fervently to help him. However, he knew Ayub would spurn his offer if he were to make him one. Shahzaib, therefore, wanted to make the most of the chance encounter.

"I have heard that you have not been keeping well, Mr. Ayub. I have been meaning to see you, to talk to you about possible assistance I can render."

"Assistance, eh? The way I assisted you, perhaps! Do you recall our conversation then, when I convinced you to stay? You stood without a thing to your name. And now I stand totally dispossessed."

"Yes, yes, that is so! That is the way of the world. But I did not contrive it."

"Ha, ha, how true! Why, of course, you did not contrive it. The contrivance had an impetus from another source. Nature, perhaps? Up and down! I have lived life on a roller coaster. So why should it be any different now."

Ayub threw up a mock jocularity, flailing his arms up and down in further mockery. Shahzaib, though, was sincere in his offer to help him pull back his life from the pits of desperation.

"Please listen to me just as I once listened to you so many years ago. Come and work with me, in your old factory."

He pointedly made his reference to working with, rather than for him. It was obvious that Shahzaib still held Ayub in great deference.

"I know I can't stay doing nothing but I am sure I'll find some work."

"I cannot ignore the fact that my good fortune is entirely due to your generosity. I will never be able to repay you but I do wish to contribute to your rehabilitation. We have not moved into your old house yet. Come and reoccupy it. I am sure my wife will not mind it at all. I have no desire to live in a mansion."

"I can never do that. You do not know what you ask. I must, however, thank you for your offer but no thanks."

"Will you at least consider my offer of work?"

The irony of the reversal of the roles was not lost on the older man and he thought to heighten it even further.

"Alright, I will come to work for you but I will work at what I always was, a skilled craftsman."

So saying, he shook Shahzaib's hand abruptly and hastened away as if unwilling to betray himself further. Shahzaib watched him as he vanished round the street, confounded at his farcical demand. The next morning Ayub showed up at the factory. Shahzaib once again offered him an executive position but Ayub was obdurate over his demand. A flustered Shahzaib was left with no choice but to play along and hired him as a technician. Ayub had conjured up an absurd situation but Shahzaib could not stop the surreal drama from playing itself out before him. In fact, it was obvious that Ayub's desire to work as a technician in his old establishment was nothing but an act of self-flagellation. He was simply seeking to punish himself for the sins that continued to torture his conscience and by this measure he must have envisioned for himself a redemption which he had so eagerly sought in his many acts of penitence.

There was yet another, more disturbing, side to Ayub's perverse inclination to demean himself. Try as he might, he could not cleanse himself of the ill feeling he had for both Myra and Shahzaib in spite of his former protégé's concern for his welfare. That ill-feeling came from the gut and even his spiritual redemption would do nothing to dilute the visceral contempt he had developed for the duo. His presence at the factory would serve as a constant reminder of the indignities he had suffered at their respective hands. By such reminders, he might have been priming himself to get even with his tormentors in a more sinister way.

"It's her money that propels him upward. How odd, here I am, working for him as a laborer and he is now the master. My factory, my house and the woman who had once consented to be my wife are now all in his possession."

As he dwelt on his poisonous notions, his state of mind started deteriorating. He would lapse into moodiness without any obvious provocation and would constantly mutter in tones betraying recklessness. Ayub's odd behavior was not lost on his fellow workers. As his moods became more morose, his speech started becoming incoherent.

"How I wish I had not taken that damned oath. Oh! How I wish I hadn't. I will go to the shrine of the saint and beg forgiveness. I will beg to be released from my oath."

Ayub kept repeating the words in a trance-like state, as if it were a mantra. His perplexed colleagues strained to understand his rambling speech and when they did understand it, they inquired about the oath. At first, they were mystified by his allusions to the overarching role of divine power in the affairs of ordinary mortals, and other such philosophical musings. They were at their wits end and demanded a cogent explanation of his reference to the oath. After much goading, Ayub finally explained his dilemma more coherently.

"In my youth I had taken an oath not to indulge in intoxication of any kind for the rest of my life. I am an old man now and I wish to seek a release from the sentence. I shall beg forgiveness from the saint before whom I took that oath."

After resolutely standing by his word for so many years, the burden of his wanton fate had so weakened his will that he was about to give in to base desires once again. In a different state, he would have remonstrated with himself for the thought of breaking a solemn oath, much less one that he had made in front of a saint he so revered. However, he reasoned that persisting in wrongdoing for which one can seek God's forgiveness is better than penitence compelled by fear.

CHAPTER 61

Noor confronted Ayub as soon as she found out that he intended to take to alcohol. She knew what this new license would do to him and used all her powers of persuasion to dissuade him from embarking upon yet another feckless pursuit. Alas, she had not been able to gauge the deteriorated state of his mind. So, when Ayub did start drinking once again, she tried her best to ease the situation by her presence. She often sat with him for hours while he pandered to his newfound fancy, even taking his arm to guide him to his bed as he walked blankly like a blind man, blabbering half-uttered words. She might have ignored his utterances as the thoughtless banter of a drunken man, yet she was alarmed at some of his pointed insinuations.

"I am a man of my word. For 22 years, I kept my oath from which I have now been granted a release from the saint. I must take another oath now. That man, that upstart has taken away everything from me, I will …"

Ayub trailed off without completing his thought. Noor was startled at the obvious allusion to Shahzaib. She knew very well how he would have completed the sentence but sought a confirmation anyway, fretful of the consequences.

"What will you do?"

Ayub did not answer her query but she was troubled just the same. She knew her father was capable of taking extreme steps and felt it was her duty to caution Shahzaib of the danger that her father posed for him; it was certainly her strong desire to make sure that no harm came to him.

CHAPTER 62

No one had informed Myra that Ayub had entered her husband's service. There was really no reason for Shahzaib or anyone else to inform her. She visited the factory only occasionally and only if she had to see Shahzaib urgently, as she did presently. No sooner did she enter the premises, she was suddenly face-to-face with Ayub, flabbergasted at his sight. Ayub's mock self-deprecating words taunted Myra, adding to her rising distress.

"Good morning, ma'am, we are glad to see you here. Your visit is always a great honor for the labor class. It means so much to us that the lady of the establishment should take a personal interest in our welfare."

Then glancing at his watch, he continued with his mockery.

"Oh! It is an hour and a half longer before we get off from work. You see, ma'am, we of the lower classes have to abide by the watch. We know nothing of the leisure that your class enjoys."

Other laborers too were present there and Myra did not respond to Ayub's madness. In fact, it was too much for her to bear and she hurried away from his presence and left the factory without seeing Shahzaib. The sarcastic encounter with Ayub frightened Myra. She trembled at the thought of what he was capable of doing in his present state of mind. She could not ask her husband to discharge him because she would have to explain her dilemma. In any case, she knew it would serve no purpose and instead decided to simply avoid visiting the factory, though that too provided her with little comfort. Her thought reverted to the letters and mementos still in Ayub's possession. She had to have those back at any cost, and immediately.

Meanwhile, the mocking attitude that Ayub displayed in the presence of Myra had become more widespread. He spared no one and often disrupted the day's normal activities on the factory floor. The supervisory staff conveyed it to the boss. During the course of his employment at the factory, Shahzaib had always been considerate to Ayub. He had even brushed aside Noor's warning of Ayub's state of mind. It was now getting more and more difficult to put up with his antics. He nevertheless continued to tolerate Ayub as long as he caused no personal affront to him. He still thought of him with some compassion because of his circumstances. Naturally, Ayub in his present circumstances would not be the man he was previously. In fact, Ayub was very much the same man, a man with devious qualities that had remained latent thus far but were coming alive with the battering he had received lately.

Shahzaib's view of Ayub started changing as his moods became more ominous. He could no longer ignore the complaints he was receiving against him, with some regularity now. Ayub was making a mockery of this staid man's business. It soon became obvious that his ultimate target was Shahzaib. He started heaping offensive assaults on him that soon increased not only in regularity but also in severity, even bordering on vulgarity. These attacks were particularly galling because Shahzaib was showing so much concern for Ayub's well-being. Shahzaib could not help wondering why he was trashing him in such venomous tones. His own moods were now becoming a victim of Ayub's rapaciousness and he would often betray a volatility that he had never displayed before.

Unsurprisingly, Shahzaib carried his moods home. Myra was quite perplexed at the change and wanted to know if anything was bothering him.

"It is Ayub. I can understand why there would be envy but I cannot see the reason for the intensity of what he feels personally. It's more like old-fashioned rivalry in love than just a bit of contention in business."

Myra was alarmed at Shahzaib's unwitting simile as he continued with an elaboration.

"I gave him employment. I could not refuse it even though I knew all along that by asking for a skilled job he was making a mockery of me. But I cannot now be blind to the fact that his actions have become so irrational and executed with such intense passion that there is no telling how he will conduct himself the next moment."

"What has he been saying?"

Myra spoke anxiously. The words on her lips were 'anything about me?' but she did not utter them. She could not however suppress her agitation and her eyes filled with tear. Shahzaib became concerned at Myra's tearful reaction and reassured her that he would control Ayub's excesses, though he did not know the nature or the seriousness of

Myra's apprehension. Nor did he know Ayub's intent as well as she did.

"No, no. It is not that serious. I can get rid of him and that would be the end of the problem. I just do not want to be harsh on him. I will give him an opportunity to change his behavior before going for that option."

Myra was anything but reassured as she pleaded with Shahzaib, now rather mournfully.

"I wish you would do what we've talked of so often. Just give up the business and let us go away from here. We have plenty of money. We can live a good life in Europe."

Shahzaib did consider the possibility strongly and was not averse to relocate, at least to another city where he could ply the same trade, if not abroad. Then an opportunity presented itself that he would not turn down. The military junta took over the government and offered Shahzaib a ministerial position. He considered it an honor for someone from the wrong side of society's tracks to be elevated to such heights and accepted it despite his wife's vehement protestations.

"See how it is obvious that we are ruled by the powers above us? I did not come to stay here but I stayed. There was no reason for us to meet but we did. There was no question of the two of us getting married but we got married. I could not have imagined that I would receive such an honor but I did. We make plans for ourselves but a higher force veers us in a different direction. If they want to make me a minister, I will stay and Ayub can rant about it if he wants."

CHAPTER 63

From then on Myra felt even greater unease. If she had not been so injudicious in her relationship with Ayub, she would not have acted as she did. In desperation, she went to the factory and confronted Ayub forcefully. In the din of the machines, no one could make out their discourse.

"Ayub, I asked you many months ago to return the letters and photographs of our past. You promised to do so but you have not yet acted on it. I insist now that you honor your promise. You know how important it is for me to ensure that our past relationship should be blotted out for the good of all concerned, including you."

"Why, blessed woman, I packed up every scrap of yours and asked you to collect it at my mansion but you never showed up."

"A death in the family prevented me from coming then. And what became of the parcel?"

He recollected that he had bundled up the letters and the photos and had left the package in the safe in his study at the mansion. Myra and Shahzaib were, of course, the current occupants of the mansion. He wondered if Shahzaib had opened the safe yet. A grotesque grin spread over his face as he contemplated a misshapen mischief. He told Myra that he could not recall right away where he had stored the parcel, while at the same time reassuring her that it was secure. He promised he would let her know the next day.

The same day he enquired of Shahzaib to see if he had come by the parcel.

"I may possibly have left a parcel in my old safe in the study. Have you found it?"

"It should be there now. I haven't opened the safe."

"It is not of much consequence to me but I'll call for it some evening when you are home, if you don't mind."

Ayub was in no hurry to retrieve the packet. In his deviousness, he may even have hoped that Shahzaib would chance upon the packet and hoped too that curiosity would take the better of the devoted husband.

CHAPTER 64

Shahzaib's marriage with Myra was a happy occasion for his mother although she might have wished that Shahzaib had married someone within her own social orbit. She was a blue-collar wife and had lived in working-class neighborhoods all her life. Her son's prospects and circumstances had soared since he came to work for Ayub and mother and son had moved to lodgings that were more suited to their new status. Myra had moved in with them after her marriage to Shahzaib. But, Myra and Shahzaib's mother were poles apart, in everything really. It was for Myra to make the adjustment and she did so ungrudgingly. Myra was courteous with her mother-in-law but never condescending and the two got along amicably if not warmly. The move to the mansion, however, was somewhat intimidating to the mother at first but she soon settled down comfortably.

The news of Shahzaib's success had reached his old neighborhood in his hometown. The fact that one of their own had made it big was a source of great pride amongst those who had known him in different circumstances. In the cultural milieu of Shahzaib's society, the unfortunate usually became supplicants of those who had managed to improve their lot. As soon as word of Shahzaib's success went around, people who barely knew him began approaching him for assistance. The requests were mostly in the way of financial assistance though job-seekers were not too far behind. Poor relatives, in particular, expected such generosity as a right. It was therefore only a matter of time before Shahzaib's father, Ibrahim, called on the mansion. After all, he was the closest poor relative and he could be excused if he thought he had a prior claim on his son's largesse.

Shahzaib had grave misgivings over his father's role in his life. He had never forgiven him for abandoning the family while he was still a child, a time when he most needed his presence. But the issue was not as cut and dry for his mother. Ibrahim had abandoned his then young wife almost as soon as Shahzaib was born but they had never divorced. He was still her husband and, indeed, quite capable of asserting his position. The father never dared approach his son directly but if he was barefaced enough to come begging at his doorsteps, the poor mother had no choice but to oblige him. Lately, he had made it a habit to visit the house often but always in the absence of his son. He would receive his pickings in the kitchen and slip out unnoticed.

Shahzaib drove home unexpectedly one day and saw his father in the kitchen, obviously waiting for his mother. He confronted his father, heaping all manner of recriminations on him while the father tried to explain the exigencies of his life.

"How dare you come to my house? You abandoned my mother and left her to look after me alone. Now that she is a little more comfortable, you seek to take undue advantage of her compassion. You shame me by your prevarication."

"I did not abandon you by choice. I swear I did not. My circumstances forced me to stay away from you though I sorely missed you and your mother. In any case, I am your father. Would you rather that I should die of hunger and cold on the street?"

"I do not care if you were to die this very moment. I will have nothing to do with you. Do not ever come to my house again and do not ever hassle my mother."

Shahzaib did not wait for his father to leave. He rushed into the house and accosted his mother, upbraiding her for entertaining his father. His mother tried to explain the contingent reality of her action but he brushed her off. He would hear nothing more about the matter. Thereafter, the father stayed away from Shahzaib's house, at least for the present.

CHAPTER 65

Ayub decided to visit the mansion to retrieve the packet of letters so dreaded by Myra. It was quite late in the evening as he left his house, primed with a substantial quantity of alcohol. Alcohol had become a habit with him once again and he found it difficult to function without it. However, he had consumed considerably more than his usual dose that evening in anticipation of the special rendezvous. A fiendish smile hung on his face as he approached the house, as though he were contemplating some enlivening form of amusement. Whatever it was that he happened to be planning was not in any way diminished by the fact that it was his first visit to the house since he lived there. The bell spoke to him in a familiar tone and the sound of the opening of the door must have revived in him the memory of the dead days of his glory. Yet he experienced none of the nostalgia that should have been such a natural part of his feelings. He was so preoccupied with his mischievous thoughts that he felt no angst at the sight of Shahzaib emerging from the doorway of his lost resplendence. Shahzaib invited him to the study, where he at once unlocked the safe, Ayub's safe, custom made precisely according to his need. Shahzaib drew the parcel and other papers and handed them over to Ayub. He apologized for not having returned them earlier.

"It doesn't matter. The fact is that they are just old letters, quite unimportant actually."

Shahzaib had no inclination to invite Ayub in but for the fact that he wished to open the safe in his presence. Shahzaib handed Ayub the parcel but made no overture of hospitality. However, Ayub had come armed with a nefarious intent. He made himself comfortable in the plush leather wingchair that was once his favorite perch and ritualistically asked his hesitant host about his wife's well-being.

"I hope Mrs. Shahzaib is well."

"She was feeling a bit weary and has gone to bed early."

Shahzaib sat down reluctantly on one of the smaller chairs. Though he was not in a mood to carry on a conversation with Ayub, he nevertheless behaved politely towards his old boss.

"Did I ever tell you about the curious chapter of my past, about the woman I was about to marry? Ah, I may not have. Anyway, let me tell you about it though it is of no consequence any more. I was all set to marry a young lady a few years ago but I had to abandon her for a higher cause. These letters are from that woman. Thank God it is all over now."

"What became of that poor woman?"

"Luckily she married and married well and so the emotions she poured out on me do not cause me any pangs, as they might otherwise have done. But just listen to what she has to say."

He proceeded to untie the bundle of passionate love letters that Myra had committed in the naivety of her youthful infatuation. He shuffled through the papers and started to read from one.

> *For me there is practically no future without you. In truth, I am so devoted to you that I cannot contemplate life without you. It would be blasphemous even to think that I can be the wife of another. I shall wait expectantly for you until the end of my life.*

"That's how she went on and on, acres of words like that."

Shahzaib, though quite uninterested and bursting with yawns, sat through it attentively, even willing to humor Ayub.

"Yes, that is the way it is with women, isn't it?"

The fact was that Shahzaib knew precious little about women, not having had much interaction of any sort really. Nonetheless, he knew enough about Myra's sentiments to detect a bit of a similarity in the effusive manner of Ayub's woman with the outpourings of his own wife. He had no way, of course, of knowing that the object of Ayub's derision and his wife were one and the same. Ayub unfolded another letter and read it likewise.

"I cannot divulge her name, of course. She is now married to another man, you know. It would be extremely unfair to her and to her husband no less."

"True, true but why didn't you marry her?"

Shahzaib asked these questions in a comfortably indifferent tone, in the manner of a man to whom the matter did not concern even remotely.

"Well, despite all her protestations of passionate love, when I finally did come forward to marry her, she was not there for me."

"Maybe she had already married another."

"Yes, perhaps."

"The young lady must have had a heart that flip-flopped quite readily."

"Oh she did! She did!"

Ayub exclaimed quite emphatically as he opened another letter and yet another, reading selected lines from each in turn, each time coming close to divulging her name but stopping short. In fact, he might have intended to do just that, to demonstrate enough of the passionate love avowed in the letters and then end the drama by reading out the name. It was a vile thought designed to heighten the woman's unusual flirtation and with it Shahzaib's anxiety. He may well have come to the house with that very thought but for some inexplicable reason, he could not now summon enough resolve to carry out the heartless deed. His intoxication was waning and with it, perhaps, his courage. He refrained from naming the woman, at least for now.

Myra had gone to bed early that evening, not knowing anything about Ayub's impending visit. In fact, Shahzaib could not have been certain if Ayub would come by that evening and so, there was no reason for him to inform Myra. However, the chime of the doorbell had awoken her. She could make out the opening of the front door and the entering footsteps. She soon heard indistinct voices and came out of bed to discover the source of the din. She put on her gown and descended the stairs, which were in the proximity of the study. The door of the study was open and, in the stillness of the night, the voice and the words were clearly recognizable. She stood mortified. Her own words, the ones through which she had conveyed her passions, greeted her in Ayub's voice, like spirits from the grave. She could hear each tone clearly. At the end of Ayub's rendition of the letters, a conversation broke out between the two men. Myra could hear her husband inquire of Ayub in a rather subdued and casual tone and Ayub's answers to those queries in an enthusiastic and animated voice.

"Is it fair to the young woman to be reading to a stranger what was meant only for you?"

"Well, you may think so but by not disclosing her name, I am merely making her an example for others such as you. I am certainly not scandalizing her."

"If I were you, I would destroy them. As another man's wife, it would ruin the woman if her protestations of love became known."

"No, I shall not destroy them."

Ayub put the letters back into a bundle. He then rose to leave and Shahzaib saw him out. Ayub could not help taking a parting shot though.

"Well, I am much obliged to you for listening. I may tell you more about her someday."

It was clearly a declaration of intent but Shahzaib obviously had no way of sizing up that intent. Myra went back to her bedroom in a state of hysteria. She sat on the edge of the bed and waited for her husband to come up. The suspense was consuming her. Had she confessed all to her husband at the beginning of their acquaintance, he might have gotten over it and married her just the same. The thought had crossed her mind but she had concluded then that it was a risk she should not take. For her or anyone else to tell him now would be fatal to her marriage.

Myra gazed expectantly at Shahzaib as he entered the bedroom, waiting to unearth his reaction. She had no idea how much Ayub had revealed. Then to her joyous wonder, he looked at her with such an affectionate smile that her fears dissipated instantly. Ayub had not revealed their secret, she thought, at least not yet. She could not hold her composure any longer and sobbed hysterically. Shahzaib could not understand her sudden hysterics but calmed her anyway.

CHAPTER 66

The next morning Myra approached her dilemma a bit more calmly. She should boldly tell her husband the truth, she thought. She dreaded that, in so doing, he, like the rest of society, would condemn it as her crime rather than her misfortune. She decided to employ further persuasion with Ayub instead. This seemed to her to be the only practical weapon left to parry his incipient attack. She sat down and wrote a note telling him what she had overheard the previous night and how very distressed she was with his antics. She asked him to meet her at a park where she usually went for a walk in the evening. In her great anxiety, Myra was throwing caution to the wind once again. She was making a move that could expose her to an even greater hazard. If Shahzaib were to learn of her secret rendezvous in a public place with an ex-lover, it would surely invite grave allegations of duplicity and at once jeopardize her marriage. However, her anxiety was such that she paid no heed to the consequences of her action.

Myra arrived for the encounter as darkness was beginning to envelop the park. She looked pale and haggardly, her hair unkempt and her dress quite rumpled. It was uncharacteristic of her to step out of her house in such a state. Normally she would take great care in her appearance. In fact, she had not slept at all the previous night. Even otherwise, her features were now beginning to look wearisome, as if ageing prematurely. Extreme anxiety had obviously taken a toll. She waited breathlessly in the dark shadows of the park as she saw the outline of a figure approaching her. It was Ayub. He stood motionless for a moment, observing her curiously. Myra could not understand the hesitation in Ayub's stride. Actually, Ayub was horrified at the unusual plainness of the woman in the midst of the eeriness of the dusk that was setting in. As he approached her, the haggardly appearance and the sadness of Myra's countenance revived in him the memory of another woman he had condemned to her fate. Ayub had lived a life full of gloom, a life overshadowed by visions of an impending doom. The sight of Myra in her present state seemed to signal even greater turmoil in his life in the approaching days. Thus, even before she spoke a word, he knew how he would deal with the situation. He stammered with unconcealed compunction as he addressed her.

"I am sorry to see you look so ill."

She shook her head vigorously, which seemed to enhance the distress on her face. She had obviously taken great umbrage to his ill-conceived sympathy for her corporeal condition when he knew nothing of the storm that was brewing inside her.

"How can you be sorry when you deliberately cause me such anxiety?"

"What! Is it anything I have done that has pulled you down like this?"

"It is all on your account. I have no other grief. I would be quite happy but for your threats. Oh, Ayub, do not wreck me like this. Have you not caused me enough distress? When I came here I was a young woman of firm features, now I am rapidly descending into raggedness."

Ayub was completely disarmed. She had come to meet him here in this compromising way without perceiving the risk she had taken. Myra was displaying the same thoughtless want of foresight that had led her into her imprudent relationship with him. That relationship was now the sole source of her agony. Such a woman, he thought, deserved pity if nothing else. He lost all his desire for her there and then and no longer envied Shahzaib his bargain. Ayub was suddenly gentle in his style.

"Well what do you want me to do? My reading of those letters was only a practical joke. I disclosed nothing."

"Return those letters to me and anything else that may reveal our association."

"So be it. I shall return every scrap. But between you and me, he is sure to find out something of the matter sooner or later. But I can only assure you that I will not be the source."

"Ah but by then, I shall have proven myself to be a faithful wife and he may forgive me. In any case, you shall then stand absolved."

"I hope he does forgive you. You will have your letters and your secret is safe, at least on my part. I will have nothing more to do with you or your new life. You have my solemn promise of that."

Myra should have been quite satisfied with the success of her mission but there was a lingering feeling in her guts that things may not go as smoothly as she might have wished. Even Ayub's favors had a way of ending in adversity.

CHAPTER 67

Alam Mirza's situation was becoming more desperate by the day. He had been searching for gainful employment but all he could find was occasional patches of work. He was known throughout the trade to be dishonest and that alone was enough to thwart his efforts, notwithstanding the fact that he was an experienced and even a competent professional. Alam Mirza had learnt his trade and had spent the better part of his career at the tannery now owned by Shahzaib and he thought he deserved another stint in it. Shahzaib knew him well by his tarnished reputation and flatly refused to entertain him. In his desperation, he thought of seeking Ayub's intercession. He was quite convinced that if Ayub were to plead with Shahzaib on his behalf, Shahzaib would not spurn the request.

Alam Mirza had never sought out Ayub since they started living together and the two met and spoke only in the common living area. However, this time he had a pressing reason to call on him. He walked to Ayub's bedroom and knocked on the door a few times. There was no response. He opened the door slightly and peeped in to see if, perhaps, Ayub had failed to hear his knock. He could not see anyone clearly and so he walked in. Ayub was not present in the room. Alam Mirza had never been inside Ayub's room but he was not at all surprised that there was not much by way of belongings in the room. Ayub had not even bothered to change the worn out furnishings that Alam Mirza had left behind when he vacated the room. He gave the room a cursory glance, more out of curiosity than as if looking for anything in particular. He saw a packet on the bedside table and, true to his inquisitive nature, proceeded to examine it.

After his meeting with Myra in the park, Ayub searched through his meager belongings for Myra's articles. He collected every scrap of her notes, letters, and photos that he possessed, including those he had brought from the mansion, and made a parcel. He aimed to be as good as his word and meant to find a way to dispatch the same to her. He left the parcel on his bedside table pending its delivery and went off to work. Ayub had no reason to imagine that anyone would enter his room without his permission, much less pilfer his belongings. Alam Mirza, of course, was the only other occupant of the cottage.

Alam Mirza opened the parcel and immediately retrieved an intimate photograph of Ayub with Myra. His eyes lit up and a menacing grin spread across his face. He had now confirmed the suspicion he had formed over time. Alam Mirza had accompanied Ayub on business trips to Europe a couple of times. He had become quite well acquainted with Myra and had observed her unusual interest in Ayub. He went on to probe the bundle further and found, to his delight, a treasure trove of letters and mementos. Then he took just one letter, the juiciest he could find, and the most intimate photograph and left the rest of the packet in the same position. Once back in his room, he rubbed his hands in glee. He made up his mind to exploit Myra's intimacy with Ayub. He reasoned that she would, at all cost, prevent the revelation of her past with the man who was more or less her husband's adversary. In fact, he had plans beyond securing employment; he figured she could be a continuous source of sustenance. Alam Mirza was a desperate man and in his desperation he could go to any length.

Ayub came home after work and picked up the parcel. He had no suspicion that Alam Mirza had tampered with the contents. He had arranged with Myra to have her collect the same near the cottage and handed over the packet to her as she sat in her car. Neither spoke a word nor exchanged a glance at each other. He returned home satisfied, having completed his end of the bargain. Myra reduced the contents of the packet to ashes within the hour. The poor soul was inclined to prostrate herself in thanksgiving, relieved that at last no evidence remained of the dark episode of her past. She felt quite confident of the future.

CHAPTER 68

Shahzaib in the meanwhile had continued to involve himself in public matters. Fresh from his stint as a minister, he turned his attention next towards his own trade body. The tanners' association was set to elect a new chair in place of Ayub and had convened a meeting of its executive council for the purpose. Ayub had resigned in the wake of his bankruptcy which saw him dispossessed of his tannery. Other members of the council had greeted his resignation with a sigh of relief. As the chair, Ayub had been an unrelenting bully rather than a comrade-in-arms. He had bullwhipped and browbeaten his fellow councilors to keep them in line and so he had few, if any, genuine friends left on the council.

This time Shahzaib was the only candidate for the chair and the meeting of the council was a mere formality. He was popular within the trade and his marriage to the wealthy and winsome Ms. Myra had enhanced his popularity. His brief stint as a government minister had further extended his influence amongst the members who felt they needed his contacts with the power brokers to lobby for the trade. The council met in the hall of its local office and elected Shahzaib as its new chairperson within minutes of being called to order. Shahzaib then took over the duties of the chair and the meeting continued.

The hall suddenly reverberated with the sound of heavy footsteps advancing along the corridor, followed before long by commotion outside the door. The door of the hall was flung open in an instant and all eyes turned towards the source of the disturbance. The sight of Ayub, shabbily dressed and looking worn out, greeted the astonished onlookers. He was obviously drunk. He entered the room and started hollering at the top of his voice.

"I see you have already chosen a new chair. I have a feeling that I should like to join you in this moment of great triumph for our illustrious new chairman."

The council members exchanged indignant glances, concerned at the dubious intrusion. Shahzaib immediately caught the mood of the council and was obliged to respond to Ayub's ungainly intervention by virtue of his newly acquired office. In truth, he would have been glad if this most unpleasant duty had fallen on someone else. Unfortunately, it was his to handle and he wanted to handle it as deftly as he could.

"It would be quite improper, Mr. Ayub Qureishi. We are conducting a formal meeting of the council and since you are no longer a member, your presence here is highly irregular."

"I have a particular reason for wishing to participate."

Shahzaib looked around at the council. The members were clearly not in favor of allowing Ayub a bully pulpit again and spoke out vociferously. Shahzaib then addressed Ayub's request.

"I think the council has expressed its opinion. I cannot permit your presence in the meeting."

"Then I am not allowed to participate."

"I am afraid so. It is out of the question."

Ayub became rowdy and spewed out expletives by the dozen, most thrown naturally enough at Shahzaib. At first, Shahzaib remained calm hoping he would simply run out of steam and leave. When that did not happen, he had to take measures to assert his authority. He called the security guards who tried to persuade Ayub to leave. However, Ayub stood his ground rigidly, barking even more venomously at Shahzaib.

"Do not forget that you have partaken of scraps from me. If it weren't for me, you would still be wasting away on pennies. You are an ungrateful mongrel to blot me out of your memory. But, I suppose that is how it should be. You have found a new patron. You are now sponging on a wealthy woman."

Shahzaib was incensed at the outrageous outburst with which Ayub had mounted a personal attack on him. He flew into an uncharacteristic rage of an intensity that he himself probably did not know existed in him. He got up and seized Ayub by his collar. He dragged him back and threw him to the ground. Shahzaib pulled himself away from the prostrated form of his erstwhile boss and warned him to leave the premises at once. Ayub's eyes met Shahzaib's and Shahzaib observed the fierce light in them. For a moment, it seemed Ayub would retaliate in kind, being the stronger of the two, but he slowly raised himself up from the ground and left without saying another word. No one had seen Shahzaib so agitated, though inside him he felt no anger, no animosity, only anguish, deep anguish.

CHAPTER 69

Alam Mirza waited outside Myra's office building. He advanced towards her as soon as her driver dropped her off at the entrance. She stopped in her tracks as she saw the man approaching her furtively. She did not recognize Alam Mirza right away as he impressed upon her the urgency of his mission, apologizing all the while for his brusque manner. He then proceeded to plead his case.

"Ma'am, I have been out of work since Ayub fired me and frankly I am in dire straits. I cannot even provide for my family. You've known me, or at least known about me, a long time. I have been loyal to the establishment that you now own. I have given it my sweat and blood over so many years. The grand tannery represents as much my effort as it does that of Ayub or your husband. I would feel much obliged if you would put in a word to your husband for my employment."

Myra responded to Alam Mirza's entreaties rather indifferently. There was no reason for her to react differently.

"You are pleading with the wrong person. It's a thing I know nothing about."

"But you can testify on my behalf. Surely, you remember I visited your office in Europe. Indeed, I first met you in your father's office when you were but a young girl."

"That may well be but I know nothing about you."

"I think, ma'am, a word from you would secure for me what I covet very much."

Myra was steadfast in her refusal to help him and spurned him rather rudely. Alam Mirza became surly and started upbraiding her for her lack of compassion. She in turn was greatly irritated at his insolence and used a few choice words to tell him off. At that point, Alam Mirza decided to use his weapon of last resort. He warned her of the consequences she would have to suffer if she did not accede to his demand.

"I know you were in an affair with Ayub. I know how lustily you carried on with him. I have documentary proof and I will not hesitate to make it public if you do not cooperate."

Myra was quite satisfied that no proof of her past with Ayub remained and was now confident that Ayub himself would refute such a suggestion. She turned around and left abruptly without bothering to engage him any further. Alam Mirza watched her as she entered the building and then went home. He sat down in the small common area of the cottage brooding over the events of the day. He felt deeply insulted at the manner in which Myra had dismissed his despair and vowed not to take it lying down. He was no longer interested in gaining fav

Ayub too had had a harrowing day and to compound his misery, he happened to walk in on Alam Mirza in the middle of the rogue's portentous frame of mind. Alam

Mirza had heard of the ruckus at the meeting of the tanners' association earlier that day and greeted Ayub caustically on the subject.

"So the council snubbed you, did it not?"

"And what if they did?"

Ayub delivered his response quite sternly, indicating that he did not really wish to engage in any further conversation on the subject. Alam Mirza continued anyway.

"Why I've had a snub too, so we are both under the same cold shade. You know how hopeless my situation is. I met Myra and pleaded for her intercession with Shahzaib to secure me a job, but she told me off very rudely. I know you cannot approach Shahzaib any longer but I am sure Myra will oblige you. I wish you would talk to her for my sake."

Ayub heard Alam Mirza's strange request and let out a hearty laugh.

"You wish me to secure a job for you from Shahzaib. You wish me to talk about it to Myra for your sake. Do I hear you right or are my ears ringing?"

Ayub suddenly lapsed into a somber frame of mind. Alam Mirza's appeal reminded him of his own concern at the relationship of Myra and Shahzaib. He started mumbling about the supposed ill-will that the couple had displayed towards him and he did it with great overtones of self-pity, oblivious to Alam Mirza's presence.

"There was a time when she submitted herself entirely to my will but now she cannot bear even to speak my name. She even wishes never to lay her eyes on me again. And what about Shahzaib? I took the upstart under my wings and nurtured him so lovingly. You should have seen how angry he looked. He charged at me furiously and hurled me to the ground. I took it like a lamb for I saw that I would not be able to settle it there. He would not have dared lay a finger on me if it were not for the security guards that surrounded him but he shall pay for it."

During the rest of the evening, Alam Mirza and Ayub sat together, drinking and commiserating with each other over their common misery. In his present state, Ayub could not comprehend how much he was demeaning himself in the company of a man of such dubious antecedents. It was hard to believe that Ayub had not understood that his success was not entirely his own but had a generous contribution of the company he occasionally kept of men whose status in life was always a notch or two above his own. It was equally hard to believe that he had not learned that his downfall was the result of the company of lowly men, weak in conscience and character. He who has chosen his friends unwisely must inevitably pay a price.

CHAPTER 70

As the evening progressed, Ayub began to lose control over his faculties, helped along in no small measure by Alam Mirza's devious exhortations. He reminded Ayub how Shahzaib had injured him as a rival in trade and love and had even snubbed him as a laborer. But, Ayub needed no reminders of what might have seemed like a somewhat distant past by now, when just that morning Shahzaib had held him by the collar in public as if he were a vagabond. That insult, indeed the degradation, was unbearable. It was not in Ayub's character to overlook an injury to his self-esteem. Ayub had learned in his formative years that if someone harmed you, the only fitting response was revenge. You gave just as well as you got--an eye for an eye and a tooth for a tooth. The company of refined men had rendered many of Ayub's perverse tendencies latent, though he had never been able to exorcise those completely. The company of men like Alam Mirza had once again brought those to the surface. Ayub could no longer contain himself and set forth to find Shahzaib.

Ayub went straight to the mansion and inquired about Shahzaib. The servants informed him that Shahzaib had not returned from work. He immediately set off for the office. It was late in the evening and the staff had left for the day. Ayub knew where to find his target and at this hour, there was no one to hinder his passage. He flung open the door to the chamber that was once his own. Shahzaib was engrossed in some paper work and was startled to see Ayub staring at him across the room.

"Hey, man. What is wrong? What are you doing here at this late hour?"

Shahzaib spoke in a tone that had just enough severity to show that he remembered the untoward encounter that had taken place at the council meeting. He knew Ayub had been drinking and that that was the immediate cause of his irrational action there. He was quite prepared to forget the whole incident and when he saw Ayub standing before him, he even entertained the thought that he might have come seeking reconciliation. Shahzaib could not have been more amiss. He had no idea of the nature of the beast in the belly of the man who stood before him.

"Now, we stand face-to-face, man-to-man. Your money can no longer protect you and my poverty cannot keep me down."

"What does it all mean?"

"Wait a bit, boy. You should have thought twice before confronting a man who has nothing left to lose. I withstood your rivalry in business which ruined me and your snub which humbled me but I will not suffer the disgrace you inflicted upon me in public."

Interestingly, even in an advanced state of inebriation, Ayub was quite careful in keeping the rivalry for Myra out of his present confrontation.

"You had no business being there."

"I had as much business as any of you, boy."

The vein in Ayub's forehead started swelling as he spoke, threatening to burst open any moment.

"You insulted the council and it was my duty to stop you."

"Damn your council. Don't forget that I was the council before anyone ever heard of you."

"I don't wish to argue with you. I know your antecedents but you are doing your past no favor with your present actions. Wait till you cool down, wait till you cool down; you'll see things the same way I do."

"You may be the one to cool down first."

Ayub's tone was grim and threatening. Then unexpectedly, he whipped out a butcher's knife from the folds of his pantaloons. He had of late started carrying the knife again, as if to keep him in constant reminder of his humble origin. It also signaled the reawakening of his latent violent streak. His violence was increasing in direct proportion to his despair and inversely to the state of his faculties. Some of his actions might even have suggested that he was on the verge of losing his sanity.

The dangerous move on the part of Ayub alarmed Shahzaib who stood up instantly. He could never have imagined even in his wildest thoughts that his rift with Ayub would come to this pass. Before Shahzaib could gather his wits, Ayub lunged at him forcefully with the menacing weapon held firmly in his hand. There ensued a struggle between the two that at times came dangerously close to causing considerable harm to the younger man. Shahzaib was no match for the brute strength of Ayub but brave men fight with their heart and Shahzaib put up magnificent resistance. Ayub eventually overpowered his quarry in a stranglehold designed to break a bull's neck.

"Now, this is the end of what you began this morning. Your life is in my hands."

"Then take it, take it! You've wished it long enough."

Shahzaib displayed remarkable sangfroid in the face of death. Ayub looked down upon him in silence, as their eyes met. Ayub's eyes suddenly turned moist and a tear dangled from one.

"That is not true, damn it! As God is my witness, no man ever loved another as I loved you once. I loved you as a son. Now, though I come to kill you, I cannot hurt you! Go and call the police and have me locked up, do what you will. I care nothing of what becomes of me!"

He then loosened his grip and withdrew, setting himself up against the wall. A look of remorse spread over his face. Shahzaib looked at him in silence still sprawled on the floor, a palpable undercurrent of relief showing on his entire person. A security guard, responding belatedly to the commotion, entered the room. Shahzaib waved him off. He then got up and went out of the room without looking back. Ayub would have wanted to call him, to apologize for his murderous insanity but his tongue failed to respond and the younger man's steps slowly faded out of his earshot. The crouching figure of Ayub was a picture of anguish and self-pity. He remained motionless for a few moments, thoroughly repressed by a deep sense of guilt. He was like a severely wounded tiger cowering in the bush, waiting to die. The sight reflected tragically on the man whose stern features were not so long ago such a remarkable sight. At length he arose, shook the dust off his clothes wearily and slowly left the premises, all the time murmuring to himself.

"He thought highly of me once. Now he'll surely hate me. He will despise me forever."

Shahzaib in the meantime descended to the street, breathless from his encounter. He decided to go on a long drive instead of going home; as much to recover himself as to consider his future course. This matter of Ayub was getting far too serious and he could not afford to neglect it anymore. For the first time he thought of Ayub as a mortal enemy, far removed from the trivial mockery that he had tolerated for so long.

The deadly incident with his erstwhile protégé caused Ayub such deep anguish that he became possessed of an overpowering wish to make amends for his behavior. He wanted to plead desperately, even prostrate himself, before the victim of his dastardly attack. He wished desperately to win a pardon for his moment of insanity. Such unsettling thoughts troubled him immensely. In the end, he had to live with his high indignation and wounded pride as he concluded that a rapprochement with Shahzaib was no longer possible. He could not continue with his hysterical denial any longer.

CHAPTER 71

Alam Mirza too readied himself for an assault on Myra, an assault much more deadly than the one that Ayub had mounted on Shahzaib. He picked up the two pieces of evidence of Myra's indiscretion that he had stolen from Ayub and went off on his dubious mission. He had decided to get the photograph and the letter inserted in a newspaper and displayed on the internet with the help of a friend who described himself as a 'freelance journalist'. Many such 'freelance journalists' earned a livelihood unhindered by the ethical norms of the profession. The newspapers and media houses paid them nothing though they might have been contributing regularly. They were simply instructed to fend for themselves. Of course, the best that someone of the stature of Alam Mirza could do was to get the scurrilous material published in a rag and to put it on an obscure website. The item did not readily come to the attention of those he had meant it for but it did get noticed ultimately. It fell to the lot of Noor to bring the same to the attention of

Myra. She rushed to the mansion and barged directly into her bedroom, breathless.

"I am sorry for the intrusion but I had to see you straightaway. Is Shahzaib in?"

"No, he is out of town and won't be back for a few days. But why are you so winded; what is the matter?

Without saying anything, Noor took out the newspaper from her bag and thrust it before her. Myra was stunned. She just stared at it and said nothing. The paper carried the photograph and the hand-written letter. The letter required strained attention but the photograph was naturally more damning in its visual appeal; it was also more salacious. The picture showed Myra sitting in Ayub's lap with her hands around his neck.

After an agonizingly long pause, Myra let out a muddled exclamation.

"It's me and him and my letter, in my handwriting!"

Ayub was never one to take pictures. In fact, he probably had no use for a camera in any form. Myra would often carry a camera or take selfies with her cell phone and even printed the ones she fancied. The posture too was quite out of character for Ayub and was the handiwork, once again, of Myra. She was, in a sense, somewhat more culpable than her companion for the existence of the photograph. Yet, Ayub could not wish away his share of the blame for the misfortune. His carelessness was the ultimate cause of the photograph becoming public.

Myra was beginning to turn pale, as if her blood was draining out of her body. Noor could see the pain that the revelation was causing her friend. The contortions on Myra's face were getting wilder with each passing moment. Yet, Noor could not have kept the matter from her. She had to bring it to her notice before some less-friendly quarters sprung a surprise on her. Noor even tried to ease Myra's pain by downplaying its importance.

"Let us ignore it for now. It is only a rag and none of our acquaintances will likely see it. In any case, no one will believe it. We will counter it effectively."

Myra was by now hysterical.

"It's no use! He will see it, will he not? Shahzaib will definitely see it. It will break his heart. He will never love me anymore. And oh, it will kill me; it will kill me for sure!"

From the beginning of her liaison with Shahzaib, Myra had been obsessed with concealing her affair with Ayub. Any young woman who had formerly been in an inappropriate relationship would naturally try to cover up her missteps. In the case of Myra, there was an exaggerated impulse to erase all signs of her past. After all, Ayub was not an unfamiliar or abstract character of her past in whom Shahzaib would see neither relevance nor rivalry. Moreover, the intensity that their business competition had assumed would magnify the matter enormously, she thought. She was sure Shahzaib would want to have nothing to do with her once he found out about the affair.

Noor was frantic. She did not know how to calm Myra down. Myra's worst fears came alive as friends and foes alike called to inquire. Word had spread. Myra continued to gaze at the newspaper, now with deepened anxiety. She started crying out hysterically.

"That is me, that is me!"

The next moment, she burst into wild, unprovoked laughter. She stood up, remained motionless for a second and then fell heavily onto the floor, convulsed in paroxysms. Noor bent over her in anguish. She realized the seriousness of Myra's condition and summoned an ambulance. She also called Myra's personal physician and asked him to reach the hospital as soon as possible. All along the way, Noor rubbed Myra's forehead gently. Myra recovered her consciousness briefly but lapsed into a fit and fell unconscious again.

The doctors at the hospital proceeded to examine her and immediately pronounced the case serious. Noor was anxious to know the actual cause of Myra's condition and directed a worried inquiry towards her personal physician, her tone even betraying an intense desperation.

"Is it a fit?"

"I suspect it could be more than a fit. It could be a stroke. In her present state of health, she may not be able to bear it. You know, of course, that she is expecting. Where is Mr. Shahzaib? You must send for him at once."

The news of Myra's pregnancy came as a surprise to Noor, escalating her concern even further. Myra's life seemed at that moment to depend upon her husband's return. Even in her semi-conscious state, she was in great mental agony, lest Shahzaib should hear of her past with Ayub only through scurrilous innuendos. She wanted to tell him the unexaggerated truth, the truth of the unconditional supersession of her feelings in his favor.

CHAPTER 72

Ayub heard the news of Myra's condition with great anxiety. He could not make out how the two items had found their way into the newspaper. He was sure he had returned every letter and every photograph in his possession and presumed that someone must have stolen the two items from Myra. Nevertheless, he did feel a great deal of remorse and wished to visit the hospital to enquire after the unfortunate woman's health. He did not think he would be particularly welcome, yet he was unable to restrain his urge and set off for the hospital. Friends and relatives had by now gathered at the hospital and regarded Ayub incredulously, as if marveling at the sheer audacity of the man in showing up at the scene of a crime he had himself committed.

Ayub saw Noor pacing the corridor frantically. He walked up to her and inquired about Myra's condition.

"How is she?"

"She is in grave danger, Father. Her anxiety to see her husband makes her frightfully restless. His presence might pacify her. Poor woman, I fear they have killed her. Oh, Father! How did she deserve the treatment that these rascals have meted out to her?"

Ayub observed his daughter curiously and that very instant he saw her in a new light. He liked the look on her face as she answered him. There was tenderness and great yearning in it. He had expected Noor to accuse him of the act, just as everyone else probably did. After all, the cause of the present situation was his photograph with Myra. It was highly unlikely that any one other than the two possess such an intimate picture. Yet, her attitude towards him seemed to suggest a compassion for his own distraught feelings and a sensitivity that the gravity of the situation demanded. Noor suddenly came across as a beacon of light in the midst of his despondency. He even entertained the hope that, perhaps, he could somehow undo the bitterness that his attitude had generated between them. He could once again come to love her as his own if she would only return the sentiment in a like manner.

Ayub quietly departed from the scene and proceeded onward to his lonesome reality. So much for a man's rivalry, he thought. Death may yet possess the prize that he and Shahzaib each had coveted, in their own turn and then simultaneously.

Ayub entered the door of his cottage and encountered Alam Mirza in the small living area. Alam Mirza asked him about the news of Myra's illness and inquired of its cause. Ayub told him what little he knew of the sordid story, not yet suspecting Alam Mirza's complicity in the affair. He could observe though that Alam Mirza was beside himself with anxiety. Alam Mirza could not have imagined the harm his mischief would cause. Ayub suddenly recalled his earlier conversation with Alam Mirza about the snub he had received at Myra's hand. The thought then crossed his mind that Alam Mirza could have snooped around his bedroom and perpetrated the crime. He abruptly hauled him up by his collar. At first, Alam Mirza was persistent with his denials but the pressure Ayub bore on him was too much. He finally confessed whereupon Ayub pounced on the mortified Alam Mirza and started pummeling him. He suddenly stopped in his tracks. The experiences of the day had worn him out, otherwise he could very easily have caused him bodily harm. In the event, he merely ordered him to pack his belongings and leave instantly. Alam Mirza was glad to do so and hastened away, more out of a fear of the consequences of his dastardly action at the hands of Shahzaib, when he came to know of it, than Ayub's reprimand.

CHAPTER 73

Myra's illness was by now the talk of the town. The distress that was the immediate cause of her condition too gained wide currency. The circumstances of her illness had greatly magnified the relationship of Myra and Ayub that may otherwise have attracted only scant and short-lived attention.

Noor informed Shahzaib of the sad event and he rushed to his wife's side immediately. He was quite upset and did not know what to make of it. The arrival of her husband soothed Myra considerably and he seldom left her side. She was still in the throes of a struggle between life and death, yet she was anxious to share with her husband her version of the secret that now lay sordidly bare before the whole world. She might have apprehended that those in her immediate company would only add to her husband's distress by discussing the subject unnecessarily and that increased her concern considerably more. She wanted to be the one to tell her husband everything but when she tried to talk to him about it, he admonished her gently. He did not want to endanger her fragile condition further, assuring her that they could discuss the matter when she was better and comfortably home. But, Myra would not wait and in the solitude of the night, she told her husband about her past relationship with Ayub. She thus unburdened herself and having done so she slipped into a coma. All efforts of the doctors to revive her were in vain and she remained in that condition thereafter.

Throughout Myra's illness, Ayub was seen lurking outside the hospital regularly, though he would not enter the premises after he had been ridiculed. He continued to inquire about her health every now and then, as if to console himself. In fact, he was there even more on account of Noor than that of Myra. Shorn one by one of all other relationships, he cherished the thought of his stepdaughter's presence in his life though earlier she had looked intolerable to him for a time. Noor's constant presence at the hospital meant that he could see her whenever he visited. It was a source of great comfort for him in his agitated state.

It was a most harrowing time for Shahzaib. Myra had now been in a coma for several days. As his wife struggled for her life, Shahzaib's thoughts were far from her indiscretions. He had obviously forgiven her, or so it seemed from the manner in which he attended to her. He had become equally concerned with another life that too was in danger if the worst should befall Myra. The doctors had warned him that both the mother and her yet unborn child would continue to be in danger unless the baby was separated from the mother. Shahzaib had gone through days of heartbreak and anxiety, not knowing if he could keep either. As Myra's condition continued to worsen, he at last permitted the doctors to perform an invasive procedure, hoping that both mother and child would come out of the ordeal alive. It was late in the night when the team of doctors operated upon Myra. The news that Myra had given birth to a healthy baby was met with an immense feeling of joy and considerable relief by the gathered company. Shahzaib was, naturally enough, particularly ecstatic.

But the joy was short-lived as Myra's condition started deteriorating. Amniotic fluid had entered her bloodstream and heart and created a vacuum. She continued to struggle for her life for days. Doctors were of the opinion that it was unlikely that Myra would survive though they continued with their efforts. Her circulation and heartbeat finally stopped. Doctors and paramedics immediately went to work on her with paddles and chest compressors to try to resuscitate her. They continued with the compression for twenty minutes or more and then on the insistence of her husband, for another twenty or thirty minutes. There was no chance of bringing Myra back to life. She had said her farewells to her husband and had delivered his child. She had no reason to linger on any longer, not even for the sake of her baby. In any case, it would have required two miracles for her to survive and live a meaningful life: resuscitation and avoiding brain damage. This could only have happened if divine providence had interfered. That, alas, was not on the cards.

Ayub remained at the hospital until dawn that night. He looked heavenwards but all that his eyes could behold was a somber darkness that rid the sky of the stars. The stillness of the air signaled a mortal serenity. A nurse walked by him. She recognized Ayub as the man who had been querying regularly about Myra. He looked at the nurse in grave silence. She shook her head from side to side; the grim expression on her face left no room for further elaboration. The unthinkable had happened. Ayub turned and left, for he knew that his presence at the hospital was now truly inappropriate.

CHAPTER 74

Ayub went back to the loneliness of his cottage but just as he was preparing to go to bed, there was a light tap on the door. It was Noor. The sight of the girl brightened his face at once. She came into the room, looking sad.

"Have you heard, Father? Myra is dead. She died about an hour ago."

"I know. I have only just come back from the hospital. It's so very good of you to come by and tell me."

"Oh, Father, what cruel joke was played on the poor soul? She deserved pity if nothing else. And now she has left another life to contend with, the girl she gave birth to shortly before she died."

Ayub was surprised at the mention of the newborn child. He had no idea that Myra had been expecting or that she had begotten a girl before she died. He was speechless as Noor continued.

"And what a beautiful child she is too, with an angelic face that matches her mother's so much. How will Shahzaib take care of the child?"

The knowledge that Myra had given birth to a child before succumbing to her torment greatly magnified Ayub's guilt that was already weighing heavily on him. He started pleading his innocence with even greater vehemence, even though Noor had neither imputed any guilt nor sought any explanation of the incident.

"You must believe me when I tell you that I had nothing to do with it. I kept my word to her to the last. It was Alam Mirza. He stole the letter and the picture from my room and committed that horrible crime."

Up until then, Noor had no idea who had committed the foul deed but all along, she had thought her father to be incapable of such indecency. She had probably read her father correctly, even though she had no persuasive reason for the supposition. The fact of the matter was that if Ayub had felt sufficiently aggravated because of Myra's involvement with Shahzaib, his code of honor would have led him to a far more stringent reprisal. He had obviously reconciled to the situation or else he would not have agreed to return Myra's memorabilia.

But Noor was always convinced of the vileness of Alam Mirza's character and from time to time she had even warned Ayub to beware of him. Even so, she couldn't quite understand the immediate reason for his vile act.

"I know you did not do it, Father. But why did Alam Mirza do it; how had she ever wronged him. I warned you about him time and again but you wouldn't hear me out."

"She had not wronged him but he perceived a slight because she refused to assist him in securing a position at her husband's tannery. He confessed it to me. I could have killed that despicable creature but I thought better of it. Now that he has fled, it is unlikely that he will ever reappear."

"But, Father, how could a person be so desperate that he should go to the extent of causing such grievous harm to someone who has done him no wrong? Was his misery so great that he became possessed of such evil?"

Ayub had no answer to his daughter's rhetorical question nor was he in a frame of mind to discuss the matter of good and evil. He preferred his own quiet introspection rather than engage in loud remonstration. After a moment of silence, he addressed his daughter.

"You must be tired sitting up at the hospital. Do stay here and rest a while."

She did as he told her without much argument and lay down on a sofa only to fall fast asleep in a matter of minutes. As for Ayub, he just gazed at her lovingly. The cruel circumstance of Myra's life had suddenly caused a great change in Ayub. He became fixated with his stepdaughter. Her filial presence was the only avenue left for his future happiness, or so he thought. Noor slept through the night uninterrupted and woke up only as the day broke. The sight of her father sitting up beside her overwhelmed her.

"Father, I fell asleep so suddenly. But you have been sitting up by my side all night, have you not? It is strange that after thinking about Myra so much all day, I did not dream of her even once."

"I could not sleep after the events of the previous day, knowing that I was in some ways culpable."

Noor kept quiet. She just did not wish to belabor the point. Father and daughter then sat down to breakfast prepared by Ayub.

"Father, it is so kind of you to have made breakfast for me with your own hands."

"I do it every day. I am alone. I live and survive, as I have always done in life, on the strength of my own hands."

She had never quite meant it the way he summed it up, a pontification of the virtues of self-reliance in general. Her immediate concern was only the present state of his existence.

"You are lonely, are you not?"

"Yes, child, I am. But it is entirely my own fault. You are the only one who has been close to me of late. But that too may change."

"Why do you say that? I will come to see you often."

"I just know. When a man has been exposed to the vagaries of life in the manner that I have, he learns to rely on his instincts."

Ayub's demeanor signified his equivocal ambivalence towards life. His mood was no longer that of the rebellious, ironical, reckless adventurer. He was now the personification of pessimism and melancholy, one who has lost all that could make life worth living or at least tolerable. In his vision, the whole landscape before him seemed like a parched desert where no life could survive except the ignoble—the scroungers and the scavengers. Later in the day as he watched Noor leave, he thought he had lost the last straw in his struggle to survive.

CHAPTER 75

Ayub was woken up early the next morning by the persistent chime of the doorbell and answered it to find, to his surprise, his daughter at the door. She asked for permission to enter and father and daughter sat down opposite each other.

"I thought you seemed very sad yesterday, so I've come to be with you. Not that I am anything but sad myself, Father."

"Do miracles still work, you think. I am not a well-read man but I have suffered enough to gain access to a bit of wisdom. Life has taught me the bitter truth; that the more one learns the more ignorant one becomes."

She could not fathom the meaning of her father's strange discourse. The sadness in his eyes caused her an inordinate amount of concern. She observed the expression on his face as he picked up a newspaper lying in front of him, the newspaper that contained the seeds of Myra's destruction.

He had mutilated the picture by a dark pen, so that her image was no longer discernable.

"Look at this image, it shows me as if I am alone. They have severed the other face from mine irretrievably. You see, the rogue's performance killed her when she had so much to live for. Yet I continue to live. And in the natural course of life, I might have to linger on another twenty or thirty years, scoffed at, or even worse, pitied."

Her father's strange suggestion troubled Noor. She was worried that her father's mental state might be deteriorating and decided she could not leave him alone.

"Father, I will not leave you alone like this. May I live with you and tend upon you as I used to do? I do not mind the present state of your dwellings. May I join you once again?"

"Join me? Do not mock me, my child. How will you forgive me for the rough treatment I inflicted upon you only recently?"

"I will. I will forgive you for every excess of the past. I want to forget the bitterness, both for your sake and my own. Oh, Father! Do you not see that I need you as much as you need me? Please do not dwell on the past with such intensity."

There was pathos in her voice, which was quivering with anticipation. Then suddenly, without waiting for her father's consent, she left to pick up her belongings and carry out the reunion. Ironically, a supposed daughter had chosen to be at Ayub's side at the hour of his deepest despair. Noor's considerate presence must have reminded him of his contemptuous attitude towards Jannat at the birth of a girl. To a father growing old nothing proves dearer than a daughter; pity the man who has ten prodigal sons but not one caring daughter.

Noor vacated the house that Myra had so graciously allowed her to live in and moved to her father's old cottage, occupying Alam Mirza's room. She could not have continued to live in Myra's house anyway.

CHAPTER 76

In due course, Shahzaib found out that Alam Mirza was responsible for the treachery that caused Myra's death. A more impulsive man might have sought vengeance to placate his sense of bereavement. However, Shahzaib pondered over the tragic event at length and the tempting thought of sorting out the perpetrators gave way to the sobering memory of his dear departed. He concluded that the only appropriate cogitation for the dead woman's memory was to regard the event as an unfortunate accident. Besides, Myra had told him enough before her death and he thought it would not be prudent to make a clamor about the matter. He had no desire to rekindle her past in the public, as much for his own sake as for her. He had evaluated his experience with Myra realistically. He understood what their union had meant and, more importantly, what it had not meant. He could not help thinking that with her death he had exchanged a looming misery for a simple sorrow. After the revelation of her past, it was hard to believe that life with her would have brought him further happiness. Consequently, it did not take him long to lighten the sorrow that her loss had plunged him in. Nevertheless, her image lived on with him.

Once he had sorted out the formalities of his personal affairs, Shahzaib's life was as peaceful as could have been under the circumstances. There was one matter, of no great urgency, that he still had to deal with though. He had to decide whether to persist with Myra's business or to pare it off. In the immediate aftermath of Myra's death, Noor had continued at the office in a more or less ritualistic manner. She was personally of the opinion that she could no longer remain with the business and had meant to tell Shahzaib that she would leave eventually. Shahzaib came over to the office for a meeting with Noor and informed her at once that he did not intend to wind up Myra's business. He also wished she would stay on with the company.

"I can think of no one who is better informed about the affairs of Myra's business than you. I think no one else will be able to run it better or more diligently. I wish you would continue."

"I am not as well educated as Myra nor am I so well-traveled. I am not sure I can run this business all by myself, though I must say I was lucky to have Myra as a mentor."

"You will have the support of our entire organization. I shall be personally available for any assistance you might require."

Shahzaib's evaluation of Noor's capabilities and the reassurance of his personal support was enough to enlist her acquiescence, though she seemed to have such a low esteem of her own business acumen.

Thus the matter of Myra's business stood settled. But the void she had left behind in the personal life of Shahzaib remained unsettled for now, though not for long. Shahzaib and Noor were destined to resume their relationship where they had left off, at the point of Myra's intrusion in it. Shahzaib was single again but his single status was now more onerous. The baby that Myra had bequeathed him would require special care. He was greatly relieved by his mother's doting presence in the house but he reckoned that the child needed a young mother rather than an aged grandmother. His thoughts revisited his fleeting involvement with Noor, which undoubtedly had some pleasant moments. The question of restoring that relationship became pertinent as he contemplated life as a single parent. He needed Noor. Noor too could not be disinclined towards such an arrangement. She had let go of Shahzaib without much remorse but a faint feeling of tenderness had lingered on. The plan that Shahzaib and Noor had prepared for Myra's business would assure a close and regular liaison with each other.

Shahzaib's mother was keenly aware of the prospect of a union between her son and Noor and was not in the least averse to the possibility. In fact, she might have wished it fervently. She had met Noor occasionally before Shahzaib's marriage to Myra and more frequently as Noor visited Myra at her home after the marriage. It was plainly evident that she was more comfortable in the company of Noor than she had been in the company of Myra. Now with Myra dead and a child awaiting a mother, she could no longer stay above the fray. Indeed, she now played the part of the matchmaker even as Noor's mother had tried and failed. Both mothers could see instinctively that the two were right for each other. Theirs was a perfect blend of temperament and propriety. Their social milieu and their native backgrounds matched thoroughly, as did their educational levels.

Noor and Shahzaib's renewed interest in each other did not go unnoticed. The wooing of the bankrupt Ayub's daughter by Shahzaib became a topic of some interest amongst gossipmongers, relishing the overwhelming irony of the proposition. However, the tattle tales of their liaison lacked the intensity that had accompanied Shahzaib's affair with Myra. One could suppose that it might have been due partly to Shahzaib's unenviable situation but also because the plainness of Noor compared unfavorably with the glamour of Myra.

CHAPTER 77

The on-again courtship of Noor by Shahzaib was naturally of particular interest to Ayub. He had grave misgivings at the renewed interest of the two in each other. It revived in him an almost dormant hostility with his nemesis. He was distraught at the thought of Shahzaib depriving him of yet another cherished companion. Any other man in his situation might have reasoned that a union between his stepdaughter and the thriving entrepreneur would not only ensure her future happiness but could even prove advantageous for him in some ways. However, Ayub looked at the eventuality with concern or even contempt. He knew that though Shahzaib might ultimately forgive him his excesses, they could never be friends again. Thus, the girl, who was his only companion now, would distance herself from him gradually. These thoughts weighed heavily on him as he conjured up a vision of yet another lonely episode in his life. He might have relented more easily had Noor chosen another man but to reconcile with a man with whom he had engaged in such fierce contention, a man who was responsible for finally breaking his spirit, was beyond his idiosyncratic faculties. A wicked thought entered Ayub's inherently wicked mind. Suppose he communicated to Shahzaib that Noor was not his child at all, perhaps even disclose that her paternity was unknown because of her mother's profession. How would that correct and ambitious man with a reputation for probity react to such information? Might he not forsake her? Ayub shuddered at his own impulse but the appalling thought stayed with him.

Ayub had imposed his paternity on Noor but he had done so at a time when he himself believed it to be true. Subsequently, when he discovered the truth, he found it more to his advantage to withhold the information from his stepdaughter. At that point, he was simply trying to ensure a continued filial association that Noor might have rejected if she had known that he was not her real father. He had done so entirely for a selfish motive. The harm he might have done to the poor child had never even crossed his mind. By not disclosing her real paternity, he had actually asked her to forsake her real father, the man who was not only responsible for her birth but who had looked after her well until his own untimely death. Ayub had been unconcerned with the emotional torment that Noor would suffer if she were to find out that she had thoughtlessly erased the memory of her real father.

Suddenly it was the latter thought that seized his imagination. The prospect of Shahzaib as Noor's husband was not germane any longer. Eventually Noor might find out her real paternity even if he chose not to disclose it. She would then know that he had deceived her into thinking that he was her real father. It would surely cause her to despise him and that disturbed him greatly. In yet another act of intemperate impetuosity, he made up his mind to tell her the truth about her paternity and thus release himself from the guilt. He would do so privately and let her decide if she wished to maintain the secret. He knew that the response that this revelation would elicit from his daughter would be too great an emotional exertion on him. He knew he would not be able to face her thereafter and so he decided to go away from the city. He had always defended his reputation for rectitude fiercely and now Noor could well accuse him of false conduct.

As soon as he saw Noor that day, he surprised the young woman by addressing her quite casually.

"I am going to go away from the city."

"Go away and leave me alone!"

"Yes, I don't much care for the bright lights and the noisy streets and the busy folks of the city anymore. I would rather be back in the countryside, back in the village, my village, from whence I came to the city. I will follow my old ways and leave you to yours. You don't really need me and I am sure you'll manage very well by yourself."

She looked crestfallen. In her estimation, this decision of her father was a direct result of her attachment with Shahzaib. However, she showed her commitment to Shahzaib by controlling her emotions and speaking out with a firmness that was obviously difficult to muster.

"It is because of my renewed interest in Shahzaib, isn't it Father? I know you disapprove of my relationship with him and I will not continue with it if you do not assent. I'll be bitterly disappointed if you should leave because of it."

"I approve of anything you desire, my child. In any case, it would not matter even if I disapproved. It is best that I go away because my presence here may make things awkward for you in the future. I wish to leave right away."

"Then, if I should marry Shahzaib you will not be able to come to my wedding. That is not how it ought to be."

"I don't want to be around. Think of me sometimes in your future life, think of me when you are living a blissful life as a wife and, perhaps, a mother and do not let the mistakes I have made in life, when you know them all, cause you to despise me. I only came to know you late in life but I did come to love you. Towards the end I loved you very much."

"It is because of Shahzaib, isn't it?"

Noor was now sobbing uncontrollably.

"I don't forbid you to marry him but promise not to forget me when …"

Ayub's voice trailed off without completing his thought. He knew that the disclosure he would make would devastate the girl. He meant to ask her for forgiveness when she found out she was not really his daughter and that he had led her on unfairly. He had continued with the charade even when he had discovered the truth.

"I will leave a note on my bedside table. Look it up after my departure but don't dwell on it too hard."

In her agitation, she promised him everything, and the same evening Ayub left town, the very town where he had arrived as a pauper and in which he had thrived to rise to the pinnacle of prosperity, enjoying the fullest extravagance of life. Noor took him to the bus terminal. She did not even know Ayub's destination as she bade a melancholy goodbye, holding him back a minute or two before finally letting go. She parted from her father with unfeigned sorrow, even lingering on at the terminal as the bus diminished before her eyes until she could no longer see it. Though she could not naturally know it, Ayub presented much the same picture when he entered the town for the first time a quarter of a century earlier. Except, to be sure, the added years and his state of hopelessness had weakened him and imparted to his shoulders a perceptible droop. Ayub had boarded the bus without even a cursory glance over his shoulder, for he had no desire to watch his daughter in despair. Soon the stony demeanor gave way to a convulsive twitch as his true emotions betrayed him.

"If I could only have had her as my companion, I would be a stronger man. Why, I am still capable of looking after her, capable of working just as hard as I did when I was younger. But alas, that cannot be. I have only added to the burden of the thoughts I entertained then and that added burden weighs me down today exceedingly. I have lost the lightness of my being irretrievably. In any case, I cannot impose on her more than I have and I must not be an impediment in her quest for some belated happiness. I deserve to go through the rest of my miserable existence alone, an outcast. I am capable of bearing my punishment without equivocation."

Ayub experienced the bitterness of men who realize upon deep introspection towards the end of their lives that the material success they had achieved was hardly worth the cost, a life lost to unhappiness and remorse, a grim calculus of the excess of the cost in relation to benefits. He had long since regretted the state of his existence but his subsequent attempt to replace the fickle fruits of his ambition by love too had failed spectacularly.

From then on, Ayub subdued his anguish and carried on stubbornly.

CHAPTER 78

Noor heaved a sigh at the sight of the vanishing bus, recovered her composure and returned to the cottage. She entered Ayub's bedroom and looked around wistfully for a moment. Her eyes fell upon a folded piece of paper lying unobtrusively on the bedside table. She picked up the paper and started reading the note. Noor was astonished at the contents. She had expected a parting note from a father to a loving daughter underscoring the pain of separation. What she found instead was a terse note revealing her real paternity. The note did not explain how Ayub had confirmed her true paternity now when he had once so strongly asserted it. It also did not say anything about her mother's past or the existence of a stepsister.

Noor had heard rumors about her mother and herself but she had tended to believe the account that Ayub had given her of the incident and so she was disposed to accept him as her real father. Now that Ayub had refuted his own account, the rumors would naturally take on more meaning for her. Noor sat down on the bed, clutching the piece of paper. She had barely overcome the trauma of her father's departure and now it turned out that he was not her father at all. Suddenly, she recognized the real reason for Ayub's hasty departure. Ayub's deceit overwhelmed her feelings. Noor was crushed by the confusion over her paternity.

Noor became less distraught as she absorbed the new reality. It was not difficult to restore her old belief in her real father. After all, she had never entirely disowned him. She had continued to shed a tear of grief whenever she thought of him and she thought of him quite often. But Noor wanted Shahzaib to know the new facts, at least as disclosed by Ayub. She was not one to withhold such secrets, no matter what the consequences. She grabbed the note and went straight to Shahzaib, anxious to know how he would react. Paternity counted for honor and society did not treat such matters lightly. However, the death of his wife had altered both Shahzaib's circumstances and his mindset. He felt it was necessary to enter into an early marriage and he had chosen Noor to be his wife. Shahzaib's mother too had become quite convinced about the choice of Noor. She had been prodding her son to marry her at the earliest for fear that he might come under the sway of another woman less suited to her own way of life, as had been the case with Myra. She need not have worried though. Shahzaib had begun to love Noor. He read the note and responded rather nonchalantly.

"You know there have been rumors about your paternity for quite some time now. As far as I am concerned, it is of no consequence. I give the news no importance now, just as I dismissed it earlier. But if Ayub knew about it all along, he ought not to have misled you."

"I said I would never forget him but I think I ought to. I cannot forgive such deception. I cannot forgive him for the duplicity with which he tried to wean me away from my real father even after he found out there was no blood relationship between us. He should not have done that. What will we do now? Should you wish to end our relationship, I will not hold it against you."

Shahzaib held Noor in his arms, trying to sooth her ruffled nerves. He assured her again that her paternity did not matter to him at all. More importantly, she had not deceived him in any way. On the contrary, she had been a victim of deception herself. If anything, he sympathized with her for the awkward situation in which Ayub had placed her. He understood perfectly well her anger at the falseness of the man but he still sought to downplay and even defend Ayub's action as those of a lonely and broken man, desperate for love. The two continued to converse on the subject until there was hardly any point in debating Ayub's action anymore. Even then, Noor remained firm in her revulsion towards the man whom she had supposed, for a time at least, to be her father.

"Come now, never mind, it is all over. Now about this wedding of ours, shall we discuss the arrangements?"

CHAPTER 79

Shahzaib's father, Ibrahim, had heeded the remonstrations of his son for the most part. Nevertheless, he did keep himself duly informed of the happenings in his son's life and learned of the death of Myra and the birth of a daughter. He at once reasoned that he had an obligation to commiserate the bereavement of his son and decided to visit the mansion. Yet he knew better than to do so with the bereaved man himself and so, he chose to offer condolences to Shahzaib's mother, his wife instead. In the process, he hoped also to revive a measure of sympathy for his own cause. He arrived at the mansion at the rear entrance, as he usually did, and asked the servants to inform his wife.

The poor woman felt she could not turn her husband away. Death and birth are two occasions that permit a visit even by an enemy. In this case the visit was occasioned by both. Moreover, she did not expect Shahzaib to come home for some time. Keeping in view the purpose of his present visit, she admitted her husband into the parlor instead of the kitchen. Once inside he made himself comfortable, even ordering a cup of tea. After mouthing sympathetic homilies on the death of the young woman and the great pleasure on the arrival of the baby girl, Ibrahim continued on to the real purpose of his visit. He needed help and he needed it urgently. His wife told him he would have to seek it from his son. She knew well that Ibrahim would not have the gumption to do so and even more unlikely that Shahzaib would relent. Soon Ibrahim's tone became somewhat threatening whereupon the harassed wife asked him firmly to leave at once or else she would have to communicate his surly behavior to her son. He got up with a start. Having failed to cow her down with his threatening posture, he now started pleading, even begging, as he bid her a simulated deferential farewell. The wife showed him towards the entrance and walked part of the way with him, more as a matter of habit than as a measure of respect for her husband. In fact, it was the first time that Ibrahim had departed from the front entrance rather than the kitchen.

As Ibrahim reached the foyer, he stopped in front of a portrait hanging on the wall. The portrait was that of Ayub. Shahzaib and Myra had barely had the time to change anything around the house since they moved into Ayub's former residence. Ayub had not bothered to come back for his personal belongings and the same photographs and paintings still adorned the walls of the mansion. Ibrahim gazed at the portrait, seemingly transfixed. Ayub's portrait appeared to jog his memory but he could not be sure. He asked his wife who the man was.

"He is the former owner of the house. You know Shahzaib bought this house at an auction by the bank. The poor soul lost everything when his business failed.

Shahzaib has never gotten around to returning his personal effects yet."

"Do you know him? I mean are you personally acquainted with him?"

"I have never met the man but he was the reason why we relocated. He was Shahzaib's boss until this great misfortune befell him and he lost everything. Noor, who is betrothed to Shahzaib, is his daughter."

Ibrahim continued to stare at the face in the portrait, his eyes narrowing as he concentrated on the image. Then all of a sudden, he yelled out a triumphant declaration.

"By god, he is Yuba?"

Her husband's incomprehensible announcement clearly baffled the poor woman and she sought to correct him.

"No, I think his name is Ayub."

Ibrahim seemed to take no note of his wife's correction as he cried out ardently.

"Indeed it is Yuba, my brother."

Then in a moment of wistful reminiscence, Ibrahim transported himself into the past. He began a journey into a period of his life that had receded into oblivion long ago, unmindful of the presence of his mystified wife.

"I last saw him when he was barely thirteen years old or so. That is when I left my family in the village. I came to the city to escape poverty but the city was no kinder to me than the village as I continue until today to grind out a living. How could I have returned to the village, to my family, when they were expecting so much from me? I did nothing for Yuba. He was my little brother and he must have looked up to me but I contributed nothing to his life, not an iota. I was of no use to anyone there and now I am of no use to anyone here."

Ibrahim had told his wife all about the family he had left behind but the uncovering of a kinship with Ayub was unbelievable. Shahzaib's mother was dumbfounded, not just at the shockingly unexpected discovery but at the inherent irony of the incredible coincidence. She stared at her husband in utter disbelief, not quite sure of how to respond. Getting together with a long lost brother would be a momentous occasion but the coincidence of the betrothal of daughter and son of the two brothers in sheer ignorance of their blood ties was miraculous. No one had informed Shahzaib's mother of the real paternity of Noor yet and the poor woman was of the firm belief that fate had conspired to bring the two brothers back together at an opportune time. She viewed the reunion of the family as fortuitous and believed firmly that it had occurred only because providence had willed it. But, contrary to the good graces of Shahzaib's mother, the moment of the possible get-together of the two brothers was anything but opportune. It could only have been contrived by the powers that be to extend the punishment of the man whose original sin yet promised to burn all those who crossed his path.

After a few moments of studied silence, Ibrahim asked his wife if she knew where he could find his brother. She replied in the negative but told him that Shahzaib might know. Ibrahim waited eagerly for his son to come home. Shahzaib returned from work late in the evening and was surprised to see his father in the parlor but before he could vent his anger at his presence, his mother startled him with the newly discovered fact. At first, he tended not to believe the story but his father managed to allay his initial misgivings. When he was convinced that that was indeed the case, it shocked him. Soon, a different view of the past dawned on him. The man who had alternately been a benefactor and bitter rival had turned out to be his father's brother. The man he saw as an adversary might still have been a friend, a mentor and an associate had the relationship been unearthed earlier. But, Shahzaib realized it was too late to make amends. Moreover, both Ayub and his father had treated him harshly and he no longer found it in him to extend his interest in them beyond the present state. He, therefore, at once bade farewell to his father.

It was now Shahzaib's turn to surprise Noor. He asked her to come over to the mansion at once; the shocking expose could not wait. Shahzaib proceeded forthwith to explain to her the reason for summoning her so urgently.

"My father came by the mansion today. In fact, he left shortly before you arrived. I told you how he abandoned the family while I was still a child. I have rebuffed his entreaties for assistance and have told him that I want no part of him. So he has been visiting my mother in my absence, extorting money by emotional blackmail. The poor woman has been compelled by her married status to comply with his demands."

"How shameful and what a pity that someone would stoop so low to gratify his needs. It must be painful for you to have been placed in such a situation, after all paternal ties cannot be severed entirely and one learns to look up to a father, not condescend."

"Yes, that is true but it is not my father's worthlessness that I wish to talk to you about. It is another, more intriguing, matter that I want to bring to your knowledge. You know of course that Ayub's photograph is still hanging in the foyer. Well, amazingly my father has identified him as his younger brother. I do remember that Ayub had mentioned his long-lost brother once and that I resembled him somewhat. That, of course is true, I do resemble my father. He had even mentioned his brother's name as Ibrahim, which is Father's name too."

"Could it really be true? What a strange turn of events. We were all once strangers but it turns out that our lives were intertwined all along. What deceit has nature contrived to bring us all to this pass? What shall we do now?"

"There is nothing to be done. We will carry on as we planned. In any case, the revelation is not of much consequence to our lives now. This event changes nothing, nothing at all. I do think, though, that I would have shown greater deference and a lot more forbearance towards Ayub if I had known of my consanguinity with him. But, we must learn to live with our past, even as we revel in our present and wonder at our future."

Yet Shahzaib knew all the while that it was not as simple as he was making it out to be. He would soon have to grapple with his feelings, to dismount the emotional roller coaster and accept Ayub as his flesh and blood, at least in spirit. Shahzaib, had caused the man considerable privations, though none of it was advertent or intentional. It would not be easy to commiserate with him now, should he even wish to do so. Shahzaib had nourished a business rivalry with the man until he capitulated. He had competed with him for a woman until he usurped her favors. He was in a fight to death with him until he downed him morally. He had wrenched the last ounce of his will by proposing as his wife the one person who could have given him hope and comfort and, perhaps, a reason to live. It was hard to believe that all along there was a biological bond that had remained hidden until nature found an opportune moment to reveal it. Yet, to the end, Shahzaib remained unaware of his role in Ayub's misfortune. He had become the unwitting instrument of the divine retribution justly or unjustly meted out to Ayub.

CHAPTER 80

Meanwhile, the man, who was the subject of the gathered company's introspection, continued on his lonely journey. It soon became clear that he was heading for the small town where he had committed the indescribable indiscretion of his youth. He was returning, perhaps, to relive the memory of that fateful evening, a memory that refused to fade away. He had never once visited the town or his village during the years of his self-imposed exile but now a mordant obsession with the past had brought him back.

He reached the town in the afternoon and, sure enough, made straight for the location of the shack. He remembered that the shack stood alone in the middle of a barren patch of land on the outskirts of the town, next to its only graveyard. The dirt road that ended at the door of the shack then was now a carpeted road and continued beyond the point where the shack might have been located. The graveyard had stood its ground, though overflowing now with the dead of the past two and a half decades, but there was no sign of the shack. There were a few open spaces next to the graveyard, which the dead were stealthily encroaching. The rest of what was once a barren patch of land was now a dense thicket of human habitation. Ayub tried to figure out where the shack might have stood almost twenty-five years ago. A partially torn down structure in one such space seemed to catch his fancy as the venue of his injudicious behavior. He started ruminating, acting out a mock pantomime.

"Yes, this must be the road that led to the shack. The shack was probably located about here. I sat close to the door, maybe around here. She came in carrying the baby. She was so sad and weary because my father had rendered us homeless. I cursed her for intruding on the rare moments of peace that I enjoyed with my friends and yet, I pulled her down roughly by my side to prevent her from leaving. I would not listen to her genuine concern all because of my cursed notion that her presence by my side was the cause of my poverty. Then I continued drinking and committed my crime. She might have stood here as she said her last words to me before going off with the stranger. I can still hear her words echoing in my ears. I can still hear the sound of her silent sobbing."

The expression on his face betrayed the immense torture of his conscience, newly resurrected by his recollection. He could see the moment pass before his eyes and hear the words she uttered as clearly as though it was only just happening. He clenched his teeth and covered his ears with both hands, as if to shut out Jannat's voice, an increasingly shrill voice that seemed to reverberated in his head like an echo in the wilderness.

"Yuba, I have lived with you the past year or so and bore the brunt of your foul temper. You blame my presence for your miseries. Now that you have plucked the thorn from your side, I do hope, for your sake, that you will overcome your present status in life. I am no longer your wife now. I too shall try my luck elsewhere. It has to be better for the baby and me."

He could not remember if he looked at his baby as the mother and child exited the shack but he somehow conjured up an image of the baby turning her head and looking longingly at her father. He did remember though that she was crying feverishly in her mother's arms as both vanished from his sight.

Ayub stayed at the venue of the shack for the better part of the afternoon berating himself on a life misspent. He presented a sad spectacle, alternately crying bitterly and laughing hysterically, sitting on a dirt grave and pounding his head with his ample hands. It was obvious that his mental state was not too stable. Having thus reproached himself, he lumbered on to his old village. It was easier to make his way to his father's mud hut since the intervening twenty-five odd years had changed nothing there. The prodigal son was united once again with the sound and smell of his native soil. Death and desertions had left his father without a companion. Ayub once again started living in the old mud hut, in worse condition now than when his father threw his family out of it years earlier. Ayub had traversed the full circle and had resurrected Yuba.

CHAPTER 81

Ayub's mental state worsened with the passage of time. He spent his days in seclusion, interacting with no one, not even his aged father. Poisonous thoughts were leading him to the brink of harrowing incapacity; he could think of nothing but his past. In truth, he was too disillusioned to nurse any further ambition in life. Indeed, he had acquired the seeds of destruction and with it, a death wish.

"Everywhere people are dying before their time, though they are cherished, loved and wanted by everyone. While I, an outcast, a burden on the very ground I tread, wanted by nobody and despised by all, live on against my will."

Soon the state of his mind began to have an effect on his body and signs of incipient decrepitude and creeping infirmity began making an appearance. At last, as he grew weaker in body, his mind too became weaker, plunging him into a vicious circle, with the body and the mind chasing after each other. Ayub had returned to the location of his indiscretion as the last act of penance and had intended to lose himself altogether. However, even the debilitating weakness of his mind could not banish the thought of his two daughters, albeit each for a different reason.

Noor's memory warmed him intermittently in an otherwise dreary existence. In a curious twist of events, the grave social aberration caused by Ayub's follies had brought out a blossoming flower of nature. Of all the wrongs committed by him in life—and there may have been many—he regretted none as much as the wickedness he had directed towards Noor. Surely, he thought, by now Noor must be in full picture of the deception he had perpetrated upon her. He could not bear the thought of how much she might have come to despise him for that dishonesty. Yet, it did cross his mind that in his agitated state he could have misconstrued Noor's probable reaction. Such thoughts engaged Ayub often during brief moments of lucidity permitted by the state of his mind but not without a reason. He longed to see Noor just one more time, eager to find out if she was happily married. He wanted to be near her once more, if only for a fleeting moment. He wanted a chance to plead his case before her, to seek forgiveness for his fraud. It would be well worth the risk even if she rebuked him for his deception, he thought. He even called to mind Noor's words at his departure; that she wished very much for him to be present at her wedding.

But his step-daughter was not the only reason for his eagerness to take a trip to the city one more time. He was passionately possessed with the thoughts of his real daughter. The real Noor had been transformed into another human form and could not now be reached. She could only be restored to her pristine form with the death of Bina. His mind reverberated constantly with the hollow sound of an imagined cry for help. It was a cry from Bina, his forsaken daughter. He thought she was crying out to her father to put her out of her misery. He was alert to a mission he had yet to accomplish. He had never lost sight of it but it had to wait until he could overcome his irresolution. The recollection of his sin galvanized his resolve.

A sudden reckless determination to seek out both his daughters overwhelmed him and he decided to undertake a journey. He even bought new clothes that he thought would place him in greater harmony with the surroundings he soon expected to be in. He then embarked eagerly on his foolhardy mission, leaving his father and the village yet again.

CHAPTER 82

It was almost nightfall as he alighted from the bus and made his way to the cottage. On reaching there, a big padlock greeted him on the gate. He was told by some youth hanging around in the street that the occupant had probably left the house permanently, having gotten married sometime earlier. The news of the marriage did not surprise Ayub though the suddenness of the event, or at least as perceived by him, took him by surprise; in truth, he had lost track of time altogether. Sadness descended on his face, accentuating the loneliness in his vacant eyes. After a moment of reflection, he reasoned that he had come to make amends to Noor and so he resolved to do so, irrespective of her wedded state.

Ayub knew exactly where to find her, the mansion that was once his own. Noor had lived there before, at times as Ayub's stepdaughter while at others as his real daughter. Ayub had cherished her presence and scorned it alternately. She had tried her hand at being the mistress of the house after her mother's death, to look after the needs of her errant father but had later thought it best to dislodge herself from the mansion to avoid his derision. He figured she would now be the true mistress of the house, the lawfully wedded wife of the master.

On entering the street, he could see the full glory of the mansion, lighted magnificently in opulent celebration. He had stumbled upon a grand wedding reception of the groom for the elite of the city, a signal that Noor and Shahzaib had consummated the union. He could observe the extravagantly lighted lawns through the wide-open gates. He could sense the festive mood amidst the glitter and glamour of the guests. His courage suddenly failed him. To enter so poorly dressed in the midst of such resplendence was to bring needless humiliation to Noor, not to mention the revulsion of her husband. The circumstances of his life had so enfeebled his once resolute personality that he now feared situations he would have once derided imperiously. However, he reasoned he had come to see Noor and decided he would do so anyway. He went instead into the street at the back of the house that led to the rear entrance, used mainly by menials and tradesmen. Ayub approached the solitary guard at the gate and requested him to inform the master and mistress of the house that a humble old friend wished to call upon them. The guard took no note of the request of the disheveled old man and tried to shoo him away, taking him to be vagrant. In the ensuing argument the housekeeper emerged from inside to see what was going on. The sight of his former master awed him and he rushed forward to greet him with great reverence. The housekeeper wanted to lead him to the front of the house but Ayub had no desire to mix with the guests and thought it best to wait for Noor in the small pantry next to the kitchen. He was in the pantry a few minutes when he suddenly panicked. He could not bear the anxious wait any more and quickly rose to his feet as if to flee a rushing torrent. He had become intensely agitated in anticipation of Noor's reaction to his presence at the hour of her greatest triumph. Noor entered the pantry just as Ayub was about to step out. He stopped in his tracks as she greeted him with a touch of disdain.

"Oh! Is it Mr. Ayub?"

Ayub turned back and moved towards Noor.

"What, Noor? Why do you act as if I were a stranger? Why do you call me Mr. Ayub? Do not scourge me like this. Call me anything but don't be so cold."

He attempted to seize her hand but Noor cringed a bit and gently drew her hand away.

"I could have loved you always, I really would have. But how can I now, when I know you have deceived me so bitterly? You led me to believe that my father was not my father. You contrived to keep me in ignorance of the truth even after you became aware of it. How can I love you again, as I once came to love you so dearly? You have been most unkind to have treated me like this!"

Ayub's lips parted to respond to her but he said nothing. He could not complain to her that her mother had deceived him until he discovered her deceit in a most disparaging manner. Besides his lie had been a desperate move. He had lied to gain her affection even at the cost of his own honor and he did not wish to defend his move, now or ever again.

"Don't be upset on my account. I do not want to see you upset, especially at a time such as this. I was wrong in coming to see you at this most inappropriate time but I had no inkling of the occasion. I accept my error but I wanted to see you, one last time, to atone for my mistakes. So forgive me and I will never trouble you again, no, not until my dying days. Good night and goodbye."

Noor was so piqued that she might have gone on with her recriminations but she suddenly remembered another matter. She calmed down and stepped forward to stop Ayub from leaving, even advancing her hand to hold his. The sudden change in her demeanor surprised Ayub though his feelings were quite vague.

"Forgive me. I did not mean to be so surly. It is just that I feel violated. Yet even though you have hurt me by your action, I cannot continue to hold that against you. I think you might have been afraid to lose me. You have lost many of your kith and kin and that reminds me of another matter that I must bring up. I happen to have stumbled upon some news regarding your brother, Ibrahim. He is very much alive and what is more, he is probably in the city even as we speak."

If the news of his brother excited Ayub, he did not show it. Indeed, he reacted in a most disinterested manner, displaying an amused expression. Perhaps, the aloofness with which Noor greeted him initially had robbed him of the enthusiasm that the news of his brother might have produced otherwise. In his cheerlessness, he could only respond mechanically.

"Oh! And where did you find my brother? I could never locate him despite my best efforts even in the early days of his disappearance."

"Your brother is Shahzaib's father. He was here a few days earlier and recognized you by your photograph which is still hanging in the foyer by the entrance."

Ayub was stunned. He had received the news of his brother with a measure of equanimity but the news of his consanguinity with Shahzaib was shocking in its implication. The irony of the revelation overwhelmed Ayub. By his own admission, he had once loved Shahzaib as his own even when he knew nothing about him. At the very first meeting with him, he had discerned a faint resemblance to his brother, faint only because of a fading memory of the distant past. If he had seen the two standing side by side, he would have had no doubt of the sameness of their blood. It now transpired that the instrument of his annihilation was of the same flesh and blood as his own.

The discovery of his kinship with Shahzaib was probably the last nail in the fortunes of Ayub, foreclosing any possibility of regeneration. If he had entertained even a feeble hope for a turn around to his now miserable existence, the hope was dashed that very instant. The knowledge that it was ultimately his own who had conspired with destiny to destroy him so comprehensively, heightened his sense of tragedy. He could clearly see the chain of events that had brought him to this pass. His character had caused him to wrong an innocent woman. He had shown poor judgment in admitting his sins into his proximity by bringing the wronged woman back into his life when he could have compensated her at arm's length. The deception of the wronged woman had made him love the daughter of another as his own. He had invited a stranger with open arms into his life and had fallen under a mystical attraction that he could only now begin to understand. Ayub just stared at Noor for a few moments with expressionless eyes. Then before she could react to his unsettled appearance, he was gone. She ran after him and called out to him but he only quickened his pace and was soon out of sight. Noor looked at the departing figure wistfully. She might have wanted to make amends for her angry impudence but that would have to await another occasion. For the present at least, she put him out of her mind and concentrated on her own affairs whose magnitude was beginning to overwhelm her, her role as a wife, a homemaker and, perhaps in time, a mother.

CHAPTER 83

Ayub had come to the city ostensibly to see Noor one last time and, perhaps, to seek forgiveness for the wrong he had committed against her. But all along he had also planned to take care of another urgent matter, irrespective of the manner in which his rendezvous with Noor fared. He had to seek out Bina and do the honorable thing by her. His latent notions of honor had resurfaced when he first heard of the past of his wife and daughter but he had bided his time. He did not wish to jeopardize innocent lives, particularly that of Noor. In that thought, he was being most ambiguous about his values though he naturally did not see it that way. Ayub now set out in right earnest towards his goal.

Ayub proceeded towards the brothel alone. He did not need the pimp anymore; he could carry out the transaction with the madam on his own cognizance now. After taking care of the formalities, Ayub entered the bedroom and waited for Bina anxiously. Bina walked in and greeted the man.

She at once took note of his condition, which had altered distinctly since his earlier visit, uneasy with his ragged state.

"What have you done to yourself? You look 100-years-old. Have you been ill? Should you even be here? I think you should leave."

Ayub remained silent while assiduously avoiding eye contact. There was a palpable chill in the air. The sadness in the old man's face somehow repressed the intensity of her initial aversion to his physical condition and she sat down next to him. Ayub slid away to avoid physical contact. Bina tried to lighten the atmosphere with small talk, seeking at the same time to fleece the discomfited old man. In his moment of effusive empathy, Ayub must have wished fervently to grant Bina any request she might have made, even one as base as seeking added remuneration for unusual favors. Ayub put his hand in his pocket, fished out a large amount of currency and handed it all to Bina without saying anything. Bina made a make-believe mockery of the man's stinginess and tried to goad him into parting with more. Ayub probably saw her move as an indicator of the character of her profession and his face was suddenly flush with a surfeit of contradictory emotions. Beads of sweat appeared on his forehead. He continued to be tense in his silence for a few awkward moments and then ventured to say something. He addressed Bina by a name that caused her great consternation but he had taken the liberty for he knew that Noor's restoration was quite at hand. Before he could continue his ungainly attempt to speak, Bina interjected rather brusquely. Even the anger in her speech could not mask the emotive tone of her outpouring.

"Don't you ever call me Noor. I hate that name. Nobody calls me Noor anymore. My mother named me Noor and called me by that name while I was still an innocent young girl but when she left me here for eternal damnation, I became Bina."

Ayub listened to Bina's furious eruption and then seized upon an intriguing element from her oration.

"No, it was not your mother who gave you that name. It was your father."

Bina was clearly amused by the curious disclosure of an arcane facet of her life from a total stranger. It only reinforced her assessment of the enigmatic caller and his outlandish calling.

"How the hell would you know such personal details about me? In any case, I am Bina, for you and for the rest of the world, at least until the end of my life. After that I might cease to be Bina and become Noor once more."

She let out a chuckle that seemed to calm her somewhat as she continued her conversation in the same inane vein as she did before her brief arousal.

"So you think it was my father who named me Noor? You'll tell me next that you even know who my father is. I knew you had a sense of humor. It only needed to be pried out from beneath your unnecessarily frigid exterior and I think I succeeded."

Ayub said nothing more, not that Bina expected any elaboration on that or any other mark of her life from the strange old man. She was now beginning to be wary of Ayub and looked at him suspiciously. She could not figure out where this unusual encounter was heading. After another moment's awkward silence, the man made a most uncharacteristic request, though a mild one by Bina's reckoning. Ayub's nervous tension was plainly palpable.

"Noor, may I hold your hand?"

Bina was beside herself in laughter at the strange request of the weird old man.

"First, stop calling me Noor. I am not Noor. I am Bina. You can hold Bina's hand but not that of Noor. You can even hug and kiss Bina but not Noor. You've paid for Bina not for Noor."

There was a sign of revulsion on Ayub's face at the suggestion of the young woman. The thrust of the woman's proposition went far beyond the simple sentiment that Ayub had tried to express. The irony of her words too had penetrated his senses though the purpose of her dialogue was clearly nonsensical. Ayub's hand started trembling feverishly but he somehow lifted it up and clasped Bina's hand tightly. Bina felt a strange sensation at the old man's move and looked up at his face. She saw tears welling up in his eyes as a tormented sadness engulfed his expression. A strange situation seemed to be developing which gave pause to the young woman, causing heightened apprehension in her. A teardrop fell out of Ayub's eye onto Bina's hand which he clasped even more tightly now. Ayub asked her to stand up. He gave her a peck on her forehead. Bina stared at the strange man, not knowing how to decipher him. Then before she could gather her wits, Ayub whipped out a butcher's knife from under his tunic and thrust the blade headlong into Bina's stomach. Bina gave out an agonizingly shrill cry as Ayub repeatedly thrust the knife in and out of her until there was nothing left for the knife to penetrate. Ayub kept repeating hysterical entreaties over Bina's shrieks as he continued with his dastardly act.

"Forgive me Noor, forgive me if you can. I had to do this for your sake and for mine, for the sake of your honor and of mine."

Bina crumbled lifelessly as Ayub buckled onto his knees under the weight of an immense mental turmoil. The knife that he had so mercilessly wielded on his estranged daughter slipped from his loosened grip as he fell onto his knees. The deep wounds to his psyche were all too evident and so was the grief that was now writ large on his countenance. Ayub started crying pathetically. Yet, although he was clearly at the end of his tether, he could not summon the courage to wrench out his own life. Perhaps, the blood of the dishonorable woman had stained the knife so virulently that he could not now use it for an honorable object. In truth, he might have wished to end his life but he had no life left in him to carry out the act and the desecrated knife slowly slipped out of his hand.

Bina's wailing shrieks alerted the housemates who rushed towards the bedroom and broke down the door. They were horrified at the ghastly scene on display. No one could figure out what might have transpired. They stood transfixed at the sight of the wilted body of the young woman and the crouching figure of the man. No one dared approach Ayub, not knowing how he would react. The police soon arrived and led him away. He was a dead man walking, carrying an impassive face on his stooped shoulders, his legs barely able to carry the burden of his guilt. His present docility was in sharp contrast to the violence of the act committed by him only a short while earlier. Ayub had performed ablution with the blood of his tarnished daughter. He was now ready for his final prayers to the Lord.

It is a strange commentary on the values of a society where honor finds an expression in an act of such foul desperation. The price of thanksgiving for the emancipation of one's soul is the sacrifice of the life of another living being, oftentimes an animal but sometimes even a woman. Rarely ever does honor require the sacrifice of a man.

CHAPTER 84

The next day the media was agog over the story of the crime. Not only was the crime dastardly in its execution, it showed a great perversion of character in one who had been so highly regarded not too long ago. A man who was once a denizen of high society had murdered a prostitute, in a brothel no less. Ayub confessed to the crime but refused to disclose the cause of his action or his relationship to the victim. There was speculation over the matter as the public memory harked back to Sheeda Pistaul's revelation. But Ayub would not add to or subtract from the speculation and so the mystery only deepened. The general opinion thereafter attributed the act to Ayub's frustrations, frustrations of a fallen hero who was down and out and desolate. Some even laid it to the doorsteps of a less worthy explanation; the frustrations of a drunken pervert vented on a defenseless prostitute. Ayub allowed such disgrace and further opprobrium to his person in order to save Noor from public humiliation. The story soon died down and Ayub slid into ignominious anonymity.

Ayub's adamant silence had shielded Noor from the true story of her mother and stepsister. But the murder of a prostitute by her stepfather was shocking in its implication, enough to cause a deep loathing for him. Noor had belatedly acknowledged Ayub as her father and might have forgiven him his excesses. Sooner or later, she might even have forgotten the deceit he had perpetrated regarding her paternity. However, she could never have anything to do with a man who had turned out to be a cold-blooded murderer. She could not understand her stepfather's motive try as she might. She did not know of course that he had murdered his estranged daughter, his flesh and blood, in the name of honor when his own dishonorable act had brought her to that pass. Nor did she have any knowledge of the previous episode of Ayub's participation in the honor killing of his sister either. Or else, on both counts, Noor's ire might have intensified even more. In any case, she refused to visit him in prison.

Shahzaib experienced none of the emotions that troubled Noor over the scandalous episode. Yet he knew he would not be able to detach himself completely from the affair. Ayub was an uncle who had been a father figure in the past even without the knowledge of their blood ties. His situation would almost certainly inconvenience him, though he felt no angst over it. So, he did what he could to make Ayub's life a bit more comfortable in prison. At Ayub's age and in his condition, a prison was hardly a desired place to be in. Shahzaib knew Ayub would reject his offer of help contemptuously and he therefore provided the requisite assistance without bringing it to his attention. Shahzaib too never attempted to visit Ayub in prison, not because he had any compunction in doing so but because he knew Ayub would not admit a meeting with him.

In any case, Ayub refused to meet anyone though there were many who wanted to visit him. He might have wished to see Noor but she had no desire to see him ever again. His brother Ibrahim finally broke the ice. He showed up at the courtroom where the prison police had escorted Ayub for a hearing. After well over a quarter of a century, the two brothers stood face-to-face. Neither knew what to say until emotions welled up in each. Ibrahim hugged Ayub but Ayub was unable to reciprocate because of the handcuffs. Ibrahim slipped the police some money to allow the brothers a measure of privacy. The circumstances of that meeting had accentuated the emotions caused by the reunion. Their first meeting in twenty-five years was taking place in a holding cell of the court with the younger of the two incarcerated for a heinous crime. Ayub at once disclosed the reason for his act to his brother, knowing not only that the secret would remain safe with him but also that he would understand his motive. Ibrahim saw nothing wrong with what his brother had done. He told Ayub that he would have done the same and far from upbraiding him, he saw him as someone who had the strength of character to uphold his honor. The approval of his brother oddly perked up Ayub and thereafter he was neither burdened nor depressed. He awaited his end with remarkable equanimity.

CHAPTER 85

Ayub's trial proceeded without any fanfare. He did not want to prolong his agony through a long drawn out trial and sought a swift end to his misery. He had already confessed to the crime during police investigation and did so again before the judge of the trial court. There was no need for a trial and the judge sentenced him to death. Thereafter, the prison authorities promptly lodged him in a death cell. The cell came with a worn-out rug to sleep on, a thin blanket, a bucket to hold water and a half partition made of stone that concealed what passed for a lavatory. The lodgings though dismal by Ayub's standard, were not entirely inappropriate for Yuba the butcher. Ayub continued to rot in the death cell as the wheels of the justice system turned slowly. The death sentence had to be appealed automatically even though the man himself wished a quick end to his misery.

Visiting day at the prison had a special feel to it. It was an opportunity for families and friends to visit their loved ones suffering the loss of freedom. The outer compound of the prison bustled with activity with men carrying food and provisions and women dressed as if out on a picnic. In a bizarre sort of way, the scene did indeed resemble a picnic. Ibrahim was the only occasional visitor as Ayub's end drew near and their encounters were always somber. Despite Ayub's exhortations and unrelenting protestations of love conveyed through Ibrahim, Noor was adamant in her refusal to visit him in prison. Her high indignation at the dastardly act was of a magnitude that exceeded her reservoir of forgiveness, or perhaps she just wanted to remember the best part of their relationship and did not wish to sully her memory with the image of Ayub as a condemned prisoner. In any case, she would not see him.

When the day of his execution drew close, Ayub managed a last word with Ibrahim. It was a message for Noor. He wanted Ibrahim to tell her what he might never have been able to say to her face-to-face, looking into her eyes. He wanted her to know that he had loved her as he had loved no one else in his life. He had loved her as his own child. He cherished the care she had taken of him as no one else had done at any point in his life, perking up his dreary existence when he had nothing left to live for. He was leaving behind nothing more precious in the world than her. He wanted her to know that he was truly sorry for the anguish he had caused her and begged her forgiveness. If Noor's remonstration at their last meeting had not subdued him so thoroughly, he might have cried out to her even as the hangman's noose was about to wrench the last shred of his life.

Ayub had barely slept in the days that preceded his execution but he suddenly and inexplicably fell asleep as he awaited the pre-dawn knock on the fateful day. The prison superintendent entered the cell and asked the condemned man if he had any last will or testament. Ayub nodded disdainfully. Prison guards led him out of his cell, his hands tied behind his back, his shoulders in a straitjacket, and through a door that opened onto a large cemented courtyard that contained the gallows. The guards guided him up the ramp and made him stand on a designated circle on top of a trap door controlled by a lever. Ayub said a silent prayer as the guards secured his legs with a leather fastener and covered his face with a black hood. He jerked his neck as the executioner placed a knotted noose around it, the jerk resulting probably out of discomfort rather than fear. If he was nervous during the entire process, he did not show any evidence of it at all. The hangman reached for the lever and the trap door opened with a thud. Ayub struggled for a few moments until his body went limp.

Even though death is preordained, one does not have a measure of its investiture until the moment arrives. But the death of a condemned man is destined to be delivered at a specified time. Yet long before Yuba died physically, Ayub had died spiritually. He had succumbed precisely at the point when he passed from prosperity to abject penury and from honor to ignominy. If his death had occurred at the height of his power and prosperity, society would have, no doubt, eulogized him with flattering soliloquy. The denizens of high society would have gathered together to extol his virtues, acclaim his success, glorify his struggle and wax lyrical over his supposed qualities of head and heart; in other words, society would have praised him to the high heavens. In the event, all and sundry probably envisioned a cozy corner in hell for the errant soul. If his death did not occur earlier, divine providence was only saving him as a symbol of great vice and unending shame. The amends he tried to make late in his life were lost sight of forever under the overwhelming weight of the original sin.

As soon as Ibrahim received Ayub's body from the prison, he transported it to the village. There he was buried beside his mother, as he had willed. In his present circumstances, he was fortunate even to gather a few pallbearers for a simple burial, with no one mourning his death. The rituals of grief so poignantly played out in that part of the world were most conspicuous by their absence. Some village folks did come to remember him afterwards but most showed no concern. Nevertheless, Yuba had returned home for good. He had now truly become a son of the soil, finally at rest and perhaps even at peace. As the darkness enveloped the village, it spread a blanket over the dead man's story.

CHAPTER 86

It was almost a year since Ayub's hanging. Noor had gone about her state as a married woman routinely, looking after the house and her husband. She had earlier been in a family way and in time, she gave birth to a beautiful baby boy. She had miscarried twice before and had become despondent over the prospect of motherhood. Her joy knew no bounds when she was able to carry her pregnancy to term. It was a momentous occasion for Shahzaib and Noor. Her good fortune, though, curiously turned her thoughts to the misfortune of the man she had once known as a father. The sadness of her last encounter with Ayub and her refusal to visit him in prison before his death had left a belated but telling imprint on her mind. She had not been able to put him out of her thoughts despite her husband's tender reassurances that none of what happened between Ayub and her really mattered anymore.

Yet, the thought of Ayub disturbed Noor immensely. She could have, she thought, made her peace with him and perhaps rendered his life tolerable but alas, it was too late for that now. So great was her regret at the indifferent manner in which she had spurned Ayub that in a brief and uncharacteristic moment of emotional incontinence, she even began to flirt with the idea that she could name the child after her stepfather if it was acceptable to her husband. At the least, she wanted to atone for her grave feelings of guilt by paying her respects to the man at his final resting place.

Shahzaib had never so passionately liked Ayub as Ayub had liked him. At the same time, he had not hated him as vehemently as Ayub had hated him either. In any case, he was the cause of his own present status and for that reason alone Shahzaib had much to be thankful to him. Besides, Ayub may not have been Noor's real father but he had been an important part of her life. Therefore, he was not the least indisposed to assist his wife in her laudable mission.

Shahzaib and Noor set out for Ayub's village, as much to pray for the soul of the dead man as to seek his forgiveness for their own sins towards him. The entourage was not without an irony, the irony of two children in their tow, one from the erstwhile lover of Ayub, the other from his supposed daughter; both fathered ironically by the man who was, in a manner of speaking, his nemesis. It was by no means easy to reach Ayub's village. After travelling for a while on a congested highway, they veered on to a country road that was in the ultimate state of disrepair, its broken surface and the frequently occurring potholes posing grave hazards to the uninitiated. After a few kilometers of the hazardous journey, the intrepid travelers finally reached the village that had sprouted the likes of Ayub. They sought directions from the village folks and finally managed to reach the mud hut. It was located in the deepest squalor of hutments, with garbage strewn all over and sewage overflowing onto narrow openings between rows of dwellings that passed for streets. The hut had been the venue of Yuba's birth, his marriage with Jannat and the very same where his own Noor or Bina, if you will, had been born. It had finally served as the last residence of the despairing and downcast Yuba. Years of abuse by both man and nature had ravaged the mud hut and left it in the present precarious condition, with bent rafters and holes in the thatched roof.

The fragile door was ajar as Shahzaib knocked on it. An old man who was barely able to hold up the weight of his body appeared at the door. His face showed marks of deep sadness as his eyes lifted onto his visitors in a distracted stare. They inquired about Ayub's relatives.

"Ah, yes, sir, Yuba! I am his father. I would ask you to come in but it may not be appropriate. How will you gentle folks squat on a mud floor."

As the old man introduced himself, Shahzaib's jaw fell listlessly. The old man was in fact his grandfather and he was straightaway in a quandary whether to let him know that he was his grandson. He decided to remain quiet at least for now. He wanted to avoid the immediate awkwardness that his declaration might cause both of them. And so apparently did Noor, though the old man was nothing to her other than the fact that he was the father of the man for whom she had come to pray. Shahzaib could not have imagined in his worst nightmare the kind of abject poverty that his father and Ayub might have endured. Whatever little he had seen of the village seemed to evoke sympathy in the young man for Ayub and, indeed, for his own father. The mean surroundings and the bleak prospects it offered its inhabitants could not but become part of the character of these people. Their attitude towards life and their ethics and mores naturally emerged from the harshness of their surroundings. The oppression of their physical being could not but oppress their minds.

Noor ventured to address the old man, faltering in her speech as she was overcome by surges of guilt.

"We have come to commiserate with Ayub's family. Are you the only member of the family?"

"Yes, ma'am, they are all gone. I am the only one left from the family that was once quite large. Yuba's mother had wished very much to see him again but alas, she died without setting eyes on him again. You see ma'am, he was her favorite child. Yuba did finally come back to the village and he was just as poor when he came back as he was when he left. We shared this crude home again as we once did many years earlier. But he would say nothing, talk to nobody. Yuba was a sick man and he could not gain strength, for you see he wouldn't eat—no, no appetite at all. He wouldn't eat because he had no reason to live. He had lost the last person whom he loved. He said so himself."

The old man paused to take a deep breath.

"He left again suddenly sometime later. Then his brother Ibrahim returned home one day—many years after he himself had left the village—carrying Yuba's dead body. The poor folk around here pitched in to give him a decent burial. He had been killed, no question about that. We saw the marks on his neck. But we poor folks have always suffered such indignities and there is nothing we can do about it."

Shahzaib's reaction was curt in its design. He could feel for himself the dispossession that the environment must have nurtured for the unfortunate inhabitants and needed no elaboration. As for Noor, she found it unnecessary to vent any further sentiments. The sadness with which the old man comported himself left little space for any further verbiage. The old man then asked if they wished to visit Yuba's grave, which was only a short walk from the hut. They went together to the muddy patch where the dead man's remains stood interred. There was barely enough land to accommodate his mortal remains and no light to brighten the approaching darkness; just a few stray dogs and a lot of sewage water. After a deep and anguished silence, Noor could no longer remain composed. She spoke her words through sad tears, all the while cradling her child tenderly. And she at last spoke of Ayub as her father once again. The harsh reality of Ayub's tragic life had no doubt resurrected the feelings of tenderness for the man she had only recently felt contempt for.

"Oh! Shahzaib, Father must certainly have met a bitter end and that too on my account! My unkindness at our last parting must have caused such intolerable turbulence within him. If I could only undo that damage and make amends, it would lessen the burden of my guilt even though my grief will never subside. But nothing can be altered now, and so it must be."

All was over at last. Noor's regrets at having displayed such hostility towards Ayub at the end of his life soon receded into the crevices of her mind, though these were sufficiently deep and sharp for a good while longer. Thereafter, she found herself in a peaceful frame of mind but never far from contemplating the turbulence of the past few years. She realized that happiness was but a sporadic episode in life that does not come of its own accord. It is a choice that requires an effort to produce. She could not stop wondering at the vagaries of nature, grateful though she was for the bounties that fate had accorded her late in life. She considered herself fortunate but could not help thinking that her good fortune had come at the expense of others.

From then on, husband and wife bequeathed a fair amount of their earnings to the village that was, in the final analysis, the source of both their lives. At the end of the day, they had their lives to live and, of course, so did the Yuba Kasais who continue to proliferate in villages all over the countryside.

THE END

Printed in the United States
By Bookmasters